BLACKOUT

THE **COLOR ALCHEMIST** BOOK THREE

NINA WALKER

ADDISON & GRAY PRESS
WWW.NINAWALKERBOOKS.COM

Copyright © 2018 by Nina Walker. All rights reserved.

Characters, names and related indicia are trademarked and copyrighted by Nina Walker.

No part of this publication may be reproduced, distributed, or transmitted in any form or by any means, including but not limited to photocopying, recording, or other electronic or mechanical methods, without the prior written permission of the publisher, except in the case of brief quotations embodied in reviews or other noncommercial uses permitted by copyright law .

Published by Addison & Gray Press, LLC.

The characters and events portrayed in this book are fictitious. Any similarity to real persons, living or dead, is coincidental and not intended by the author.

ISBN# 978-0-9992876-5-1

For Alma and Holden

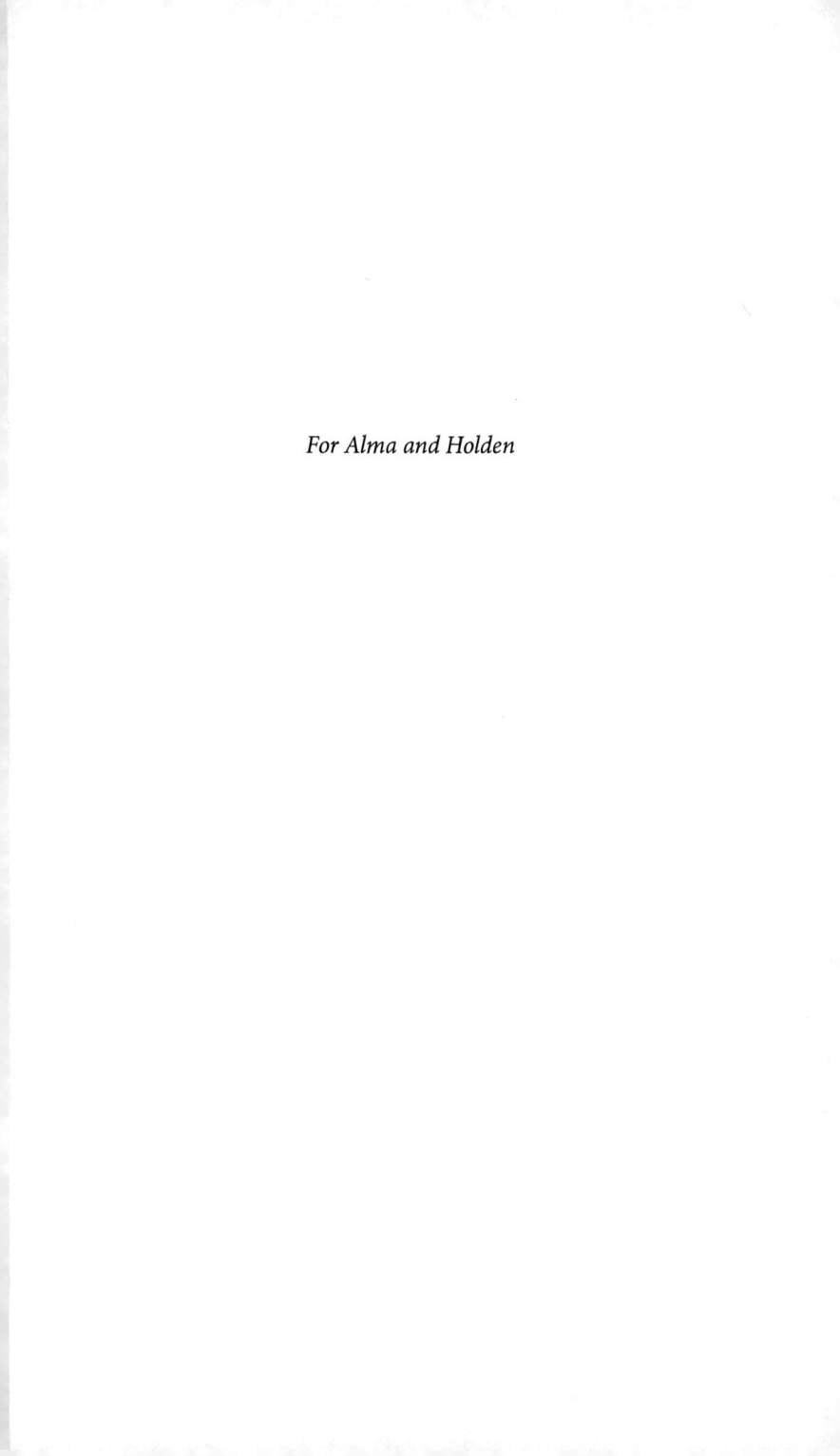

ONE
SASHA

My head whipped back as the officer's knuckles cracked across my cheek. Pain exploded from the impact, jarring my consciousness. I sucked back a strangled cry, gritting my teeth and blinking rapidly. *I refuse to beg for relief.*

The coppery taste slid down the back of my tongue, thick as syrup.

"You're wasting your time," I growled, spitting the blood onto the concrete floor. It splattered like ink on paper. I shifted in the uncomfortable metal chair, careful not to tug at the handcuffs. They'd been biting into my wrists for far too long. Red rings of angry flesh wrapped around each, stinging like crazy. "I'm not telling you anything."

"Again," Faulk remarked coolly. I glared up through puffy eyes at where she stood in the corner of the small room. A punch landed in the next second, the same spot as before, doubling the pain. I held back a sob as something in my face gave way. The crack rang through my head and my vision blacked out for an excruciating minute.

"If you break my jaw, then I really can't talk," I gasped.

The officer struck again, unperturbed. I yelped, tears burning my eyes, and scowled at the man. He held no emotion. His expression was stoic, a machine ready to strike on command. No, it was Faulk who was causing this, even if her hands weren't exacting the blows. Blood was splattered across his white uniform. Hers was pristine, but she was anything but clean in this matter.

"Oh Sasha, don't be so naïve." She grinned, stepping closer. Then she cackled, a strange sound for such a hard woman. "I'm sorry, perhaps you'd prefer to be called Francesca? Oh wait, no…that's not right. I seem to recall you went by Frankie. You always were a bit of a tom-boy."

I turned away. Her boots clomped across the room until she was face to face with me, leaning down to glower. Wrinkles spread around her eyes. Her lips were thin and her complexion ashen, but something in her eyes gleamed. Didn't she ever get tired of this?

"Wake up, you fool!" she spat. "If we break your stupid jaw, we can have a guardian heal you. And then we can break you all over again. And again. And again. And again."

Of course, I knew that! Still, hearing it spoken aloud sent a shiver of fear down my spine.

Bam! Her fist slammed against my jaw, and my vision blurred. I gasped and fought the urge to cry. No, she would not get the better of me.

"You'd be better off to talk now." She leaned close and her icy cool breath swept across my burning face. "Before we try…other means. You know, eventually you will talk. And you know what our alchemists are capable of."

I glared up at her through wild strands of hair hanging limp in my face. She was right. Without any color to grasp onto in this prison cell, I couldn't pull on my magic. And enough blue sent my way would have me talking. I didn't even want to think about what they would do if and when they made Jessa use red alchemy on me.

It would all be over.

I shook my head. "There's nothing to tell," I rasped. "You caught us! You won. Now move on."

"Don't patronize me." Then she pranced toward the door. She lifted her hand to push her way through and turned her head nonchalantly to call back to her hulking underling. "Again."

There was no time to brace myself. His fist pummeled my face, my rib cage, my arms and chest, over and over. He was huge, muscles bulging, teeth bared, and he held nothing back. A guttural cry escaped my lips as the pain enveloped me, tormenting me in a never ending agony. The overwhelming stench of blood became too much, and soon, I choked on its heaviness.

What did I hate more? The pain? Or my own weakness? I didn't know anymore. I couldn't think anymore.

The darkness spilled over.

▼

A barking cough echoed through the room, waking me with a start.

I blinked rapidly, focusing on the source of the noise.

Christopher.

The lights were bright this time, assaulting my vision. My scream caught in my throat when I saw him, sounding helplessly in my head. He was Christopher, my father, but his face was barely recognizable under the immense swelling and cacophony of colorful bruises. He'd been beaten to a pulp. He sat hunched over on his own metal chair, also handcuffed.

"Are you okay?" I winced as the skin around my mouth stretched the wounds that had accumulated, one on top of the other.

He sat up, an agonizing groan escaping his swollen lips. He took in the full extent of my injuries, and sadness filled the space between his puffy eyes. Finally, he nodded. "I'm alive. We're alive. That's better than what I was expecting. Frankie, I'm so sorry…"

I froze, the use of my real name sinking in deep.

"They could still kill us, you know." I sighed, still stuck on the "we're alive" bit. I wasn't holding out hope that would still be the case once they got what they wanted from us.

"True." He swallowed hard. "But as long as they need information from us, then we're still breathing. We have to hold onto that."

I scoffed. "I guess so." While being beaten to within an inch of my life was technically still living, it wasn't what I'd had in mind when we'd first raided the palace. We should have known better. Of course, the whole thing had been a trap. Richard wasn't going to let us walk in and take the place.

"I'm sorry," he said again.

"For what?" But I already knew.

My teeth ached and it hurt to talk, but somehow, after everything I'd endured over the last couple of days, this conversation felt like salvation.

"For not listening to you. For coming in here unprepared. If it hadn't been for me, you'd have gotten out with your friends."

I wasn't about to argue with him. "Well, they caught a bunch of us, didn't they? It's not all your fault."

He shifted in his chair, the legs grinding on the concrete.

He was dressed in the prison gray cottons, same as me, dried blood also splotched across the overly starched material. The collar of his shirt was torn, revealing the sweaty sheen of his chest. Swollen eyes squinted from his bruised face and bits of flaky blood crusted his wispy head of hair.

"But I heard the guards talking before they moved me in here with you," he said, the bruises stretching like taffy as he talked. "The other alchemists don't know the exact coordinates of the resistance camp. They killed Cole's guys and mostly everyone who got trapped in there. I was spared, you, some alchemists…"

"What's your point?" I really didn't want to relive our terrible failure. We almost had him. Cole had his gun pointed right at Richard but then…

The image of his body jerking and blood spraying outward from the impact of the bullet flashed through my mind. I closed my eyes and pushed it away, despite the rise of vomit that burned in my throat.

"My point is, I don't even have all the details they need to find the camp. I wasn't told all the specifics, I just know we were in Canada. You're the only one they have who knows exactly where the camp is. I think that's why they decided to stick me in here." He leaned forward, his arms also shackled to a chair, and glanced around the small gray room, eyes landing on the door. The room was empty except for the two of us and our godforsaken chairs.

"Figures," I muttered, glancing up. The lights burned bright as I stared at my distorted reflection in the metal ceiling. My attention turned to the gray walls, the floor of polished concrete, and the singular metal door. I fought hard against the rise of panic in my chest, but it was starting to get the better of me. I was trained to handle this kind of situation, and it still was wearing on my faith.

They knew who I was. They knew everything.

"What happened to you?" Christopher asked. I jumped, startled by his voice but more than that, I was nervous to answer him. *Doesn't he deserve to know? If you don't tell him, someone else will.*

I rolled my lip between my teeth for a moment and then spoke. "I'd originally been a color alchemist at the palace. After I got sent away from home." I couldn't meet his eyes when I said that part. The shame was still buried deep. "But I had been rescued from the Guardians by Hank and Tristan. It was while on assignment when I was only ten-years-old. That's how we'd ended up in the camp in the first place."

Silence stretched between us and I finally met his eyes. His were filled with regret. Even with the bruises and cuts, I could see that clear as day. "I came back into New Colony about six years later, undercover with a new name, Sasha. It worked, too. I eventually came to the palace and worked directly with Jasmine."

"Jasmine?"

"She died," I ground out the two words that hurt just as bad as the pain in my jaw. "Anyway, I had to blow that cover in order to help someone." That someone was Jessa, but I knew better than to say that here. She was still undercover. "Once I disappeared, I'm assuming the officers dug into my past and figured out who I really am. Faulk knows my real name, and that you're my father."

A lone tear fell down his face. "I'm so sorry," he said. "None of that should have been your weight to bear."

I shrugged and looked away.

The officers also knew I was a red alchemist. Well, I used to have that curse. I'd been able to successfully block it for years, but that wouldn't stop Richard from trying to rip it out of me again.

"I'm here because I'm their leverage," my father said, bringing me back to the moment. "Little do they know, I don't mean anything to you anymore."

"That's not true," I snapped.

He stilled, and I refused to say more. Yes, I was still mad about my past. But in light of everything that had happened, I was realizing that maybe I actually did want to be part of a family again.

Maybe.

I wasn't making any promises.

The door swung open, and Faulk strode in with an ugly conspiratorial smile ruining her face. "Of course you still mean something to her," she said to Christopher. "You are her father. No one could ever replace you."

"So then why take me away from my family? Why do that to little children?" I yelled, anger swelling as I tugged on the cuffs. The need to punch Faulk right in her beaky nose overwhelmed me. I imagined her crumpling to the cement floor, her head smacking it with a thud. I'd jump on top of her and match every single blow that she'd ordered on me and my father, until she begged for mercy.

The scene played out before me, but reality?

Reality sucked.

She glanced at me briefly, smiled, and then turned back to Christopher. "How are you feeling this morning?" She chirped. What was this? Good cop, bad cop?

I growled. "Morning? How long have I been passed out? Forget that, how long have I even been in this prison?"

She didn't bother to look at me as she ignored the questions. Living inside a gray box was not a fun thing for anyone, let alone an alchemist. But still, I hoped it had been days. My friends needed to get out of that camp. Innocent people would be caught and punished because of my stupid mistakes. Faulk was right: eventually she would get to the truth. But I would do everything in my power to make sure it was too late when she finally did.

"What do you want?" Christopher and I asked Faulk, at the same time.

She moved further into the cramped room, and a couple of her henchmen followed. They slammed the door shut and the space got tighter, the air thick and hot.

"Don't play dumb." She sighed. "You both know what I want. Sasha is going to tell us where the camp is."

"No, she isn't," Christopher said just as I snapped, "No I'm not."

I nodded my quick approval toward the man.

"We'll see about that," she purred, then flicked her bony wrist toward Christopher. Two hulking men strode toward him, arms raised, preparing to strike. He didn't cower.

"This is Jose," she pointed to one of the men. "And this is Carter." She pointed to the other. "They are two of my best officers, known for their fighting ability."

I glared at the men and quipped, "Pleased to meet you."

"It's not really a fair fight, though, is it?" She winked at Christopher and shrugged. "Oh, well."

"Wait!" I snapped.

She paused and turned, a smile playing at her lips. My eyes shot to Christopher, who was shaking his head. "Don't…"

"Just kidding." I smiled. "I'm only messing with you. Go ahead. Beat him. Beat me. Do your best, but it won't matter. I'm not telling you anything."

Crunch. A fist pounded across his face, and he cried out, ragged, as the men delivered punches that fell one upon the other. I flinched, but held my ground. It was what we both wanted. Besides, they could heal him if they needed to.

"Enough," Faulk said.

The room grew quiet, and she glared at me, her gaze cold and calculated.

"Bring her in."

The man she introduced as Jose threw open the door, and Jessa stood frozen on the other side. Her face was white as paper. Her eyes widened as she took in the extent of our horrible wounds. We were in huge trouble.

"What have you done to them?" she whispered and wiped at the tears that had immediately sprung to her eyes. They fell down her pale cheeks as she ran toward Dad. *Get it together, girl!* Jessa was apparently the emotional one in the family, but now was not the time

"They're traitors," Faulk replied. Jessa already knew that. Not only was she a part of our Resistance, but she was well aware that her parents and little sister had fled New Colony months ago. *My* parents and little sister, too.

And she knew who I was. Faulk had already brought her in the first day I'd been locked up in here to rub the news in everyone's faces.

"They have information we need," Faulk explained, "and, as you can see, we've exhausted our traditional means of extracting that information."

"And that's why I'm here?" She questioned, her voice squeaking. "But it could hurt them."

Red alchemy. How long could we drag this thing out? Would I be able to resist Jessa? I didn't have access to any color, and I wasn't able to do anything with white. I wasn't that talented.

Lucas, on the other hand…if only he were here. Leave it up to the prince to never be in the right place at the right time.

"Think of it this way," Faulk said. "If you don't do it, they'll only be hurt more. If you do what you're meant to do, what you were just initiated to do, then not only can we all move on with our lives, but we can heal their wounds."

"And then what?" I asked. "What happens to us then? You're not just going to let us go. Jessa, think about it." I turned on her. "Once they have what they need from us, we're as good as dead."

She glanced back and forth between us, her eyes somehow even wider than before. She was beautiful and sweet, to be sure, but at that moment, all I saw was weakness and I wanted to slap her for it.

"Don't do it!" I begged. "Refuse. She can't make you!"

"Shut up," Faulk roared. She motioned to her officers once again and this time, the pair separated, one coming at each of us.

The pain was nothing this time. Actually, it was awful, but it was nothing compared to the knowledge that I was right. I closed my eyes as Jose's fists pummeled me, forcing my mind into silence.

"We. Can. Take. It," Christopher gasped out between blows. "Sasha is right!"

"You have sworn an oath of loyalty to the royal family over all else!" Faulk yelled at Jessa. "Take this knife and take care of it, immediately!"

The pain kept coming, but Jessa did not. She'd backed up against the far wall, covering her face as she silently cried. Her tall, slender frame shuddered with her sobs as the emotions overtook her.

"Do it!" Faulk walked right up to her and dragged her back to us. Red splotches blossomed across Jessa's cheeks as she continued to cry. Faulk was right up in her face now, ready to explode.

"No," Jessa replied, finally ripping her arm free from Faulk's angry grasp. "I can't! Not until I have confirmation that you won't hurt them anymore, that you won't kill them."

Faulk laughed, shoulders bouncing, head down, and the sound anything but entertained. "I can't do that."

"Then I can't use red alchemy. I won't!"

"That's my girl," Christopher muttered. The officer that had been beating him responded with a punch to his face so hard that his body went limp. His head tipped, his arms dangled at his sides, the cuffs scraping against the metal chair.

I glared up at the two men, memorizing their faces. One day I would repay them for what they'd done, Faulk being first in line, of course.

Jessa was screaming and had crawled to Dad's feet. "Stop hurting them!"

"You know what we need. Get it, or we will beat them until they are dead!"

"No you won't," I challenged. "You need our information first!"

"I only need one of you," she replied, "and I'm guessing that one is you. Tell me why I shouldn't just end this man right now and get it over with?"

"Because"—Jessa jumped up and stood nose-to-nose with Faulk—"because he's my father. You're sick! You know that? You're truly sick to use him against us like this. I'll help you, okay, I said I'll help you, but I need a guarantee first."

"And how would you like me to do that?" Faulk spat.

They were toe-to-toe, wills battling. Faulk had the leverage, but Jessa was the one with the power. They needed her, and if she refused, what could they really do?

"Get Richard," I interjected. "Get him to agree to it."

Another fist slammed against the side of my face, followed by a ringing penetrating my head. I fought to regain control, to keep present in the moment.

To keep fighting.

Jessa stepped back from Faulk. "Sounds good to me. Let's get the king. You know he's my future father-in-law, right?"

Did I hear that right? I shook my head, trying to follow.

Faulk's cool exterior had cracked. She huffed before grabbing Jessa by the arm and dragging her from the room. I caught Jessa's determined expression and knew this wasn't over. The two officers followed like trained dogs. The door slammed, the lights cut out, and I was left to catch stilted breaths.

▼

The ambush came masquerading as mercy.

A light tugging on my hair caused the pain to heighten. I blinked, willing the exhaustion away. Something warm and wet slid across my face.

"Careful—" I sputtered, before she hushed me with the gentle press of her finger to my swollen lips.

"Hold still, we're going to get you cleaned up and healed in no time," Jessa said. Her voice was soft as comfort, like a mountain breeze. Just the thought made me long for home, for the pine scent and the stillness of the air.

Wait…

"What happened?" I forced myself back into the moment. I'd been dozing off when Jessa and another girl dressed as an alchemist shuffled into the cramped room. They had kneeled down before Christopher and me, warm rags in their hands. Rags now soaked through with blood.

"Shhh," Jessa said. "We're here to take care of you."

"Did I talk?" I asked. "Did something happen? Why are you here?"

It had to be. I must have been victimized by red alchemy

and ordered to forget the whole thing ever happened. Why else would these two be in here helping us after the way Faulk had dragged Jessa out earlier?

Oh, no. All those people…

"Maybe we should heal them first and then we'll finish cleaning them off." The girl spoke with a gentle meekness that was unusual for a guardian. Her blonde, curly hair caught the light, creating a halo effect around her heart-shaped face. She wore thick-rimmed glasses that glinted as she turned a tentative smile my way. A familiar knowing flickered between us. She was one of the nicer teen alchemists I'd met during my recent time at the palace. Her name was lost to me now.

"Good idea." Jessa nodded, and the two girls hauled a potted plant over to us. It landed with a thud between Christopher and me. I longed to reach out to the green for relief. But, as I tried to lift my arm, the sharp pain in my shoulder felt like a million knives ripping it apart. Christopher was still unconscious, slumped in his chair, battered and beaten to someone now unrecognizable as my father.

"And after we get you out of here," Jessa said, putting one hand on the plant and reaching out to rest the other gently on my shoulder, "we'll get you changed and you can take a proper shower. I bet you're starving, huh? And when was the last time they took you to the bathroom?"

I shook my head. I had no idea but that didn't matter right now.

"Jessa," I begged as the magic worked its way into my body, filling me with healing energy. It was warm, wandering through my veins and calming all the hurt places. "Why are you allowed in here? What did I do? Did I talk?"

She paused then whispered low, "You didn't talk. No, it's not that. It's King Richard. He wants all the new alchemists down here in the prison to come up and meet him."

A glance passed between her and her friend, who was now busy taking care of our father's wounds and subsequent healing. I had to assume the girl didn't know the full extent of what was happening here, even though she could probably make an educated guess. I mean, she knew I had pretended to be someone I wasn't, everyone did by now. Jessa raised her eyebrows at me, her blue eyes bugging out. She didn't want us to say more in front of the girl. It would have to be enough for now. At least I hadn't talked.

I think. Maybe? Ugh, this is all getting to be too much.

Christopher stirred, and Jessa turned her attention on him. They hugged and talked quietly between each other while we waited.

A few minutes later, the four of us were escorted out of the prison and up into one of the finer areas of the palace. Armed guards swarmed us. In fact, they seemed to be everywhere, more than I'd ever seen here before. They normally blended in with the shadows, eyes always watching. But now they were patrolling, walking up and down the halls, guns at the ready.

Jessa, Dad, and I were brought into a generic but tastefully decorated suite, and dumped behind a locked door.

"Now what?" I asked, turning on Jessa.

"Now you two need to hurry and shower, eat, and get ready to meet with the king," she replied simply.

My chest hurt even considering the idea of facing Richard again, especially with Christopher here. But my stomach far outweighed that. The scent of cheese caught my nostrils and I dug into the tray of food while Dad took the shower first.

Chewing on a few raisins, I moved to stand by the window and stared out. It felt wonderful to see the sun, to have the pain gone and my belly full. But the undercurrent of fear threatened to take all that away any second.

The worry plagued me as I showered and dressed in the familiar black guardian outfit. Richard was up to something. Whatever it was, it couldn't be good.

The three of us left together, ready or not, to find out what that something was.

The second we stepped from the sanctuary of the room, we were met with opposition. "You can wait back here, please Sir," an officer said to Christopher. I recognized him as Jose, a man who's fists I knew sickeningly well. "You're not an alchemist." To know he'd beaten us only hours earlier, and was now tasked to guard my father, angered me completely. A shrill scream of anger threatened to escape me. More than anything, I wanted to beat this idiot down to a bloody mess.

"But if it concerns my daughters, it concerns me," Christopher challenged, his lips set in a grim line.

"No, sir, you are, under no circumstances, permitted to meet with the king today," the officer replied, stepping to stand in front of Christopher and block his path down the palace hallway. The two men glared at each other. Similar in stature, neither was about to back down. One had a gun, but the other had two magical, badass daughters. So really, if anyone asked me, there was no contest.

"It's okay, Dad," Jessa said, her voice calm and collected. "I'd rather you weren't there for this, whatever *this* is. I'll come find you afterward."

He gave her a stiff nod and sauntered back into the suite.

As Jessa and I walked down the hallway, escorted again by a pair of armed officers, I picked out other alchemists who were also being escorted by officers. They were the ones who had trained with me back at camp and joined in on the attack. Not all of them had been captured, but there were enough to leave me feeling ashamed. They avoided eye contact with me, their pace steady as they walked ahead. At least they looked clean and healthy. Hopefully, they'd been spared the pain I'd endured these past few days. These people were innocent and knew nothing that could help Faulk.

But that didn't mean she wouldn't punish them, or that Richard wouldn't ruin their lives. They'd stood against New Colony, and there would be a price to pay.

We were herded to the back of a ballroom. It was different from where we'd been arrested. It was much smaller, probably meant for more intimate gatherings. Just as decadent as the rest of the palace, with a gold chandelier that immediately caught the eye. It centered the room and dripped in gaudy crystals that reflected against the white marble floors. Gilded mirrors lined the walls, giving the room an endless look. I peered at the familiar faces, counting seven of us dressed in black, not including Jessa.

A pang of guilt gripped me as I locked gazes with the young Sam. Her black hair blended in with her clothing. She held her small frame in the same haughty stance, and her eyes pinned me down with a mixture of equal parts distrust and hope. Part of her still saw me as a leader. But most of her knew I wasn't even close to holding that title anymore.

The energy in the room stilled as two guards opened a large set of doors with a soft swish. Richard strode in, his steps purposeful, his dark eyes set on our group. Lucas followed a few steps behind, his head bowed, but his broad shoulders confident. He glanced up and looked directly at Jessa. Oh, yes, he was the same gorgeous guy I remembered, but he looked different somehow. Harder. Sadder.

Definitely sadder.

Wait, hadn't Jessa said something to Faulk about being engaged to Lucas right before I'd passed out? I made a mental note to ask Jessa about the status of their relationship as soon as I got the chance.

"It's been a long day and I'm tired of playing games, so I'm only going to say this once." Richard stood tall. "The sole reason you're still alive after attacking my family in my own home, is because you are alchemists. Perhaps, in West America, you were forced to endure savagery. Perhaps, they forced you to come after New Colony as if you were their child slaves."

There was a long pause as his words sunk into the group.

His lip curled into a smile and he continued. "In my kingdom we treat alchemists with nothing but respect."

Jessa had inched closer to me. She reached out and squeezed my hand. I waited. The urge to speak out and correct him burned inside, but Jessa tempered it with her steady grip. She was right. Play it cool. I didn't want to get kicked out before Richard got to the point of this showy speech.

"In New Colony, our citizens are well taken care of. We're prosperous, happy, and we're stable." Richard brushed off the collar of his velvet jacket, the gold buttons catching in the light as he began to step closer to us.

The room stirred, curiosity buzzing.

"I'm inviting you to choose one of two options," he continued. "You can join us, train with us, and pledge your loyalty to New Colony. If you choose that option, you'll renounce any and all affiliation with West America. And you will never want for anything again. You will live in our palace and enjoy your magical gifts the way God intended."

Oh, what does this man know about God? I dug my heels into the floor.

"What's the other option?" someone called from the back. The group stirred uncomfortably as the King frowned.

"The other option is you remain a prisoner of war."

Silence. I squeezed Jessa's hand so hard she had to pull it from my grip.

"Either way we're prisoners," I said, bursting forward, unable to listen to his lies any longer. I shook my head in fury. *He really thinks he can schmooze us over so easily?*

"Oh, Frankie." Richard replied, casually walking forward to meet me, "how I've missed you. Though I must admit I could do without the sass. It's too bad you never grew out of that. I was so angry at myself for not realizing who you were the first time you came back to us." His eyes traveled the length of my body, and my stomach churned. "But you really have changed, haven't you? All grown up and as feisty as ever. No worries, we'll wear that out of you eventually."

"Tell them what you did to me," I said, motioning to the group. "Tell them how you took me from my family as a child, how you forced me to work for you, to manipulate and *kill* for you."

"Oh, are you talking about that poor boy that you pushed off the roof?" He asked with a tilt of his head.

A wave of prickling guilt washed over me. "I didn't push him."

"Oh, right," he replied, "semantics."

The memory of the officer in training who'd jumped to his death the day I got away was something I'd never been able to get over. He'd tried to stop us and was willing to do anything to make that happen. My red alchemy had been too strong, and I'd accidently killed him.

"You were untrained and powerful," Richard sighed with sympathy. "Your training was for your own good. And those deaths, they were an accident, an unfortunate result of an unknown alchemy." He smiled again. "Let's put the past behind us, shall we?"

"Never," I replied.

"Very well. Anyone else want to join her in the prison again?"

I spun around. "You can't trust him. He'll ruin your life."

But the sea of faces were awash with pale fear, and even some indignant anger. Nobody moved. "Seriously," I cried, "he's evil. You can't agree to work for him. He'll use you to kill innocent people. He did it to me!"

"Get her out of here," Richard ordered, and within seconds I was yanked from the room. Jessa's sorry blue eyes were the last things I saw as the doors slammed behind me. Dressed in black, and with no color near, I was dragged back through the palace and into the stale prison below.

"Hello again," I said bitterly to the walls of the same forsaken, gray prison cell.

"I hope you rot in here," said one of the guards who'd so generously led me down here. I glanced back to glare as he spat on the floor and slammed the door.

Dramatic, much?

I huffed and sank to the floor. In his eyes, Richard had offered me "redemption" and I had refused. There would be retaliation even greater than anything I'd experienced before. I prayed there had been enough time for the camp to have cleared out. Tristan and Mastin had gotten away that night of the attack. I was certain they'd gone back to help everyone flee.

It will be okay. They still have time, even now.

I relaxed against the wall and waited for the inevitable. Sure enough, not even an hour later, it came.

The door flew open with a gush of cool air, and Richard barged in. Lucas, Jessa, Faulk, Christopher, and a few officers followed. The room was filled beyond capacity, but at least this time I wasn't handcuffed to the stupid chair. It was across the room, and I wished it was closer, just so I could throw it at the king.

"What do you want?" I snapped, though I already knew. I stood, arms folded.

"Tell us what we need to know this minute," Richard barked. "And don't you dare lie. We have helicopters in the suspected area. We're armed and ready. We'll know soon if you're telling the truth."

"Oh, and what is it you want to know?" I asked sarcastically. My voice was cool but already I was scanning the people in the room, looking for a shred of usable color.

"Don't play cute." He stepped close and stared down at me with hate-filled eyes so dark they were almost black. "Tell us where you've been hiding. Where's Hank Reynolds? Where is your mother, and little sister, and whoever else is with them?"

"I'm not telling you anything!" I yelled right in his face. Changing my tone had startled him and I smirked.

"Tell us now or I will kill this father of yours without a second thought." He reached out and Officer Faulk handed him a black handgun. His fingers curled around it, and he pointed it right at my father.

"No!" Jessa and I screamed together.

"Don't tell him anything," Christopher said. He moved his hands slowly above his head and kept his eyes on me. Richard *would* kill him if he had to. Richard would do anything to get what he wanted. We both knew it.

"Father, there's got to be another way," Lucas said, voice cracking. He moved from where he'd been standing next to Jessa moments earlier.

"Nice of you to join us, Lucas," I growled. I owed him nothing.

"Lucas, if you're ever going to be able to live up to the responsibility of being a king you've got to learn how to make people obey your commands," his father said. "Frankie *will* tell us everything."

Christopher met my eyes again and nodded slowly. It wasn't confirmation for Richard. It was confirmation for me. I wasn't saying a word. Richard grabbed Christopher and shoved him to his knees between us. He went down without so much as a cry. Then, Richard held the barrel of the gun to the back of my father's head.

I needed to think, to find a way out of this. But panic began to overtake me as I realized there was nothing I could do.

"Tell me now or he's dead."

I caught the determined gleam in my father's eye, recognized the acceptance, and I knew, I just knew. He would sacrifice himself to save his wife and daughter back at camp. It wasn't even a question for a man like him. Hot tears slid down my cheeks.

"Please, no!" Jessa begged while Lucas held her back, one arm tight around her torso. She clawed at him and her breath became ragged as she lost control of her emotions.

Richard glanced at me one more time before his sure gaze landed on Jessa. "It seems I've been going about this from the wrong angle." He chuckled to himself. "Or I should say, wrong sister."

"What?" I shook my head, but he was fully turned on Jessa, completely ignoring me. He kicked Christopher to the ground in front of her.

"Okay, Jessa," he said, "I'll save your father *and* your ungrateful sister if you do one simple thing for me."

"Anything," she whispered between gasping sobs. Her bloodshot eyes shone back at him in eagerness.

"Use your red alchemy," he said. "Get your sister here to tell us what we need to know and they'll both get to stay alive. I won't touch them."

"Don't do it," I shouted, but it was too late. She nodded once, pulled out a dagger from a holster on her belt, and turned on me with bared teeth.

"What are you doing? Jessa, no!"

"I'm sorry," she said, "but I have to. I can't let them kill him."

"Don't do this. Think of the consequences." I slid back against the wall, squatting low and hands fisted, ready to fight her off. "They need more time. Jessa, your mom is there. Lacey is there!"

"It's been two days. Wherever they were before, they're gone by now. They have to be!"

"You don't know that!"

"Please try to understand." She narrowed her eyes, the knife glinting against the bright light. "This is the only way."

Everyone began to descend upon me, with Jessa a viper at the forefront. Quick as a flash, she slashed the dagger at me. I jumped out of the way, narrowly missing her. But when she tried again, it connected in sharp heat against my side.

"Get away from me!" I bellowed, but it was too late.

Her hands were pressing against my shirt and the wet blood already soaking through. The magic shot through me like a feathering of poisoned needles.

No!

"Tell us where they are," she said, her voice steady and calm.

My mind slowed, becoming heavy, and all emotion flatlined.

The truth spilled from my mouth.

TWO

JESSA

Tears burned my eyes, trailing down my raw cheek. I held on tighter to my emotions and focused on my footsteps clipping the polished floor. Back in my room, I softly closed the door and fell to my knees, curling in on myself in a crying heap. Was Sasha right? Had I really just condemned innocent people to death, including my mom and sister?

No. I have to hold out hope that Mom and Lacey got out of there in plenty of time. I can't think about the alternative, not right now.

The clawing doubt threatened to choke me, but I breathed through it.

Tap. Tap. Someone knocked lightly on the door, and I grimaced.

"Who is it?" I called out. The last thing I wanted was to talk to anybody. I had to be strong— and I was anything but strong right now. My weakness needed to stay hidden in this place, but this was becoming more and more impossible. If King Richard discovered how much he'd affected me today with his threats, he would know exactly how to control me.

Too late, Jessa.

How long until he used Christopher against me again? The memory of violating Sasha like that, slashing her open and taking what I needed, was something I'd never be able to erase. It was as if a piece of my soul was lost.

Just like the night Jasmine died.

Oh Jasmine, I'm so sorry. I miss you so much.

The tapping at the door continued. "Who is it?" I called out again. Couldn't they have answered the first time? I wasn't in the mood for games.

"It's me." Lucas's velvet voice filtered through the door.

Speaking of games!

I lumbered to my feet and brushed myself off. Seriously? Lucas was the last person I wanted to talk to but still, I threw open the door anyway.

"What?" I clipped.

"Are you okay?" His hands were deep in his jean pockets and his shoulders slouched in a blue cotton shirt that complimented his eyes. But dang it, I was not okay!

I bit back my incredulity and forced myself not to laugh in his face. The whole reason any of this happened was because of him! Had he already forgotten? If he hadn't told his father about the Resistance's planned attack, it was likely Dad and Sasha wouldn't be in this mess.

Sister. It was still *so weird* to think that Sasha was Frankie.

"Am I okay? I don't know, Lucas, what do you think?" I glared at him, but still something inside me fought it. It just wanted to erase all the pain and jump into his arms again.

Traitorous feelings. There was no forgiveness here.

He scrunched up his nose, something I used to find adorable, but now only found incredibly annoying. He wanted to say more, but stayed silent.

"Really, what do you want, Lucas?"

"I want to talk."

"There's nothing to talk about." I glanced around the hallway where he stood. We knew alchemists and officers lurked at every corner. It wasn't completely safe to talk inside my small room, but I pulled him inside anyway. The touch of his hand in mine sent a rumble of emotion through me.

Get over it. He can't be trusted!

"You traded in *my* secret because of *your* bad decision. It's not my fault you chose to get engaged to Celia. I wanted to get married to you one day but not if the *only way* to get your father's blessing was to betray me. What were you thinking?"

He opened and closed his mouth, red creeping up his cheeks. He was a man who rarely blushed; this was affecting him. Then something hardened in his expression, and he shook his head. "I told you. I did it for us."

Was he serious?

"Well guess what?" I scoffed. "I don't want to be with somebody who would do that."

The anger that spread through his gray eyes reminded me of an icy frost, killing everything beneath. "Okay," was his only reply.

Okay? That's all he has to say for himself?

"I never would've agreed to it." I looked away, unable to stand the sight of him for a second longer. "I think you knew that, and that's why you went behind my back."

He didn't respond. He didn't move, drop his head in apology, or even try to look regretful. He didn't do *anything*.

I was right. And the truth of it burned deep inside my chest. He'd willingly broken my trust in such a terrible way. Jasmine and many others were dead because of it. The Resistance? Gone. And my family, the people I loved more than anything, were in more danger than ever.

And why? So Lucas and I could be engaged?

My stomach turned over.

"You should leave," I said, about to be sick.

"I just wanted to talk to you." His eyes were hard slits. How was it that his strongest emotion was anger when he was the one who'd hurt me?

"Okay, so we talked, now go away."

He stood there for a long minute. I studied him carefully, the planes of his jaw where stubble was growing through his smooth skin, the slight wrinkling of his brow. The pain in my heart nearly doubled. He finally relaxed, shaking his head, and stepped tentatively toward me. "Can I at least show you something?"

I didn't want to be around him any longer. It was too painful. What could he possibly show me that would matter at this point? But my curiosity was piqued, so against my better judgment, I nodded.

"One second," I said. I dashed to the bathroom to quickly wash my tear-stained face and brush my mess of hair. The curls were wilder than normal after my breakdown on the floor. For a moment, I stopped to study my blotchy cheeks and red-rimmed eyes, the blue irises bright with emotion. So much anger, sadness, and fear shone back at me. I shook my head and went out to meet Lucas, the boy who was responsible for most of that pain.

"This had better be good," I said, irritable as we rounded yet another corner. We'd long since left the GC wing and were in the belly of royal territory. The decadence of the marble floors and gold crown molding brought back memories of the night Lucas and I had become engaged, then the initiation the very next day when everything had fallen to ruin. I swallowed and shook away the memories.

We were nearly at the royals' private apartment, and the

heightened security set me on edge. Guards swarmed the area. I was used to at least two practically anywhere I looked in this place, but the numbers were through the roof today. A particularly huge guard with bulging muscles sneered at me and I stumbled. I was seconds from turning tail and running. If Lucas was bringing me to see his father, I would officially lose it!

"In here," he said, opening thick double oak doors and ushering me into a shadowed room.

"I hope I don't regret this," I murmured, but followed him in anyway.

Someone was standing in the middle of the room, her posture oddly familiar. *What is–?*

"Madam Silver," I shrieked. I ran into the outstretched arms of a woman I thought I would never see again. She squeezed me tight, and I melted at the scent of my old ballet studio. The worn wood floors, the baby-soft fabric of the shoes, the balsamic fumes of the cleaner. They were all there, intermixed with her floral perfume. I cried out at the shock.

"What are you doing here?" I asked, stepping back and looking her up and down. Her dark hair hung in a bob cut around her chin, her eyes so dark they were almost black, her skin pale and ageless as ever. She carried a sophisticated attitude everywhere she went, but I knew her better than that. I'd been her student for years. Underneath the cultured exterior was a woman with a heart of gold and a deep love for her dancers. She was like a second mother to me.

"I've missed you, too." She shifted back to look at me and her ruby red lips moved into a smooth smile. "It hasn't been the same without you, Jessa. We've all missed you."

"It's been so hard to be away from dance," I whispered and hugged her again.

"You're telling me? You were my prized pupil. You shocked

us all when you turned out to be an alchemist." Her voice rumbled against me, and a prickle of shame overcame me. I'd let her down. I'd let them all down.

"I shocked myself."

I frowned and took a few steps back, putting distance between us. Was she scared of me? Did she hate me for my magic? She must have sensed the worry in my expression because she shook her head and sighed.

"Too much talent for one person," she said with sadness. "It's not fair what happened to you."

She has no idea.

"You still haven't answered me. What are you doing here?" I turned to Lucas and raised my eyebrows. "What is she doing here?"

"I think you're ready to start dancing again," he said simply, the shadows in the room hiding his expression.

Joy burst through me like a sunrise. I was going to get to dance ballet again, and with my favorite teacher! A sense of peace warmed me just thinking about it. No matter what had happened in my life before coming to the palace, I had always had ballet. It was my salvation, the one thing I could do to calm the emotions inside. It was my outlet. My best friend. But I'd had to let it go in order to train as a color alchemist, and I had mourned that best friend every single day since.

"Are you going to work with me? Even though I'm a Color Guardian now?" I spun back to Madam Silver. I hated that I doubted her. But I did. She was normal, and I was the complete opposite. Normal people feared those like me. I'd learned that the second I'd accidently manipulated my stupid lavender ballet costume and the crowd of people had run away in horror.

Of course, the royals hadn't been horrified. They'd seen

the opportunity and took it for their own.

"I would be honored to work with you, Jessa." She smiled, the kind that lit her eyes. I practically tackled her when I hugged her. Her petite frame shrunk under my height, but she only laughed.

"When can she start?" Lucas asked.

Madam Silver moved out of my embrace and peered around the space, her professional eye assessing the room. It was nearly perfect. The floors were hardwood, and all the furniture had been cleared. It wasn't quite as big as my old studio, but it would do just fine.

"I can get one of those bar things installed and some mirrors," Lucas continued, moving through the room and pointing to the walls as he talked. "I would like to get her in as many classes as you can fit in your schedule, and of course, we'll pay you double your regular one-on-one fee."

I began to wander around the room, imagining the studio it would become.

"You're very generous," Madam Silver replied. "I would be happy to meet her here three days a week for two hours each session. How about Monday, Wednesday and Friday afternoons from four to six, will that work?"

"Yes!" I whirled on them. "That's perfect!"

I couldn't believe it! I would not only get to dance again, but to study independently with the best dance teacher I'd ever known. I couldn't hold back my smile, it burned on my face like a brand. Sure, this wasn't the same thing as being in the Royal Ballet, nothing would ever replace that life-giving experience, but it was something. It was better than something! It was the best news I'd received in months.

Automatically, I began to move my body in long dancer's stretches that were ingrained into my body. Lucas and Silver began to discuss more details of the specific equipment and where to install it. Leaning over to stretch my leg, my mind wandered to the reality of my situation. I wouldn't forget my work here in this palace. I would still find a way to take Richard down, maybe rebuild the Resistance if I could.

I switched to the other leg. But this? This would make my stay in the palace at least bearable.

"I wish we could start today but I'm afraid I have other engagements. Can we start next week?" Madame Silver asked Lucas. "I trust you'll have this studio outfitted by then? She'll need to be fitted for proper shoes of course, and leotards. I'll send someone to meet her here Saturday at noon to take care of that. Does that work, Jessa?"

I nodded eagerly.

"And it's called a barre, with an 'e.'" She winked at him.

"B-A-R-R-E," I spelled it out for Lucas, and when I met his eyes, a confused feeling of gratitude washed over me. I wasn't going to forgive him. He'd ruined everything, and this wouldn't make up for it. I hated him. Or, something like that...

"Darling, I must go now," Madam Silver said. She gave me a quick hug before sweeping from the room, as gracefully as a professional ballet teacher would be expected to leave a room. I stared after her, the joy still dancing within me.

"Thank you." The words fell softly as I looked up to meet Lucas's gaze.

His expression was unreadable. He stood across the room, completely still, just watching me. The room was dark, the only light coming from the afternoon sun peeking through a partially shaded window. Long shadows were cast over his hooded eyes. Finally, he nodded slowly. "Can you do me a favor?"

"Depends." I bit my lip.

"Remember all of this." He motioned to the room that was

to be my new studio. "Tomorrow night, I will escort you to meet with my father again. He will make his next move, and whatever it turns out to be, please just, remember I did this for you. No matter what, Jessa, I care about you. Everything I do, it's for you."

But that was the problem. He *still* believed that. What he'd done to betray my trust had been for him, not for me.

Tears filled my eyes. I wanted to nod, wanted to agree and just forgive him and be with the man I'd loved so deeply. Still loved. But the sting of betrayal was too hot. I didn't say a word. I couldn't. It was all too much. Instead, I turned around and left him there, closing the door behind me.

▼

I'd tried to check on my father and Sasha, or I guess her name was Frankie, but I wasn't allowed to see them. I had no idea if they were okay, or even alive. I'd spent the next day in a complete frenzy, trying to find out information but getting nowhere. I didn't even care about being discreet, either. I'd asked guards, officers, anyone who would talk to me, but nobody had information. Eventually, I'd had to give it up and get ready in the dress that had been delivered to my door. True to his word, Lucas had come to deliver me to his father.

I held his arm lightly, but kept my mouth shut and my eyes ahead. The day spent trying to help my family, who were still prisoners, had left me feeling helpless and angry. We walked into a ballroom that was lit with twinkling lights and black and white linens on tables scattered throughout the room. There were long-stemmed white roses in the center of each. In fact, it looked like everyone had been outfitted in elegant black and white, as well. We were instantly surrounded by tuxedos and exquisite dresses of all lengths and styles, but the colors were the same.

The crowd opened for us as we walked, everyone staring. I was sure we looked like a perfect pair. Lucas was styled to perfection, his suit crisp, his hair dark and gelled back, and his face clean-shaven. He smelled of ocean salt and citrus, a combination that made my mouth water. And I was wearing a full face of makeup. My hair was pulled back and adorned with crystal pins, and my sleeveless dress wrapped around me perfectly in crushed black velvet, fanning out around my hips and traveling all the way down to the ground. I hated everything about it; Richard had likely been the one to assign it to me. But I had to play along.

I planned to talk to Richard about my family tonight. Maybe I could work out some kind of deal to get them better accommodations.

"Ready for this?" Lucas whispered low in my ear.

I didn't reply. I wasn't sure what "this" was, and being here on his arm, against my wishes, made the wound between us fester even more.

He led me to a raised platform where his father sat relaxed on his throne. As we ascended the stairs, I noticed the media cameras set up again, a long row of black equipment with people buzzing around it. Last time the media was invited here was for the execution of Officer Thomas and subsequent proclamation of war. Not to mention Celia had been the one on Lucas's arm that night. My stomach flipped.

Celia. The woman was still in the palace. I'd seen her from afar a couple of times, and she'd barely even seemed bothered by her broken engagement. She was the same stoic, glossy, gorgeous redhead as always. But she was no longer set to be the next Queen. How did she feel about that? And why was she still here? I glanced around the room, but didn't see her here.

"Hello, my dear Jessa." Richard smiled coolly as we approached. "I am very excited for you to see what I have in store for you, little girl." His use of "my dear" and "little girl" made me want to spit in his face. I curtsied and smiled carefully.

"Hello, Your Royal Highness," I replied.

"Please, call me Richard." He smiled. "I am to be your future father-in-law, after all. I would say you could call me "Dad", but even Lucas doesn't do that anymore."

Lucas was watching the exchange between us without revealing an ounce of emotion. His eyes kept flicking to me as I talked to his father, but that was the extent of it. He waited for me to nod my agreement to the King and then he cupped my elbow and led me to a chair, one that looked like a mini-throne with its red velvet seat and high back. He gently sat me down and sat beside me.

The mixed crowd of alchemists and officers turned to watch us now. Their faces were a mass of curious eyes and hesitant smiles.

Richard leaned toward his son. "It's showtime, boy," he said, his heady voice a mix of threat and anticipation. He stood. No blue alchemist to bolster him, I noted, as I looked around for one to pop into the picture. How long until Reed came back from the war? I bet Richard was missing his particular set of skills.

The King strode to a podium and pointed to the line of media with their row of black cameras. They adjusted with a few buttons and gave him a series of nods. He stood at the podium, rolling back his shoulders, his back to us. The spotlights were hot and bright. I resisted the urge to squint as the rest of the room was sent into shadows. Everyone quieted as Richard swept his arms wide and began to address his kingdom.

"My beloved New Colony, thank you for your attention tonight. It is with great pride that I can announce our war efforts against West America are succeeding. We've taken over vast amounts of land and continue to gain ground every day." He paused, the light reflecting off the gold ornate crown on his head. He rarely wore it, but when he did, it meant business. "Thank you to those who've volunteered to help, and of course, many thanks to those men and women in the field, risking their lives for our freedom. I trust that because of these heroes, I will soon have good news." His voice was smooth silk, practiced and confident. He didn't need Reed tonight. The crowd of alchemists and officers were nodding along with every word, as—I was sure—were the people at home, watching from their various slatebooks.

"That is all I can say for now without giving too much away to our enemy, but rest assured this continues to be our number one priority here in the palace. We will not let you down," he continued, straightening his shoulders, gold embroidered patches on each. He also had a red sash-looking thing across the outside of his suit jacket. There were tassels and shining buttons, a slightly more elaborate get-up from Lucas's. "West America has committed many crimes against us, from the tragic death of our beloved queen, to a public attempt on Lucas's life and my own. An act that, unfortunately, killed innocent people. West America will not get away with it. We will not rest until we've destroyed their evil ideology and taken back what is rightfully ours."

He paused, only for a moment, before the crowd exploded in applause.

"Thank you," he said, after they'd quieted. "I also have to thank the Guardians of Color and the Royal Officers." He motioned to the media, and on cue, they pivoted their cameras to face the crowd of guests, in all their finery. None of the small children were in attendance, of course; they rarely were. It was teens and adults, as usual.

"I know we have kept the vast majority of what we do here hidden from you," Richard said to the cameras as they swiveled back to him. "We made that choice to protect everyone involved. What we do with magic here at the palace has stayed classified from our enemies and we wanted to keep it that way. But I've come to realize that, while we should and will continue to keep some of what we do under wraps, it's not in your best interest to be blind to the advantages of color alchemy. This ability is the very bedrock of why we're so prosperous. It's high time you learned the basics of what it is and why it's so important to cultivate. For example, our alchemists who help to make crops grow are the reason our citizens have healthy food on their tables tonight."

The crowd cheered again. A distrustful feeling washed over me as he continued to speak of alchemy so openly to the press. People at home must be glued to their screens! Color alchemy had always been such a mystery. Seeing it was as rare as snow in July. Very few ever met an alchemist. Why was he talking about it now, when for decades, it had been mostly kept secret?

Bile rose in the back of my throat. Something was coming. Lucas reached out and grasped my hand, but it did little to calm my nerves.

Richard continued, "It's with this revelation that I've decided to hold a series of public exhibitions to showcase the power of color alchemy. It is my hope that you will understand not only why it's so important to willingly send alchemists to train with us, but for you to have faith that with these people heading our war efforts, we cannot fail. The exhibitions will be publically broadcast and a lottery system will select a small number of you to have the opportunity to watch live. There will be three of these events, one here in the capitol, one north, and one south. More information will be coming soon with exact times and locations, so please stay tuned for updates."

I glanced at Lucas. His eyebrows were pulled together in intense focus as he studied the back of his father's head. Did Lucas know about these exhibitions? Could it really be that the King just wanted to be open about alchemy all of the sudden, or was there something else going on?

"And finally," Richard said, his voice turning from smooth and serious, to amused. "I have one more item of happy news to share. I know, there's more!" He chuckled to himself, and even though I couldn't see him, I was sure he was smiling from ear to ear. The cameras shifted and slid back. Another tug of nerves gripped my stomach. They were filming Lucas and me. "As you can see, my son is joined by someone other than the pretty redhead Celia you've all come to love. I hate to say it, but truth is, I wanted that marriage more than the two of them. Poor Lucas, he's such a wonderful son, he'd do just about anything for me. But these last few weeks since the engagement, I've been feeling overwhelming guilt about it. You see, I knew it was another girl who had captured his heart. I fought it because I didn't know this girl well, and I already thought Celia was best for Lucas. But I've taken the time to get to know this beautiful girl you see seated here tonight and I've decided to let my son choose her as his bride. I'd like to introduce you to Jessa Loxely." He turned to us, no longer facing the cameras; his gaze was as sharp as ice.

Lucas grabbed my hand, and together, we stood.

I froze, a million questions running through my mind. I didn't want this. I should pull away. But I couldn't, not with the King's eyes pinned on me. He had my family downstairs in his prison. There was nothing I could do but play along. Besides, I *was* engaged. That was the whole point of why Lucas revealed my secrets, destroying the Resistance in one night, my dear sweet Jasmine gone with it.

I'm engaged but this makes it official. Time to buckle up and smile, Jessa!

"You two lovebirds can sit down now," Richard said with a wink. I fell back into the chair as my knees gave way. I smiled through it, somehow. Lucas placed a hand on my leg to temper the shaking, and when it didn't stop, he frowned slightly and removed it. I ignored the immediate sense of loss.

Richard had returned to the podium. "Part of why I'd like you to understand color alchemy better is because of Jessa. You see, there's something rather remarkable about the girl besides the fact that she stole Lucas's heart."

He paused, and I could feel the slight shift as the cameras zoomed in on my face. Was I breathing funny? Frowning or smiling? I couldn't even feel my cheeks anymore.

"She's a color alchemist," he declared. "One of the most powerful we've ever seen. It is my hope that you will accept her, knowing that not only does she make your prince happy, but she can potentially bring in a new line of remarkable power to our royal bloodline."

More cheers. More fluttering in my heart.

"The wedding will be a joyous affair in the midst of the tremors of war, but life must go on. Their wedding will be broadcast upon the completion of the three exhibitions. The wedding date is set for the first day of the new year."

I held my breath to keep the tears from falling. That wasn't even two months away! It was everything I had wanted, but had come in the worst package. I loved Lucas, I couldn't pretend otherwise. But I also saw too much of his father in him, too much greed and deception. I couldn't do it.

I have to find a way out.

Lucas squeezed my hand, and I smiled wide for the cameras and leaned over to offer him a quick kiss. On the outside, any tears in my eyes must have added to the presentation of the announcement. I probably looked so overcome with happiness that I was brought to tears. If only that were true.

"Thank you again, my dearest friends, for all you do," Richard continued. "I know there's a lot of change in the air right now, but rally with us and we will come out stronger than we've ever been before. Goodnight."

There was another blast of cheers followed by a pause and a release of air. The media began to take down their equipment, and Richard strode over to greet us.

"Congratulations again," he said to us and grabbed my hand, pulling me into a hug. The buttons on his suit coat dug into my chest and my whole body went rigid at his touch. He smelled so much like Lucas that I had to hold my breath. This man was a monster. And now he would be my father-in-law? The fact he could fool the kingdom so easily frightened me most. He could charm everyone at a moment's notice, all while killing anyone who got in his way. Was this an attempt to get closer to my red alchemy? Was it something else? I had a sinking feeling there was more to this charade than I knew. Even if I married Lucas, I would still be a prisoner.

Maybe even more of a prisoner than ever before.

"Enjoy the party." He released me and patted his son on the back. "Both of you. This is your engagement party, in case you didn't figure that out already." He laughed jovially, but it did nothing to quiet the fire in his eyes. They flickered between us for a moment. "You will behave," he threatened, then turned and briskly walked away, a flurry of people in his wake.

I followed. Now was not the time to be timid. "Wait, please, what about my sister and father?" I had to ask. I wanted to ask so much more. I wanted to know about the camp as well. Where were Mom and Lacey?

"What about them?" He continued to stride away, never bothering to look at me. We were nearing the back of the room, as if he was trying to get out of here before he was bombarded with guests wanting their moment with him.

"Are they okay?" I pressed. "If I'm to be royalty now, can't I help them?"

He stopped and whirled on me, expression hard, his eyes beat down on me with disdain. "There's nothing I can do for your sister, she's made her choice. She will remain in the prison for now."

I sucked in a shuddering breath. *For now?* Did that mean he would execute her? And if so, when?

"Your father, on the other hand," he continued, his voice dangerously low, "was smart enough to comply with our wishes. As long as he continues to stay out of our way, he can stay. He's already been set up with accommodations next to what will be your suite in our royal wing. Tomorrow you will be moving from your dorm and beginning preparations for your upcoming nuptials."

I nodded. What else could I do? Once again, I would be moved, like a piece on a chessboard. I was used to it now. "And what of my mother and little sister? Did you find them? Are they alive?"

I shouldn't have asked. I knew that, but I couldn't help it. And now I would pay. Rage was filling his entire body, his eyes widening and a purple vein bulging in his forehead. I stepped back, regretful. My knees began to buckle again.

Warm arms caught me and Lucas pulled me against him.

"Jessa," he said, loud enough for Richard to hear, "be careful how casually you address my father. He is your King. You must not make demands of him."

Richard's eyes danced between the two of us and he nodded, the anger fading slightly. "Quite right," he quipped, then pushed through the back door and disappeared.

I shifted away from Lucas and turned on him. "Since when do you talk to me like *that*?"

His eyes narrowed. "Your mother and sister weren't at the camp. Nobody was. They got out," Lucas said this wonderful news, emotionless, as if he was reading a math problem. "Now, let's do as we're told and go mingle with our guests."

He never answered my question about why he'd talked to me like that in front of Richard. Was he saving me from Richard's wrath, or was he really his father's son?

I followed him, no longer caring about having to feign happiness in front of all these people. I was elated! A swell of gratitude threatened to bring me to tears all over again. Sometimes it bothered me how quickly I was brought to tears, but that moment was not one of them. Mom and Lacey had gotten out! I had no idea where they were, of course, but they had to be okay. And maybe, just maybe, that meant there was still a chance.

Maybe there was still a Resistance.

THREE

LUCAS

I held Jessa close, breathing her in as we danced. It broke me.

We spent the evening dancing, making small talk with everyone who crowded us, held hands every moment. It didn't matter. She wasn't with me. Emotionally, she'd shut me out, not a single crack left in her exterior. She currently rested her head on my shoulder, the soapy lilac scent of her shampoo wafting through the air between us. I closed my eyes briefly and scoffed at my naiveté.

This meant nothing to her.

I'd hoped the ballet studio would soften her. I recognized the longing in her, knew how much she'd missed dance. When I'd seen her eyes light up at the presence of her old teacher, I'd thought, *this is it. She's going to let me in. She's finally going to understand our relationship is what I value most of all.*

Wishful thinking. She'd taken the gift and closed the door even tighter on me. I gritted my teeth, annoyed at my continued wishful thinking when it came to this girl. I'd always been such a cynic until she'd come along.

Lost in my thoughts, I hadn't realized I'd stopped leading her in our dance. We were now standing in the center of the dance-floor, curious eyes surrounding us.

"What's wrong?" Jessa asked, shifting back to look at me straight on.

My chest burned. I wanted to kiss her. So badly, I wanted to kiss her. But it wasn't what she wanted.

"Nothing," I muttered, then swept her back into my arms.

I never would have told my father what I knew about the Resistance, had I known it would backfire so badly on her family. Didn't she realize that? I couldn't have known that her father was going to show up. Or Sasha.

"How much longer do you think this thing is going to last?" she asked. "I'm getting pretty tired."

I sighed. *Tired of me, more likely.*

"I'll walk you out." I shifted to hold her hand and began to maneuver her through the room.

I noticed a couple new faces standing together in a corner and watching the two of us with distrust. Recognition passed between us as I locked gazes with one of them. They were some of the alchemists who'd originally attacked the palace with the Resistance. I was certain they saw me as the enemy. They had no idea that they could have succeeded if not for my intervention.

I only did it because Richard was already suspicious, already planning something. Telling them about the attack gave me the leverage to get to this moment with Jessa. It had worked. And then it had backfired.

I gently tugged Jessa through the crowd, stopping every few steps to thank yet another group of people. They swarmed on all sides to congratulate us, some taking photos with their slatebooks. It wasn't so much the Guardians or

Royal Officers who cared, but my father's many friends.

"Thank you so much for saying that." Jessa smiled at a particularly pushy couple. "Richard picked it out," she said, gesturing down to her dress. It fit her in the right places and dropped to the floor.

"Actually, I picked that one out," I said. Since when did I care about getting credit?

Her expression faltered as she peered up at me, her smile slipping. She'd barely met my gaze all night, but now our eyes locked and heat flashed between us.

You may be fooling everyone else here, but you're not fooling me. I know you're too stubborn to forgive me. I know this isn't what you want. By the way her wide eyes turned into a hurt glare, it was almost as if she could hear the thought.

See? We're so connected you can read my expression and I can read yours. But you're still choosing to hate me.

She huffed and turned back to the couple. "I do like this dress," she said. "I just *love* how everything in my closet was picked out for me by someone else."

Touché.

Seeds of anger, long planted, were beginning to take hold, spreading, wrapping their roots around my nerves and pulling my heart in opposing directions. When had she *ever* chosen me first? I thought she loved me, but I'd never wanted love to feel this way. Love wasn't supposed to be one-sided. We were both supposed to want it, to fight for the other one's needs.

She isn't fighting for me. I buried that thought down deep because it hurt almost as much as her refusal to look me in the eye.

I shook my head and shifted so she was even closer. She'd come around. She had to. We were getting married; no way Richard was going back on that grand announcement.

He'd never allow two canceled engagements. That would embarrass him, and embarrassment was not something he tolerated. This wedding was happening. It's what Jessa *had* wanted not too long ago, and maybe one day she'd want it again.

Once again, we moved through the crowd, almost to the door. Maybe I was ready to be done too. Sleep sounded amazing. At least then I could avoid the pain.

"Congratulations to the beautiful couple," Sabine said, sidling up next to me and smiling coolly. A prickle of heat ran down my spine. I did not want to have this conversation, but the inevitability of it was staring right at us.

Sabine's husband Mark, and thier daughter Celia, stood just behind her, eyeing Jessa with equal parts distrust and hatred. They wore smiles on their faces and expensive black dress clothes on their bodies. They nodded along with Sabine and portrayed a happy family in all its perfection. But there was something wrong with that picture.

"Umm–thanks," Jessa said softly.

They returned the smile tenfold, and Sabine stepped forward to shake her hand. I didn't like it. After following the group a few nights ago while cloaked behind my white invisibility magic, and seeing Sabine and Mark interact with Faulk and my father, I was beginning to think it wasn't Mark who led his household after all.

No, Sabine was the puppet-master behind her powerful husband.

"Thank you," I added as I cleared my throat, matching each of their heavy gazes one-by-one. They may be intimidating, but I wasn't intimidated. That was a distinction everyone in this little party needed to understand.

"That is very gracious of you to say," I continued, my voice hard. "Considering the circumstances." I refused to feel an ounce of guilt over getting out of that prison-sentence of an engagement with Celia. The whole thing had been for their benefit and not mine. No one had cared that Celia and I barely knew each other and certainly weren't in love. All they saw was the crown.

"You're very lucky," Celia said to Jessa, gesturing to me with the lift of her white-gloved hand. Her dress matched, accentuating her auburn hair. "I hope he doesn't drop you as quickly as he did me. He is such a fickle man, I've discovered."

"Celia," Sabine said low, her tone thorny. "Please, dear, none of that tonight." She wore a regal black number and was just as done-up as her daughter. She struck me as the kind of woman who agreed with the old adage that revenge was a dish best served cold.

"The girl does have a point," Mark said, glaring at me behind his thick lashes. I supposed that was what fathers were supposed to do when their daughters got dumped. "I believe Celia is owed an explanation."

Jessa tensed under my arm as silence spread through the room, both of us knowing the conversation had begun to travel. I inwardly groaned. Most of these guests would do anything to be privy to a royal scandal.

"It's fine," Celia chirped and looked away, her cheeks flaring red.

Jessa's body was still tense as stone when she spoke. "I completely agree with you, Sir." She nodded toward Mark. "Lucas does owe your daughter an explanation."

Heat prickled up the back of my neck, and I fought the urge to roll my eyes.

"Honey, why don't you dance with Celia and explain it to her?" Jessa purred, smiling at me. She was the picture of the blushing bride-to-be and I froze. Her eyes were flush with indignation. She wanted me to suffer in the hands of Celia and her family.

My jaw clicked as I held her stare, each of us urging the other to be the first to look away. The first to stand down. *Fine, if that's how she wants to play it.*

"Sure." I nodded, meeting her challenge, and turning a devilish grin on Celia. "I'd be happy to dance with Celia and have a little chat about what went wrong. I *do* need a chance to apologize."

"But what will you do?" I asked Jessa. I wanted to be the one to walk her back to her room.

She laughed. "Don't be silly, I have other friends." Then she slipped from my arm, spun on her heel, and joined a group of alchemists I'd seen her with a few times before, two teen girls and a boy. They walked off together and immediate worry replaced my frustration. I needed to get to know these alchemists and decide for myself how much they really cared about Jessa. If there was one thing I'd learned during my eighteen years in this palace, people usually weren't what they seemed.

I reached out my hand, and Celia placed her cold fingers in mine. We strolled to the dance floor. She gripped my knuckles so tightly that I assumed she was seething mad. She didn't want to dance with me just as much as I didn't want to dance with her. And her father, well, he would have punched me straight in the face if I wasn't the prince. But it was her mother I needed to watch out for. She was still scheming, still plotting, I was sure of it.

"You don't have to pretend to care about me," Celia said as I brought her into my arms.

"Good," I replied, flat, "because I don't."

She let out a huff and narrowed her eyes. "Wow, Lucas, tell me how you really feel."

I was fed up with the games and didn't need this.

"Fine." I shrugged. "I really feel like you're a social-climbing, gold-digging, crown-obsessed socialite who cares less about me than I care about you. Don't pretend like you're heartbroken; this is all about the status and we both know it. But I am sorry if your feelings are hurt, whatever *those* may be."

"I can't believe you," she growled, her voice hushed. "You think you're the only one who has powerful parents, huh? Did you ever stop to think that I was also pushed into our engagement?"

Pushed into an engagement with the prince? She'd run right into it. She wanted it, and now she wanted to play the victim.

To what end?

I paused and studied her face, searching for any sign of truth to her words. People danced around us, the orchestra playing a waltz anyone of high birth would know well. As we moved around the room, tears had formed in her eyes, and her cheeks were twice as red as they were only moments before. Her feelings could be boiled down to embarrassment, but that was nothing like heartbreak. I knew heartbreak inside and out these days.

But still, a pang of guilt lingered.

"Okay fine." I sighed. "Maybe I'm being too hard on you. But try to understand, I was already in love with Jessa when I met you. I didn't have a choice about you—that was all my father. What would you have done in my situation?"

Her brow rose. "Fair enough," she grumbled, "but you could have at least warned me, or broken it off with me yourself. For heaven's sakes, Lucas! Not only did you ignore me during that entire attack, but you got engaged to another woman without even breaking it off from me. I had to hear it from your father. How do you think that felt?"

"I'm sorry. But, it's done now."

"It sure is." She dropped her eyes and turned away, a curl whipping through the air between us.

By now, the crowd of dancing couples around us were doing little to hide their gawking expressions and wide eyes. A flurry of whispers circled the room as the gossip spread like wildfire. The phenomenon wasn't unusual for me, but it had to be far worse for Celia. Maybe I really had mistreated her.

But if she wanted me for me, she wouldn't have offered Jessa the opportunity to be my mistress. That was proof enough that she put the crown before the person actually wearing it.

I was done playing into the manipulations of her family. However it had happened, I was over it. I had my own life to sort out.

"You should go home now." I dropped my arms and stepped back. "There's no need for you to stick around the palace."

She shook her head, a sickly smile creeping across her crimson lips that bore a striking resemblance to her mother.

"Oh, you hadn't heard?" She cocked her head to the side. "I'm staying in the palace until further notice. The King wants me and my parents to help with the exhibitions, among other things."

"What other things?"

She leaned forward and whispered in my ear, the movement sudden. "You and your little girlfriend better watch your backs, Lucas, because we certainly are."

Was that a threat? I shook her off and glared down at her. "She's not my girlfriend, she's my fiancé, and soon, she'll be *your* queen."

Her face fell, the color washing away. I turned briskly and

strode away.

They were "watching us", huh? I wasn't even surprised; already Sabine and Mark had jobs with my father that went far beyond what they told the rest of the kingdom.

Obviously, some kind of undercover operation. They could watch me all they liked but they had no idea who they were dealing with. It was *them* who should be watching their backs. They might be working for my father, but I was working for myself, and I wasn't going down without a fight.

▼

The echo of my shoes filled the musty stairwell as I descended to the prison. I stalked down the dimly lit hallway, noting the guard and an officer leaning against the wall. They jumped up when they saw me, bowing low.

"I want to talk to her alone," I said gruffly to the two bleary-eyed officers. They blinked rapidly, probably because they were bored out of their minds and fighting sleep, until I interrupted them. I'd chosen to come down here in the middle of the night on purpose. Anyone with a vested interest in Sasha was presumably asleep.

"Uh, I'm not sure you're authorized to go in there alone, Sir." One of the officers stared at me and scratched at his stubbly neck, his young eyes squinting. *Good, I'm glad they put one of the younger guys down here; they were always the easiest to manipulate.*

"It's Your Highness, not Sir," I snapped. "I'm the prince, what more authorization do you need? If you'd like me to drag my father down here in the middle of the night, I'll do it. He'll be raging mad, but I don't care, I need to talk to that traitor *now*."

"Of course. Please forgive me." The other officer nodded

to his cohort who unlocked the door with a quick flick of his wrist. The keys moved in and out of his pocket in a flash, and I smiled.

"Thank you," I said. "I won't be long."

I slid into the darkened room. Sasha lay fast asleep on a cot. No blanket, just her legs tucked up against her body. Her face was bruised and swollen, as I was sure the rest of her was as well.

Why though?

We'd gotten to the Resistance camp and torn it to shreds looking for evidence. But maybe because it had been empty, Faulk thought it fair to continue punishing Sasha. Not getting what she'd wanted had warranted another beating, knowing Faulk. Shame burned in the back of my throat, and I loudly cleared it, the abrupt rumble filling the small gray cell.

Sasha stirred, rolling over. I pushed up the solo chair and sat down to face her.

"We need to talk," I said quietly. I pulled a blue stone from my pocket and slid it into her palm. She knew what to do. She'd used blue alchemy as a means to keep our conversations private before.

She blinked a few times and sat up. "Water," she croaked. She sounded so broken, her voice so scratchy that it was jarring. This wasn't the Sasha I knew. My spine stiffened. What had they done to her?

"I'll get you some water as soon as we're done," I said. "I promise."

Her eyes narrowed as she focused on me. It was mostly dark, but I could still make out the mistrust that shone in her searching eyes. After a moment, she nodded, the stone hidden in her hand working its magic.

"We have to be quick," I continued. "I wanted to run

something by you."

"What do you want?" She leaned back against the wall and rubbed one of the bruises on her jaw, then winced.

"I want to help you," I whispered, my voice low.

She laughed, a desperate sound.

"I'm serious. I want to get you out of here."

"Why should I believe you?" She glared beneath the shadows. "Jessa told me what you did. This is *your* fault. Years of hard work and planning were wasted because you had to tattle to your daddy." She punctuated her words with the quick flick of her wrist. "I'm not doing a thing for you."

Guilt ripped through me, but I forced myself to stay calm. Now wasn't the time to hash out the details of that night.

I shook my head. "Who else do you have? Getting a lot of offers for help in here, are you?"

She paused and looked me up and down. I could feel her distain for me, hear it in every word she uttered. "Why should I believe you? Why should I even trust you? You know, I could tell them *your* secret. Did you ever stop to think about that?"

I had. Which was a big part of why I was here in the first place.

"Look," I said, "if you stay here, Faulk will kill you. Maybe not today or tomorrow, but eventually, it will happen."

"Jessa will stop her. She'll figure something out." She leaned back against the wall, pulled her legs up against her chest, and closed her eyes. Even in the darkness, I could make out a rip in the knee. Her flesh shone in the dark, scraped and bloodied.

"Do you really believe that?" I scoffed, exasperated. "Christopher is staying upstairs. All the other alchemists, too. You're the only one Faulk has to beat on at the moment, in case you didn't know."

"You think I like this?" she hissed. "That psycho keeps having them heal me only to hurt me again. She's sick. I already told them everything thanks to that ridiculously emotional sister of mine."

I needed to change tactics.

"They got out." I leaned back in the chair and crossed my arms over my chest. "The people at your camp. They got out."

She chuckled, a coy smile filled her face, and for the first time I caught a glimpse of the Sasha I remembered. "Where'd they go? Are they okay?"

"West America," I said. "That's all we've been able to figure out so far. As you can imagine, Faulk and my father are pretty angry about the whole thing. I think they're taking it out on you." I smirked, despite my better judgment.

I expected her to punch me or something, but she didn't.

She grinned even wider. "Let them. I don't care anymore. I'm just glad those people got out. Now the alchemists here on the other hand, they're complete idiots for giving in to him so quickly."

"I have to agree." I nodded. "And the thing is, it won't be long until Richard comes for you, too. If Faulk doesn't kill you, what he'll do will be much worse."

"What's that supposed to mean?"

"What do you think it means? Think about it, Sasha." I paused. "Frankie? He remembers you as that powerful alchemist. He's going to get over his anger with you eventually. The way I see it, either Faulk kills you with one of these beat-downs, or Richard forces you to come out of this little hidey-hole and do his bidding."

"Red alchemy?" she groaned. "No, I don't do that anymore anyway."

"So you've told me. But don't you think he'll try?"

Her eyes shut tight in annoyance.

"Yeah, me too."

Her eyes popped open, and she cocked her head at me. "Fine. So what's your plan, Lucas?"

"Go along with whatever Richard asks of you."

She laughed. "No way!"

I shushed her. She really needed to keep her cool, and keep it down, just in case her blue magic was rusty.

"Yes," I whispered. "It's the only way we'll be able to get enough leniency to get you out of here. I think I have an idea. I'm not sure of all the details yet. But when I come for you, you have to trust me and do as I say."

She held my gaze, the silence stretching between us.

"Fine," she finally grumbled and shook her head. "I can't believe I'm agreeing to work with you, of all people."

"Yeah, yeah, I'm such a traitor," I sighed. "And yet, I'm your best chance of getting out of here."

"And what about Christopher and Jessa?"

"I'll try to get him out with you, but I'm not sure about Jessa. Not yet."

What I didn't add was that I was too selfish to let her go. I wasn't sure I could do that, even if part of me had accepted I might have to. I knew getting her out of here would probably be the only way she'd ever forgive me.

But then she'll be gone. What did you expect?

I pushed the thought away to deal with at a later time.

"I need to go now," I said. "If anyone asks about me being in here, tell them I threatened Christopher. That I said you needed to cooperate with my father in exchange for me looking out for your dad."

"Fine." She nodded. I reached out and she dropped the warm stone into my palm. "Good luck, Lucas," she said. "I think you're going to need a lot of it."

I rose and slipped the stone into my pocket. "Me too."

I didn't want to count on something so fleeting as luck, but it was all I had left. I turned back to her just before I reached the door. "One more thing," I said. I could barely make her out in the darkness now.

"What?"

"About my secret," I said. "If I'm going to be able to help you, I'm going to need to keep it *my* secret."

She chuckled sweetly, a stark sound against her ragged appearance. "No kidding."

I smirked and shook my head. "No kidding."

▼

"Are you going to tell her, or should I?" My father leaned back in his chair and smugly placed his boots on the desk between us.

I'd come to him here with my latest idea. His study was filled with books, paperwork stacked neatly on the desk, and a map plastered across the wall. Little pins spread across it. A photo of Mom sat in the corner of one of the shelves and my eyes kept flicking to it, despite my efforts to ignore it. Seriously, being in here with *him* wasn't something I was excited about, but I hoped my idea would help Jessa in the long run. I wasn't sure she'd see it that way, but lately nothing I did would turn her on to my way of thinking anyway.

"Actually, you better tell her." He threw back his head and laughed, gleaming white teeth reflecting the overhead light. "She's going to have to learn that's the way things are going to be in your relationship. You make the rules."

I held in an angry breath but didn't repeat the thoughts brewing inside my head. Richard didn't seem to even notice, or if he did, he didn't care. He just went about his business as usual, plopping his feet back down and returning to his paperwork. I was next in line for this job. Would the power consume me the way it did him? I shoved my hands into my pockets, shaking my head, just watching him.

After a minute, he stood from his oversized oak desk and restacked the already neat pile of papers. He gathered them into his hands, straightening them against the desk with a click.

"What are those?" My curiosity was piqued by the sheer amount of paperwork. I'd seen him labor over paperwork before, but never so much of it.

"The latest reports from the front lines," he replied.

"Anything important?" I asked.

He raised an eyebrow as if carefully considering the question. "Everything was going well, but we're at a bit of a standstill at the moment, neither side making a move. That won't last long."

Of course it wouldn't.

"They'll be expecting a retaliation," I stated, matter-of-factly. They'd attacked us in our palace. Even though they'd failed, it was only logical they would be bracing themselves for the backlash to come.

Even I was bracing for it.

He nodded. "And they're going to get it," he said. "But not in the way they expect."

I raised an eyebrow and waited for him to explain further, but he didn't.

"Go tell Jessa the plan," he said gruffly, changing the subject. "I want to get started on this immediately. Faulk will work out the details."

I stood from the leather chair and left in search of Jessa.

I hated this part. I didn't want to go along with any of this, let alone be the one to orchestrate it, but I had to think of the bigger picture. The endgame.

She was my endgame.

Brushing my balmy hands against the thick denim of my jeans, I willed myself to take on the persona of the old me. She'd liked the old me…

Since when did I care so much about what women thought of me? Since when did I bend over backwards for someone who didn't do the same for me?

Since Jessa, you idiot.

I scowled at my internal battle and knocked on her door with a heavy fist. I was tired of it. Nothing I did would be good enough, so I'd just have to do what I thought was best and hopefully, in the end, she'd finally understand.

"Lucas." Jessa swung open the door. The sound of my name on her lips buried me. Her cheeks flushed pink when her eyes met mine. Her lips quirked before she frowned. I wanted nothing more than to run my hand through her wayward curls.

"Why are you here?" she asked.

And that was the problem. As soon as I saw her, felt her presence, she changed me. The hard exterior I'd built during my walk over fell away in the space of a single glance of her cobalt eyes.

"Can I come in?" I asked.

She drew her eyebrows together but nodded and opened the door wider. A few days ago, she'd been moved back into the royal wing. Even though she was officially a Guardian of Color now, royalty took precedence.

Her suite was one of the nicest in the palace and was just next door to Celia. I hated that Celia was even still here, but my father wouldn't even talk about the matter with me. It pissed me off. After Celia's threat, she had no right to be here.

"Do you want to sit down?" Jessa asked, moving through the room in her usual dancer's way, her limbs long and elegant. She sat in a striped, pale yellow armchair. It matched the rest of the room—a room almost sickly sweet in its decoration. Her black Guardian's uniform stuck out with its practical uniformity.

I settled into the loveseat across from her. "You're not going to like this," I sighed.

She closed her eyes tightly. "Just tell me."

"You're going to start training the other alchemists in red."

Her eyes popped open. "What? How?"

"Well, you're going to try, anyway. You'll show them what you do and help them try to replicate it."

She shook her head slowly from side to side. "I don't think it will work."

"I hope it won't. In fact, I'm betting it won't."

We sat in silence, a silence so thick and awkward and long that a sudden urge to do something drastic overpowered me. *Do something. Kiss her. Yell at her. Something!*

I did nothing. I stared at the floor, like a coward, my hands fisted in my lap.

"Is that all?" she finally asked, her voice tepid. I looked up to find her also staring at the rug like it was the most interesting thing in the world. Like nothing we'd just talked about had an effect on her anymore.

No, that wasn't all! I wanted her to fight with me like I had expected. In the past, if I had come to her and told her she would be doing something she didn't want to do, something as dangerous as this, she would have challenged me. She would have gotten in my space, her eyes sparking, her temper flaring, and I would have met her there. She would have demanded something of me. But today she wanted nothing.

The loss sunk me. First, my mother. And now, Jessa.

"Yeah, that's all," I replied and excused myself from her

room. She didn't bother to watch me leave.

Had she really given up? Was she so done with me in all aspects that she wouldn't even argue with me anymore?

The hurt suffocated me from the inside out. She might be ready to give up on me, but I wasn't ready to give up on her. Or on us. *And when will you be ready?* The question lived in the back of my mind. Despite how many times I buried it, it was still there. Still asking. Still waiting for me to face it.

FOUR
JESSA

Ice crystals crunched under our boots as we ventured outside. I tried to relax into the cold, but couldn't hold back the shivers.

"It can't be that bad, can it?" Callie asked with a friendly laugh as we walked further out onto the patio.

"Are we talking about the cold now or are we still discussing my sad lack of friends here?"

She quirked her lips. "It is that bad."

"Yes, trust me. You're the only alchemist left in this place that still willingly talks to me," I said. "After you saw what the red can do, even I'm surprised. I don't blame the others for avoiding me."

"Hey, it's not your fault." She smiled. A fog had coated her glasses, hiding her caramel-brown eyes. She took them off and rubbed them against her top. "It's not like you made the King do that." She glanced around and then whispered, "That was crazy. And all on him. It wasn't your fault what he *made* you do."

She was right, of course, but I couldn't allow myself to

agree with her.

I bit my lip and looked down into the steaming mug of hot chocolate warming my fingers. I didn't even know what the drink was. I had certainly never tasted it. After Callie had seen me wandering around the GC wing with nothing to do, she'd invited me to try what she called "heaven in liquid form".

But first, she'd said, we would have to take it outside. Apparently, by her logic, I needed to be cold to get the full effect of the hot chocolate's goodness.

"Ready?" she asked, nodding toward our mugs.

My mouth watered as I sniffed the drink. I took a small sip. It stung at first, the liquid hotter against my tongue than I'd expected, but the taste that washed through my mouth was equal parts calming and amazing.

I closed my eyes and let it warm me from the inside out.

"Well," her voice teased. I popped open my eyes and grinned back at her. "What do you think? Good, huh?"

"It's incredible," I said. I wished I'd had something like this growing up. All those snow days, hot chocolate would have been something to make the freezing, wet cold totally worth it. But chocolate wasn't easy to get for my family. Or really, any family that I knew. Our status allowed us enough money to buy the essentials. It was usually those of the Royal Court who had the best jobs and subsequently, the highest quality of life.

"One of the perks of living at the palace," Callie added, as if to make my point.

I nodded. I didn't know what to say to her that wouldn't make me sound ungrateful. The palace was nice. It was beautiful, decadent, filled with magic, and parties, and more food at each meal than I'd ever seen. But I would trade it, hot chocolate and all, for one more normal day with my family.

The winter air that had been nipping at me was starting to eat me alive. "Okay, I'm officially freezing, let's go back inside."

"Wait," Callie said, gripping onto my black coat. "I wanted to ask you a question."

I studied her expression, careful to keep my own relaxed. So, this wasn't about hot chocolate…

"What is it?" I asked.

"There's a lot of rumors going around about you," she said. I sucked in a breath. "Sorry, it's not like that," she rushed to add. "It's just, I wondered if you'd set the record straight for me. Since we're friends and all."

I hoped we were friends. In fact, if we were, she was my only one, at the moment. But that didn't mean I wanted to answer her questions.

Still, I slowly nodded.

"So, okay, you're engaged to Lucas. No surprises there, the guy has been following you around since the day you arrived. But your sister is apparently Sasha—"

"I didn't know about that until pretty much everyone else did," I interjected. I didn't want her to think I was hiding that because I wasn't.

"And then you've got this crazy powerful, albeit terrifying red alchemy thing going on," she continued, her eyes round orbs behind her thick glasses. I looked down on my friend with her wiry blonde hair framing her earnest face. I wanted to trust her, I did, but I was uneasy.

"Yeah, I didn't know about that part either, until pretty recently," I relented.

"Well." She faltered, orb-eyes shifting around us. "I guess I'm wondering if you're actually loyal to the crown. Like, do you even want to be a Guardian? I know you were initiated and all that, but something just doesn't feel right to me, like there's something you're hiding still."

"I don't know what to say to that," I croaked, hoping to sound calm, but I probably sounded guilty. "Of course I want to be a Guardian." My stomach flipped as I forced the lies from my mouth, and suddenly the hot chocolate sloshing around in there didn't seem so amazing.

"Because the thing is," Callie continued, "I wouldn't blame you, you know? That attack on the palace, the one Sasha was caught up in?"

"What about it?" I asked. My eyes flickered away from hers and toward the palace just behind us. This was a dangerous conversation.

"I can't help but wonder if you knew it was going to happen. I mean, the way you reacted when Jasmine died."

The image of Jasmine's blood flashed through my mind, and I fought back the urge to scream.

"You were pretty intense. You really loved her, didn't you? But if she was a traitor, why did you have such a visceral reaction to her death? It's a little confusing." Callie and I were standing side to side now, looking out at the snow-covered lawn. I wanted to shake her! This was not safe. But what choice did I have but to answer?

"She was my teacher and my friend," I replied, my voice faltered. "She killed herself because of what I did." I stepped back. I shouldn't have to explain that to her.

"No." Callie shook her head, turning on me. "She killed herself because she got caught, because she was about to reveal who else was working with her."

Was this how all the alchemists interpreted that night? Just no big deal because Jasmine had turned out to have a traitorous secret?

"What's your point?" I asked.

My body was so still, the cold penetrated deep into my

bones. I wanted to run away, anything but deal with these questions and the burning shame they brought to the surface.

"I think there's more to your story with Jasmine. And the thing is, I don't blame you."

My eyes shot to hers. "Be careful what you say here."

She nodded. "I just want you to know, that if you ever need help with anything, I want to help. If you know something more about what happened to Jasmine, or who she was working for, you can tell me. It's something I've been wondering about for a long time."

I held back the urge to nod, to pull her into a tight hug and tell her everything. Unloading these secrets would be such a relief. But I couldn't.

Reed had been a spy.

Even my old maid, Eliza, had been sent to spy on me.

Sasha was actually Frankie. Lucas was actually an alchemist.

No, I can't tell her. I barely know the girl.

I cleared my throat and rocked back on my heels. "I don't know what you're talking about," I said. "Let's go inside. It's too cold out here."

She sighed, her eyes sparked with disbelief, but she followed when I turned away. Her energy, a static curiosity, circled me as we walked back to the dining hall to return our empty mugs. She wasn't giving up on her theory, whatever her motives. And I was left to worry that either way, if she really did want to be part of the Resistance, or if she was another one of Faulk's spies, I was about to lose my only friend here.

▼

Their eyes followed me as I entered the classroom. The flurry of quiet whispers that followed was like an unexpected gust of wind. The other alchemists had seen me as a threat, at first. But their fear had settled over time and just when I'd started to fit in here, I'd shown them what I was truly capable of. It was no wonder they went right back to hating me.

I was so alone; even Callie couldn't fill the void. And Lucas, he left me loneliest of all. He was always around, escorting me to dinners with his father and their friends, helping with the wedding planning, checking in on the ballet classes. But yet he was farther away than ever. He wanted me to forgive him, to force his way into my life, but it wasn't that simple.

I sighed and found my seat in the classroom, keeping my head down. The industrial room had orderly desks pushed together in pods. I was sitting in an empty pod, well aware that everywhere else was filled with cliques of alchemists. Most of the classes had people my age, but today there was a mix of ages in the room. I ignored the awkward loneliness inside and stared at the row of crystals and potted plants on the far wall.

Someone audibly cleared their throat. I looked up to meet Faulk's impenetrable eyes.

"Did you not hear me the first time, Loxely?" she asked with a sneer that curled her thin upper lip.

I shook my head. "Sorry," I mumbled.

"Get up," she growled. "Have you not prepared anything for today?"

I blinked, confused. "Huh?"

"Figures," she huffed. "Lucas said he told you but who really knows with that boy. We never should have trusted him to get the job done when he treats you like you're made of tissue paper."

"What are you talking about?"

Her blonde hair was pulled back in her usual bun, enhancing the sharpness of her cheekbones. Her white uniform gleamed as she stalked to the front of the simple classroom. "I said get up," she barked over her shoulder.

It was Monday afternoon. We always worked on blue on Monday afternoons. Even if most of us couldn't do much of anything with it, we were still expected to try. I'd never had much luck with blue, but that didn't warrant her yelling at me. Blue was rare.

I stood to face her, and she spun on me with a look of complete annoyance, like I was the dumbest person she'd ever met.

Well, geez, nice to see you, too!

"You're starting your lesson on red alchemy today," Faulk said. "Or did you forget already?"

My stomach flopped. "That's today?" Lucas had warned me, but he said Faulk was supposed to let me know the details first.

"Yes, it's today. Did you not get the date?" She grinned slowly.

I scowled. What did I expect from Faulk? She was enjoying my discomfort.

Didn't matter. She obviously wasn't going to wait for me to tell her my *legitimate* excuse because she turned and continued her angry tirade. "If you're not prepared to teach red alchemy, then I'll have to help you along, won't I?"

I swallowed. Was she serious? Last thing we needed was that sadistic woman pushing us into attempting anything to do with red. I reminded myself to play nicely with Faulk. That would piss her off more than challenging her, which had to be the reason why she'd sprung this on me. But a little planning would have been nice.

"What did you have in mind?" I asked and shifted to face

the alchemists sitting in the room. There were about forty, all ages, but two of the youngest children sat in the front row, gaping up at me. My hands began to sweat. I didn't want to let anyone down. But I also didn't want anyone to learn red alchemy. I wouldn't curse this magic on my worst enemy.

"Let's start with a question and answer period, shall we?"

I shrugged, and several keen hands shot into the air.

I pointed to the youngest of the lot.

"Hi, Jessa. I'm Charity." The child smiled. She reminded me of Lacey, and my heart dropped. "I was wondering if it's just blood that you can use, or have you tried other reds?" Her tiny voice was so sure, and her eyes lifted in complete fascination.

"No, I haven't been able to get anything besides blood to work," I replied. "I've tried, but it's just blood that has power so far."

She nodded enthusiastically, and I forced her into my peripheral vision to call on another raised hand. To think that a child wanted my power, my horribly damaging power, made me want to run far, far away from this classroom. I blinked and tried to focus on the next question.

"What do you feel when you do it?" a boy about my age asked. "When you make someone do something like that, make them do what you say, what does that feel like?"

I carefully considered the question. The kid's black, shaggy hair hung in his hooded eyes, but I could make out the sparkle of anticipation in them just the same. I recognized him, we'd been in several classes together, and he'd once teased me about dating Lucas before we'd been official.

"It feels amazing," I answered honestly, "but also, it feels terrible. Scary. Like I'm not actually in control of anything."

His smile quirked, the desire to learn red rose in him, like this power was our drug. And for him, red alchemy would be the ultimate fix to satiate his addiction. I shivered. Not because he scared me, but because sometimes, I scared myself.

"That's enough for now," Faulk said, stepping to the center of the room. "Let's try it, shall we? Everyone grab a partner, a dagger, and a plant." She motioned to the wall of tools. "I want you to take turns trying to pull the red from each other's blood, healing when necessary."

The room buzzed with activity as the students set out to work. I stood on the edge, arms crossed over my stomach, half worried someone would succeed. After several rounds of the alchemists' failed attempts, however, I began to relax. No one was even close, and the blood was beginning to get messy. I hoped this would be over quickly. I watched the minutes on the clock as they ticked away. The frustration was growing within each person, only a small mirror to that of Faulk's. I forced myself to appear neutral.

When class was scheduled to end and nobody left, I began to get antsy. I found myself making eye contact with Faulk and frowning.

"That's enough!" Faulk finally snapped. "That's all for today, we'll try again next week." Then she strode over to me, her boots clipping on the polished concrete. "You better come prepared next time," she snapped. "Better have something to offer us." Then she stormed from the room, slamming the door behind her.

Maybe you should have told me about the proper time and place and I would have done that today, you stubborn cow!

My body eased, and I hurried toward the door. *So glad that's over.*

"She's right, you know," someone called out over the stir of conversation. I turned to face the boy who'd questioned me about what red felt like. Silence descended as every pair of eyes locked on me. He continued, his voice dark and filled with the same frustration that had built over the course of the lesson. "You need to try harder, Jessa. If you don't, we'll wonder why you're so selfish."

I froze, shame gluing me to the spot.

Then he added, "No one wants to bow down to a narcissistic queen."

The edges of my vision blurred red, and the anger filled me so completely, I felt as if I would explode. Why was I feeling sorry for myself, trying to fit in with these people?

He was being selfish, here.

"What's your name?" I asked.

"Dax." He stood.

"Well, Dax," I said coolly, walking closer, "next time I sit down to dinner with my future family, I'll be sure to mention your concerns to the King. I'm sure he'll be delighted to know all about the alchemist blaming the future queen for his own failure."

His face stilled, bright red, as he glowered. I regretted the come-back immediately. It wasn't me.

"You think you're better than us," he replied darkly, reaching out and putting his hand on my upper arm.

I shook him off of me immediately. "You have no idea what I think, so don't pretend to know the first thing about me."

So, why don't you enlighten me, Jessa. His voice echoed through my head. My eyes flashed to the purple stone strung to a black leather cord around his neck. I stepped back. Purple Alchemy…rare. I hadn't met many who could do it. But this was a challenge, a show of his own power.

He can only hear what I want him to hear. He shook his straight black hair out of his face and smirked. How far did his power go?

"No," I said forcefully, then turned and marched from the room.

▼

You shouldn't have goaded him on like that!

I groaned and fell back against my mattress. All I wanted to do was crawl into a little ball and hide under the thick comforter for the rest of eternity. *Okay, but that lesson had actually gone great.* Nobody had shown an ounce of ability in red alchemy. Letting that guy get the best of me had been the one downfall.

I rolled over and stared at the yellow wallpaper. It was hideous, truly.

Okay, it wasn't hideous by everyone's standards. Just mine. Someone probably thought it was beautiful, but to me, it was not only my least favorite color, it reminded me of where I was. It was way too fancy. Of all the rooms I'd stayed in, the dorms had probably been the best. My room there had been nondescript, simple. This one was dripping in the trappings of royalty.

Not to mention how I was next door to Celia. I saw her more than I wanted lately. She'd always smile at me sweetly, but her eyes were daggers and she never said a word. I was bracing myself for some twisted form of retaliation.

So far? Nothing. And that didn't make a whole lot of sense. Maybe she was only here to spy? Maybe she was waiting for me to disappear so she could get Lucas back? There was nothing for her to wait on, not really. The Resistance, what was left of it, hadn't made contact with me since Jasmine died. I was merely surviving until the day I'd be married off.

There's got to be something I can do to get out of here.

I needed to think. I needed to stop feeling sorry for

myself, stop complaining, and start making a plan. That's what Jasmine would have done. That's probably what Sasha *was* doing, even in her terrible circumstance.

My father was practically locked in his room, but at least we'd been permitted to visit each other. I'd gone to see him every evening after dinner, and tonight was no exception.

He let me in his room and wrapped his arms around me in a tight hug. "You're bored out of your mind in here, aren't you?" I said as we went to lounge on the couch.

He shrugged. "They gave me some books to occupy my time. If I mind my business, Faulk said I'd get more of a role in your life here."

"You trust her?"

He shook his head, his smile faltering. "Nope. She makes me nervous."

I needed a plan for both of us. I stood and paced the room. His was an exact copy to mine, just in navy instead of yellow.

"What's going through that head of yours, Jessa?"

I shrugged and plopped back down onto the sofa.

The plan had to be kept secret from him. I knew there were royal officers always outside the door. I glanced around the room, past the built-in bookshelf, the thick rug, and the huge picture window, my eyes landing on the potted plant in the corner.

"Practice," I breathed.

"What?"

"I need more practice."

Today, Faulk had made the alchemists practice something they didn't know how to do. Granted, it hadn't worked, but that was common in *all* my alchemy lessons. We practiced, day in and day out. We tried over and over again to master all kinds of magics that seemed impossible. But we did it anyway. We tried. And sometimes, we got better.

Sometimes, we discovered *new* abilities.

"That's what I've been missing," I said, looking back to Dad.

His eyes narrowed. "What are you talking about?"

I leaned over and closed the space between us, hugging him. His familiar woodsy scent washed over me. I pulled back and met his gaze.

"I gotta go," I said. I kissed him on the cheek. "I'll see you tomorrow."

Before he could argue, I sprinted from the room, out in the hall, and back to my own suite. This wasn't something I was ready to do in front of anybody, even my Dad.

Sure enough, the identical potted plant stood tall in the corner of my room, as well. "Hello there," I whispered, kneeling on the floor at its base.

There was something unique about me besides red. All the focus had been on red, but what about that other thing I had done all those months ago?

The memory rushed back. Dancing on that stage, when I'd had so little control over what was happening to me, I'd done more than just access purple alchemy. I'd separated the color into its primary colors—red and blue.

How had I done that? And more importantly, *what did it do?*

As far as I knew, nobody understood it. But what if that kind of magic was even more important than red alchemy? If I could figure it out without anyone else knowing, I might be able to use it to get us out of here. Lucas had done the same with white, another mysterious alchemy.

I picked a long, smooth leaf. It snapped from the stem. Then I split it between my fingernails, the green color oozed out and into the air in the space of a heartbeat. The swirling magic twisted into the air like thick smoke, eager for instruction. Normally, I would send it to heal someone, but instead I imagined the color separating.

Yellow and blue. Come on, yellow and blue.

Nothing happened.

I sighed as the color dissolved into a mist. Ruined. There was no salvaging a leaf that had the color stripped away.

I went to the closet and rifled through the garments, my eye out for something purple. Spotting something workable, I removed a dress from its hanger. It was made of silk, slipping through my fingers. I considered the material, knowing it would be harder to manipulate this way than if I had a plant to work with. But I'd done it before. I could do it again. I made a quick mental note to get a rainbow stone necklace as soon as possible. Now that I was officially a Guardian of Color, I was pretty sure I could get myself one without any problems.

Moving to my bed, I held the shiny fabric on my lap. I willed something to happen, but the magic wouldn't answer my call. I laid back with a huff. What was I missing?

I remembered that performance and the dance. I focused on each move, reciting it all in my mind's eye. Connecting with the passion, with life-purpose—that's what purple was all about. I allowed that passion to overwhelm me as I imagined the dance over and over. My muscles knew the movements by memory, and I ached to move. A tear leaked from the side of my eye.

Still, I missed it. The thrill of performance, the natural way I felt on the stage. It felt like home.

I blinked, forcing the tears away. *Get a grip, Jessa.*

Just above my body, the purple swirled in clouds of iridescent magic. I gasped and sat up, allowing it to envelop me.

The purple urged me forward, to reach out and connect.

Could I connect with someone's mind again? Or maybe I could even do what Lily had; maybe I could use it to predict my future.

But instead, I imagined the colors separating into blue and red.

Unlike the green, the purple opened up in an instant. The color seemed to relax as it shifted into a bold cobalt blue and a fiery red. I reached out, willing the new colors to do *something*. I wasn't quite sure what, as I'd never gotten to color this way. This magic was different. It buzzed in a frenzy, as if it were restless.

When the red touched my fingers, it zinged away from me and vanished. I grabbed at the blue and the same thing happened.

Why can't I touch it?

A tide of exhaustion overwhelmed me, like a heavy flood pouring over my body. I blinked, fighting it, but there was no use. It pulled me under.

I almost had it! The excitement inside drowned, my body succumbing to the need for sleep.

Practice. I held the thought in my mind as my eyes closed.

I'll practice again tomorrow.

FIVE
SASHA

My soul longed for magic.

So, when I woke to a clicking at the door, I assumed it was my restless imagination and rolled back over to the comfort of sleep.

"Hey, wake up," a voice whispered against my ear.

I flipped over and shot my hand out into the darkness. Nobody was there.

Okay, now I'm really losing my mind.

I had been so bored in this drab prison, that it wasn't the first time my mind had played tricks on me. The ebb of sleep nudged at me again.

"It's me," the voice said. "It's Lucas."

I sat up, blinking against the darkness. My mind was foggy, but I was sure I'd heard something that time. I squinted. Still, nobody.

"White alchemy, remember."

I shook my head, annoyed for not catching on quicker. White alchemy. A magic no one else had, that I was aware of, except for Lucas. He had used it to make our entire helicopter invisible once. The magic had both shocked and relieved me. I'd always wondered if white had power, and the shielding magic made sense to my logical side.

"What is it?" I asked, clearing my throat from the sleep. I'd been out like a light, the kind of sleep so heavy it felt like swimming through quicksand to wake up.

"Here," he handed me the blue stone and I immediately used it to shield our conversation from the possibility of listening ears.

"Okay." I sat up and stretched my neck. "We're good."

"I'm going to stay invisible. I think it's going to be safer that way."

I stood and stretched my legs. "Out with it, Lucas," I sighed.

"It's time to get you out of here," he said. My senses kicked into overdrive, the buzz of adrenaline shooting through my veins.

"Let's do it."

"I've been invisible since I left my bedroom, so nobody should have been able to follow me down here. I'm going out on a huge limb to get you out of here, I think you understand that."

"I do. I promise, I'll keep your secret safe. Now, are you going to turn me invisible with you or what?"

"At the right time, yes," he said, his voice soft in the darkness. "Security isn't as tight tonight. My father has the first exhibition planned for the morning and most of the officers are currently en route. He and I are flying out first thing tomorrow."

"So what's the plan?" I asked.

"There's no time to explain. Just follow my lead."

Oh, that sounds awesome! "Okay, fine."

"And Sasha," he said, "I might need you to try red alchemy

again."

I froze. I hadn't done it since breaking free of New Colony years ago. I wasn't even sure I could do it now, but even if I could, I didn't want to! "You've got to be kidding."

"Do you want to die in here or what?" he snapped. I couldn't see him, but I could imagine his face as his frustration grew. "We don't have to tell anyone about your red. But if you want out of here and if you want to go find your friends, you're going to have to get over it and do what needs to be done."

"Fine," I snapped back, partly knowing he was right, the bigger part of me hoping I could prove him wrong. I wouldn't use red unless I absolutely had to. If red even worked!

"Let's get you outside and then we'll use invisibility to travel together to wherever you want to go."

"We have a Resistance safe house not far from here," I said. "Get me there and I can do the rest."

"Let's go."

"What about Christopher and Jessa?" I asked. He was silent for a long moment and my stomach flipped. "We have to help them, too," I pleaded, worried about what the silence might mean.

"I know," he said, "and I wanted to, but unfortunately my father insisted they joined him at the exhibition. They left earlier tonight."

"What?" I sputtered. How did he think *now* was a good time for me to go then?

As if reading my mind, he answered, "I'll try to get them out later, I promise. But for right now, this is the best chance I have at helping you. Even Faulk is gone. Most of the officers and alchemists have left as well. It's now or never, Sasha."

I almost corrected him. *It's Frankie.* But I just nodded and walked to the door, steeling myself but ready to do this.

"There's only one guard outside right now, with security

being what it is at the moment. I'm going to open the door," he said, "and I want you to take him out. It should be easy; considering he's asleep at the job. I had no problem lifting the keys off him five minutes ago."

I huffed. *Idiots.* If I were running this place, I'd have the alchemists guarding the cells, not morons. Faulk was going to be so angry. She just might lose her job over this. But still, only one guard? Something about that didn't seem right.

Lucas placed a hand on my back and I nearly jumped. "Here, I have more," he said, opening my hand and dropping a gemstone necklace in my palm. It had all the colors I would need. I quickly strung it around my neck. "I'm ready."

He swung the door wide with a bang, and the guard jumped up, blinking the sleep from his long face. I recognized him as the one who'd spit at me.

"How'd you do that?" he asked gruffly.

I didn't answer and I certainly didn't give him a chance to make the first move. I attacked. I'd been training in combat for practically as long as I could remember. It kicked in without a second thought. I charged him and brought him to the ground, then punched him right in the nose. The shifting crack of bone made me smirk but didn't slow me down. I continued the pay back for all those times he'd stood idly by while someone did the same thing to me.

He didn't even get a chance to retaliate as the yellow alchemy flowed through me. The magic was a sensation akin to coming home, so familiar and calming, the magic sweeping through me like warm water. I smiled, administered one perfect blow to the guard, and sprightly stepped over his slumped-over body.

"Remind me not to piss you off," Lucas's voice whispered, and I laughed. The guard would have a terrible headache and some intense bruising, but he'd live.

"Where to?" I asked.

The next several minutes we navigated our way through the dark palace, our footsteps soft. As we came near the entrance of the prison, I jumped into action and quickly took out the two guards. Up the stairs, we slowed at the first corner. There was always someone awake in a building like this, so we had to tread lightly, especially near the kitchens and laundry. The low rumble of nightshift worker's conversation, clang of dishes, and hum of machines did little to calm my pounding heart.

"This way," Lucas whispered and, "right" "now, left" were my only indication of where to go. At one point I had to jump back into a dark alcove as a few palace guests passed, and a minute later, a guard on patrol. But it wasn't long until Lucas and I were on the main level next to the gardens, a door unlocked and waiting.

No red alchemy needed, thank you very much.

We broke out into the cold night, the snow falling in heavy flakes. The cold immediately seized me but I didn't mind. I grinned and reached out to let a snowflake melt on my fingertip. The frigid air smelled like freedom.

"Over here." Lucas grabbed my arm and pulled me to the side of the palace where the gardens grew thick in the summer. Now it was all sharp angles, the trees devoid of life. He pried open a gardening bin where he'd stashed some boots and a huge black coat. The area was quiet and still, as was his voice. "Get these on and then I need to make you invisible, too."

He didn't have to ask twice.

"Do you have enough energy for that?" I asked. He'd struggled with the helicopter and no way was I making out with him to keep him awake. Any misguided feelings I'd had for the prince were long gone. *Where's Jessa when we need her?*

"I've been practicing and I can go up to three hours by myself. With you invisible, too? I think I can half it. I hope that's enough time to get you to the safe house and to get me back to my room before I have to be up for my flight."

It was jarring not to be able to see his expression, not to be able to see him at all. I could feel his presence, hear his steady breath, and even smell his clean scent. But not to be able to see him left me feeling a tad skittish.

"That's enough time." I nodded, trying to relax. I hoped I wasn't about to make a huge mistake. Trusting Lucas could be the last thing I do. Maybe I could take him out and go on my own, but that was also a huge risk. "It's actually pretty close."

"Of course it is," he mumbled, then reached out to take my hand. "I really hope my father doesn't figure that out one day."

"You're telling me," I replied, distracted. My body, with its gray prison clothes and now, black puffy coat, was turning into nothing but air. As I faded, the panic began to rise. I shook my head. *Unbelievable! I really need to practice white.*

"Is this why you insisted we wait to do this outside, just to be certain nobody saw me go invisible?"

"Yes," he said. "Now, let's go." His cold hand squeezed mine, and together we ran headfirst into the storm.

▼

Sharp guilt twisted in my chest as we trudged through the wet snow. Bringing Lucas to the safe house was never part of the deal I'd made with the Resistance. Especially after he'd abandoned the cause. And even more so after he'd turned on Jessa and ruined our plans. The streetlights cast disapproving shadows across the city streets, a stark contrast to the darkened alleyways. I'd considered ditching him in more than a few of those alleys. But the closer we got to the address, the more I realized I couldn't do that to Lucas. He'd helped me and was still helping me. The urban skyline gave way to the first of many neighborhoods, and it was too late to change my mind. We'd arrived.

I approached the yellow door, centered on the redbrick house, two square windows on either side. The layout reminded me of a smile. It was a small craftsman, in keeping with the neighborhood, old, but well kept. I longed for "what might have been" as I looked at it, but shook the thought away. The Resistance would rise up again.

Right now? It's time to focus so that it has a chance to happen.

The elderly woman who lived there was named Sally. Jasmine had recruited her and her late husband. I'd had her address imprinted on my brain for a few years, hoping I'd never have to use it. Knowing, realistically, I would.

A prickle of doubt peaked the closer we got to the quaint home. What if this was a trap? What if I'd told Faulk about this place already, sometime during that interrogation with Jessa?

We continued up the short drive, the night silent as a dream. Our feet crunching against the snow, our breathing heavy, as the emotions continued to rage.

The porch light flicked on, illuminating the falling snow. We froze.

"Motion sensors," Lucas whispered.

I inwardly cursed and bit my lip. The wind had started to pick up, and my jacket was quickly losing its warmth. I shivered, no longer enchanted by the snowfall. I peered around. There still wasn't a soul out on the streets, just as there hadn't been the entire journey over. Our long tracks that were left in the snow had quickly been swept away by the storm.

"Come on." I tugged him up the steps. I knocked three slow knocks then two quick ones on the yellow door.

We hunched together, still invisible. I felt Lucas's energy begin to fade. No surprise as to why he'd slowed his pace significantly in the last few minutes, his footsteps lagging, his body leaning on mine. He needed to get back and get some rest. Morning would be here before we knew it and there couldn't be an ounce of suspicion against him.

The old woman opened the door, squinting into the night. Her bathrobe wrapped around her, pink and fuzzy, large circular glasses sat atop her nose giving her an owlish stare. Wrinkles lined every inch of her pale face in deep lines of age.

"Are you Sally?" I asked.

She startled, her mouth popping open. "Who's there?"

"Are you Sally?" I repeated, louder this time.

Her eyes grew wide, and she nodded, taking off her glasses and putting them back on again, blinking several times. "Yes, I'm Sally."

I took a deep breath. "I'm a friend of Jasmine's. I'm with the Resistance."

She began to turn her head from side to side, peering out into the darkness, obviously trying to locate the source of my voice.

"I'm going back now," Lucas whispered in my ear. Before I had a chance to react, he released my hand. Immediately, my body returned to visibility. Sally yelped.

"Are my eyes playing tricks on me?" she asked shakily. "I didn't see you there."

I decided not to explain.

"Can I come in?" I asked, eager to get off the street as quickly as possible. I lifted my arm to shield the porch light from my face and tucked my head down.

"Of course, dear," she cooed. "You're a friend of Jasmine's? Poor thing, I heard what happened to her. Such a shame. Just tragic. Come in, come in."

I stepped into the warmth of her home and shut the door behind me. Her front room was small and cozy with matching red furniture and the remnants of a fire in the hearth. The whole place smelled faintly of sugar and butter, like she baked regularly. All of these clues, and the proximity to the palace, pegged her as a wealthy woman. She was old now, but either she, or her late husband, must have been assigned high-level jobs before hitting mandatory retirement age. She shuffled ahead, her slippers cupping her tiny feet, as she led me into her kitchen.

"What's your name?" she asked.

I didn't hesitate. What would be the point? "Sasha, or Frankie, I guess."

"You guess?" She chuckled. "Well, Sasha Frankie, let's go get you something to eat. I think you'll be pleased with the company. You're not my only visitor tonight."

The kitchen was filled with white cabinets, a white and black tiled floor with a square oak dining table right in the center. My heart slammed in my chest as my eyes settled on the man sitting there, his body taking up the space with his familiar height. He looked up with black sparkling eyes and stood with a smile spread across his face. The chair tipped backward as a moment later his towering frame enveloped me into a tight hug.

Suddenly, the world, tipped off its axis, righted itself.

"Tristan," I breathed, the oxygen about all squeezed out of me. "What are you doing here?" Tears prickled.

He stepped back and looked me over, up and down several times. He then peeled off my heavy, now dripping, coat and ran his steady hands along my rib cage. My body purred against his touch. "Are you okay?" he asked, his smile thinning into a grim line. "What did they do to you?"

"The wounds have all been healed," I replied, "if that's what you're asking."

"I'm so sorry." He choked on the words. "I never should have left you there."

"It's okay." I glanced away, not wanting to go into the details of how they'd tortured me. "I'm okay."

"Did they hurt you?"

I guffawed at the question. "What do you think?"

When our eyes met, his were brimming with hatred. "I'll kill them."

The silence spread between us. Sally cleared her throat. "I'll just go hang this up." She peeled the coat from his hands and waddled from the room.

We sat at the table, the wooden chair catching my weary body. Letting out a tired sigh, I frowned at Tristan. Excitement made way for confusion. "What are you doing here?" I asked the question again.

"I came back for you," he said, leaning close to slide a warm hand down my arm. "I just got here a few hours ago, actually. I was going to find a way to get you out of there."

I shook my head, staring at him in disbelief. "You wouldn't have been able to."

"I had to try." He shrugged. "You'd have done the same."

He was right. I would have. I leaned my head against his shoulder for a minute, breathing him in. His arm flexed as he nudged me closer.

"Thank God, you're okay." His breath burned against my temple. "How did you get out?"

I sighed, sitting back up. "Lucas helped me."

He squinted at me, shook his head, and ran his hand through his hair, as he thought it over. I caught the scent of a fresh shower and it took everything in me not to climb into his lap and melt into him right there. "I honestly didn't think he was still on our side."

"Guess so," I replied. "Though, I do wonder if he has help that he didn't tell me about. He got me out of there pretty seamlessly."

"What do you mean?"

"Maybe there's still Resistance at the palace. Maybe they followed him, helped him get me out somehow? I don't know, sounds stupid when I say it out loud."

"There is still Resistance at the palace," Tristan interjected.

"Who?" I wracked my brain. Jasmine had been my contact, but surely there were others.

"I only know one personally, a trainee when I was in Royal Officer school."

I shrugged. I'd never met anyone like that through Jasmine.

My limbs still shook from the mix of adrenaline and cold. That funny sensation of being light-headed was creeping in. I closed my eyes, pushing it away. "Lucas was the reason we failed before," I said. "He's the reason the King knew we were coming. Jessa told him about the plans and he told his father. She's furious with him, and I guess he thinks helping her family out will make things better between them."

"Fat chance." Tristan whistled.

I laughed, but didn't say more. I didn't want to get into it. Lucas was in deep and he had to find his own way out. But that was his problem. I had my own to contend with, starting with the obvious.

"So what's the plan?" I asked. "How do we get out of here? Actually, first, explain how you ended up here?"

"Don't get mad." Tristan raised his hands and leaned back in the chair. He'd been holding my freezing hands in his warm, rough palms, and the release of them left mine aching. "When we got back to the camp we evacuated immediately. Mastin led the group out and I chose to travel back here on foot."

I gaped at him, lips parting and shame flashing through me. "You traveled by foot in the winter? Through the shadow lands? How?"

A journey like that was absolutely crazy. What had he been thinking? He could have been killed. *Should* have been killed. The shadow lands were a barren wasteland, not to mention, everyone in New Colony was on the lookout because of the war.

He only shrugged. "I packed plenty of food and water and I know how to take care of myself. The shadow lands were a little tricky but I managed to make it out all right."

I ground down on my teeth, breathing in slowly. "You could have died." Saying it aloud only caused the fear inside to grow. He should have never taken that risk.

"And you could have died in that prison," he replied as he squeezed my hands. "I will never leave you behind again. I'm always going to look out for you." He added, "Don't you know that about me by now?"

My heart leapt in my chest. It was true. Starting when I was only a gangly preteen kid, he'd gotten out of New Colony with Hank, and at the last minute, he'd risked everything to bring me along. He didn't even know me then, and yet he'd recognized the torment I carried with me. He'd saved me.

I let the image of him trekking through the shadow lands to sink in. The cold bitter air, the barren landscape, the snowstorms. It had to have been a couple of weeks since that night we'd been separated. He must be far more exhausted than I was after completing something so reckless.

"Let's get some rest," I said, "then we'll figure out how to get out of here."

"I have to make contact with Mastin," he said. He was wearing a black hooded sweatshirt with a pocket on the front. He rummaged around it to pull out an industrial-looking slatebook. He held it up. Military grade. And not ours. "I have a secure line to communicate with him. He said he could help us out of New Colony once we're ready. We even have a location picked out."

Wow, my boys had planned all this just for me? I grinned, glad that I hadn't been forgotten.

"Where are we going?" I asked, thinking of camp. My heart still ached to know it was long gone now. I could never go back.

"West America," he said. "We have asylum. It's too dangerous for us here."

"He's right." Sally waddled back into the room. "You two are welcome to stay with me but there will be a kingdom-wide search for you soon enough." She pointed at me, her eyes alight with mischief. "You broke out of that palace, Missy, and that makes you a fugitive."

She didn't say more, just busied herself making a pot of tea, as if it was no big deal that she was entertaining what was left of the Resistance.

"I'll let Mastin know we want to be picked up as soon as possible," he said. "We're going to have to travel on foot tomorrow to get to the drop point. It's not safe in the capitol city, for obvious reasons."

As if any of this is safe.

We sat in silence for a few minutes, listening to the teakettle. First the buzz of water boiling, and then the high-pitched whistle as the steam built inside. I felt like that teakettle, like I too was about to burst open.

"You ought to head out tomorrow. The snow will keep most people inside and the exhibition is happening down south. That's a pretty good distraction if you ask me." Sally said with a cackle. She smiled conspiratorially and joined us at the table, placing piping-hot mugs in front of us with a soft thud. The sweet scent of lavender and chamomile filled the air. I took a deep breath and wrapped my shaking hands around the mug. I needed to relax, really think this through.

As much as it terrified me, Sally was right. Tomorrow was our best chance.

I nodded, meeting her honey eyes, and took a long sip. I allowed everything to sink in just as the hot tea warmed my thawing body. "Tomorrow it is. We'll leave at first light."

▼

I should have known it wouldn't be easy. Getting out of the palace was simpler than I would have imagined. Tristan already being at the safe house was the last thing I'd expected to find there. But life wasn't easy, and I knew better than to assume luck was on our side. I leaned back against the seat and gripped the seatbelt strap that cut across my chest.

Our truck ambled along the snow-packed road. My heart raced at every turn, sure that we were going to hit ice and lose control. Tristan kept his eyes glued in front of him and his hand squeezing my knee. Somehow the torturous snow had become our salvation.

"How are you doing back there?" Jerry asked.

"Just fine," I muttered.

Tristan was more amicable, as was his way. He leaned forward, his face right behind Jerry's left shoulder. "Hanging in there. How much longer?"

"Oh, I'd say another hour, at least." Jerry was a weathered man. He had cracked knuckles and calloused hands from years of manual labor. He was also an old friend to Sally, and an ally to the Resistance.

"Good man." Tristan patted the back of Jerry's seat before sinking down into the cracked bench seat where we'd hunkered down for the journey. It was slow going, the snow picking up every now and then, flying past our window. As soon as it would start, it would stop, but that did little to relieve my stress. The roads were beyond anything I'd driven on before.

Sally had been able to connect with Jerry as soon as we'd made our decision to meet Mastin at the drop point. The hardest part of our journey had been the walk. We'd had to amble through the city streets for two miles. Public transport would have been simple, but that wasn't an option, so it was on foot to meet Jerry and hope he turned out to be someone we could trust.

The three of us had been in the pickup for four hours, Jerry at the wheel. There wasn't a lot of chitchat. Not because we didn't have anything to say, I could have talked Tristan's ear off. It was Jerry. I didn't know him. He was a necessary evil, someone I didn't want to let in on any extra information. Not to mention, the terrible roads kept my anxiety at maximum level. Tristan seemed to handle it like a pro, but me? I was jumpy and stiff all at the same time. It made my stomach ball into a tight knot by the time Jerry pulled off the road.

"This is it," he said. "These are the coordinates you gave me."

"Thanks man," Tristan said.

"Good luck."

Tristan swung open the door with a loud squeak and we jumped out of the tall truck. Our boots sunk into the snowdrifts, the cold wrapped over us once again, and we trudged into an open field. There was nothing here but snow.

Jerry didn't wait. With a quick salute and nod, he backed his truck around and drove away. The fumes of exhaust were all that was left, and soon, even that was gone.

We huddled close and waited. *What if they don't make it? What if we freeze to death out here?* The thoughts circled my mind like vultures.

Something faint sounded in the distance. A thudding echo.

"There!" Tristan pointed to a black speck in the otherwise white sky.

The West American chopper came in fast and low, until it was right above us. A door slid open and a ladder rolled out in uneven movements, the end landing at our feet. The noise of the rudder screamed through the landscape as I took the ladder first, Tristan close behind. We toppled into the belly of the chopper and a bulky soldier slid the door closed behind us.

"Ready to go?" he yelled.

We nodded and fell back into the seats, strapping our harnesses as the helicopter swooped up and away.

It was all so easy. Again, I should have known better.

I sat next to Tristan, my head resting on his warm shoulder, watching the landscape fly by in a stream of endless white. There were two other men, West American soldiers, and a pilot up front. They'd introduced themselves, but I'd quickly forgotten their names, too overcome with exhaustion to retain much. My body was still cold, and now that the anxiety of the day was melting away, the heat of my nerves was easing as well.

Mastin isn't here. I studied the thought in my mind, turning it over. Why did it bother me so much? Why did I care that he hadn't come along?

My stomach gave a little tug. It was stupid. Not important. He had other things to do and these guys were certainly capable. They'd picked us up on time, hadn't they? Still, the thought bothered me. And it bothered me that it bothered me!

Something pinged off the side of the chopper with a clatter.

"What was that?" I asked, but before anyone could answer, it happened again, louder.

One of the two men next to us drooped forward, blood pouring from the side of his face. Or...what was left of his face. Adrenaline flared through me as I scrambled to undo my safety restraint.

Gunfire!

"Get down," Tristan yelled. Not that I had a choice, he was practically on top of me, pushing me to the bed of the chopper.

"We've got a tail," the remaining soldier called out to the pilot.

"Hold on," the pilot yelled back. The chopper took a deep swerve to the left and dipped, knocking us all off balance. The pilot moved us even lower to the ground in a quick move that sent my stomach flying.

The moment we steadied, Tristan rolled off of me and reached for the guns strapped above the seats. He tossed one to me, and we scrambled to the back, around the slumped body. The remaining soldier had already opened the back window. He hunched over a gun much than ours, firing a barrage of bullets at our enemy. Army trained, the soldier maneuvered the thing like it was an extension of his body. An ounce of comfort warmed me, but I pushed it away. Tristan and I readied ourselves on either side of him.

Just behind us, a New Colony fighter jet zoomed in and

out of our wake.

We were in big trouble.

Still, I waited for the perfect opportunity.

When it came, I didn't hesitate. I pulled my trigger and let out a round of ammunition. It ducked, slowed a fraction, before gaining speed.

"Oh, hell no!" The soldier let loose a string of profanities as he let his firearm loose on the jet.

Ping. Another bullet flew through our machine. The man next to me collapsed, his gun still firing. Tristan jumped on top of him to get ahold of the weapon. I continued to shoot, but something seemed off about this whole thing.

"Shouldn't they just be trying to bomb us?" I asked. "Kill us all?"

"Not if their orders are to bring you back alive," Tristan growled.

Horror flashed through me.

"We have backup on the way," the pilot hollered back. "ETA one minute. Hang in there."

We glanced at each other, eyes wide, hair blowing wildly in the freezing wind. It was them or it was us, and I wasn't ready to die, nor was I ready to lose Tristan. He gripped the huge gun and pressed the trigger. His muscles fired along with the bullets as he followed the path of the jet. I pressed my body even further to the cold metallic surface and steadied my gun again; one eye closed as I took aim. As I shot, my mind returned to the man beside me. He was splattered with blood across his face from the other fallen men, and I thanked God he hadn't been the one in their place. I didn't even know if I believed in God, but if He was real, I thanked him for keeping us alive and prayed it stayed that way.

And then I chastised myself, guilt overwhelming me.

Those two soldiers had come to help us, and they'd died for it. Someone would mourn their loss just as much as I would mourn Tristan if he had been in their place.

"They're here," he called out. I glanced up and watched three combat planes drop into the sky, seemingly out of nowhere, shooting at the enemy, taking the jet down in a matter of seconds. It fell in a roll of fury, a blossom of fiery orange in the otherwise white landscape.

I choked back a sob as relief washed over me, quickly ducking my face. As I sat up, Tristan pulled me in to a hug. My body gave way.

Our chopper took a sudden dive, and our bodies flew apart. Alarms blared. Lights flashed. My eyes shot to the pilot, slumped forward in his seat, his head covered in a dark blossom of blood. The inertia of falling overwhelmed me. We slid with the fall, moments from death. My scream pierced the world as I dove for the controls.

SIX

JESSA

The train rumbled beneath me as my head bobbled on Dad's shoulder. I stretched my neck and I sat up, limbs stiff, bleary eyes on the changing landscape outside the foggy window.

"You doing okay, kid?" Dad said, shifting in his seat as he rolled his neck from side to side. He smiled softly when he caught my eye.

I nodded, my stomach instantly raw with hunger. It growled and Dad stood, reaching out a steady hand to help me up from the seat I'd just spent the night in. I was a breakfast person, always had been, which he knew. I'd always envied my friends who could skip it, no problem. That would make starting the day easier than only being able to think about my stomach. Oh well.

"This way," Dad said, opening the door to our tiny cabin and stepping out into the narrow hallway. I brushed off my clothes, standing to shake out my legs. I ran my fingers through my mess of hair and grimaced. No use. I joined Dad and we ambled down toward the dining car. Now that the day had started, the bustle of others waking carried through the train, a soft undercurrent to the worries lumbering around in my head.

The exhibition was to be in the southern part of New Colony, an area I'd never traveled to before today. That was normal. Most citizens lived their whole lives in the same cities.

Many of the officers and alchemists still in the palace had been summoned to the event. I thought I'd be staying behind, but just as everyone was getting ready to load up and head out, Faulk came for us. She said Richard wanted to parade me around to the country. "The main reason he's even doing these exhibitions is to get the people to accept an alchemist as their future queen, so you better behave," she'd threatened. Her words had stirred me in a way I didn't like. I was on display now? At least I got to bring Dad along for the trip.

We'd loaded up and had a simple dinner on the train. Faulk had announced that Lucas and Richard were travelling separately by air, something about their protection. I no longer cared. Finally, after a late night of conversing with Dad, I'd fallen asleep, my head pressed awkwardly against the windowpane, another snowstorm raging on the other side of the glass.

After breakfast, we retreated back to our private cabin. The snow was long gone by now. We watched the world outside whirl past us in silence. A few hours later, the train slowed, signaling our arrival.

"I think we're just outside of Marthasville," Dad said, pointing to the skyline of an urban city in the distance. "It used to be called Atlanta."

I nodded. I already knew this from school. Marthasville was one of the original colony names. Everything got a new name when New Colony rose to power. Or, in most cases, an old name restored.

Peering out of the window, I looked for similarities to the Capitol city that I knew so well. The land here was different. The air was thicker and the buildings older. There was none of the shine that the Capitol boasted. But it was much greener.

"Ready?" Dad asked.

"No," I sighed, but I put my hand in his anyway. He squeezed it once and then we exited the train together.

"The air," I muttered.

Dad looked at me, eyebrows raised.

I smiled. "It's so much cleaner here."

"Over here," Faulk barked, pulling me from my thoughts. She motioned to us, and we went to her, because what else were we supposed to do?

We were formed into lines and then escorted into a hotel just across the plaza from the train station. I marveled at the size of the trees. They were double our own, with gnarled knobs and stringy moss that hung like curtains. It was slightly chilly and the breeze had a bite, but that was nothing compared to what we'd left behind at the palace.

Royal Officers surrounded us, their guns at the ready. They eyed the onlookers with suspicion. No surprise there, not after the terrorist attack at Queen Natasha's funeral. But the crowd didn't seem fazed. Some gaped curiously, some clapped, and many had expressions twisted in fear as they followed us with their suspicious eyes.

They're not afraid of the guns. They're afraid of the magic.

"Boo!" Dax, the kid from my disastrous class earlier, yelled at one of the gawkers. The crowd jumped back, and he laughed, a dangerous ring to the sound. A few of his friends snickered along with him, as if taking pleasure in making fun of regular folks. "Did you come out to see the show?" he called back to them as we continued our walk.

I rolled my eyes and Dad and I shared an annoyed look.

Faulk shot over to Dax, grabbing him by his upper arm. She began hissing quiet instructions in his ear and his body deflated, moving toward the center of the Guardians. He didn't so much as look at the crowd after that.

"Shouldn't have teased them," Dad whispered low. "Not when King Richard wants the people to accept alchemy."

I glanced back at Dax and saw his lips set in a grim line. He caught me looking and glowered.

"That's her!" someone called out cheerfully over the buzz of the crowd. It took a moment for me to realize I was the "her" they were so excited to see. The alchemists around me seemed to split, taking their distance from Dad and me. As they did, the Royal Officers moved in closer.

"Jessa!" Another voice yelled, this time frenzied.

I studied the crowd, noticing the camera crews. The media was well-controlled by Richard, so I had no doubt he wanted my face plastered across slatebooks all over the New Colony. I smiled and waved politely, inwardly groaning to myself.

Be good. Stay in line. Go along with what Richard wants. And then when he least expects it, make your move.

That was the plan. But as I was surrounded by my fellow Guardians, all of us dressed in our black gear, with hordes of armed Royal Officers gleaming in white uniforms, and a crowd of everyday citizens surrounding us, that plan felt beyond impossible. It was as if it was on one end of the world and I was on the other.

"In here." Faulk strode up next to me, a rare smile on her face, as she pointed to the front doors of the hotel. Her blonde hair gleamed in the sunlight, making her look younger. What kind of woman would she be if she weren't an officer? Would she be happier? But her smile was for the cameras, since she wasn't the type to smile, and the thought made me a little sad. "We've got you and your dad a suite. You'll be expected to smile and say only positive things while you're here. Always assume you're on camera."

I laughed, grinning beautifully. "Got it." I nodded.

"Let's go inside, then," Faulk replied.

"Hold on." I pushed past her toward the crowd. I used to be just like these people. Before coming to the palace, I was living comfortably enough, on the outside of magic and not asking questions, but curious. Always curious.

Did they feel the same way? I wanted to see who they were. See if I saw myself in them.

I approached a family. A mother, holding the outstretched hands of two identical twin boys not much older than Lacey. A man with a full beard stood behind her, one hand resting on one of his son's shoulders.

"Hi!" One of the boys grinned up at me. He had a hole where his front tooth should be, smooth brown skin, and black, curly hair. He was adorable.

"Hi there," I said, squatting to meet his gaze. I reached out to shake his tiny hand. "I'm Jessa, it's very nice to meet you. What's your name?"

"I'm Theo," he gushed. "You're so pretty."

I blushed. "Thank you."

"Are you really magic?" he asked, his eyes lighting up.

"Theo!" His mom chastised him. "Be polite."

I grinned at her, meeting distressed eyes. "He's all right. I don't mind the questions," I said, and she visibly relaxed. I studied the twin boys, both now smiling at me with wonder that danced in their eyes. It wasn't my engagement that had them interested in me, it was my alchemy, and something about that felt satisfying.

"Yes, I am magic," I said. "It's a very special thing. Will you be at the exhibition tomorrow, so I can show you?"

"We didn't get tickets," the dad said in a gravelly voice, "but we'll be watching from home, won't we boys?"

They nodded, their heads bobbing.

Faulk choose that moment to come up behind me and tug on my arm. "It's time for the lady to go," she said to the family. They nodded along with her, eyes wide as saucers. It probably wasn't everyday an officer of the court addressed them. The crowd had started to cram around the family, every person seemingly eager to hear our conversation. A cameraman stood off to my left, trained on the whole exchange. I gave it a little wave and the crowd cheered.

"Faulk," I said, "can we please get this nice family tickets for tomorrow's exhibition?"

I turned to meet her steely gaze, her fake smile still plastered on her face. It didn't stop me from adding, "please," in a feathery sweet voice. By now, I'd become used to being on Faulk's bad side. The crowd liked me, so did the camera. They oohed and awed over my question, my public support of a simple family.

"Unfortunately, we already vetted the exact number of live attendees," she said slowly.

"Oh, but there must be something I can do," I challenged with a coy smile, winking at the family. I added, "I am Prince Lucas's betrothed, after all. That has to count for something." The crowd laughed jovially. The camera slid closer.

There was a long, weighted pause as everyone waited for Faulk's reply. Finally, she nodded. "Fine. I'll see to it that they get four tickets." She smiled out toward the onlookers, "But no more." They laughed, and she leaned in toward me, "Now, it's time for us to go."

"Oh, thank you so much," the mother called as we walked

away. Her boys waved their hands so wildly, I was sure they were going to smack someone in the face. I beamed and waved back, following the last of the group into the fancy hotel. Dad laughed under his breath.

"What?" I asked him quietly.

He shook his head, the smile soft on his lips. "I'm proud of you. You'll make a fine queen, if it comes to that."

If it comes to that. My heart burned in my chest, conflicted.

The moment we were away from the cameras, Faulk turned on me. "What was that?" she seethed, eyes bulging, that youthful smile now twisted into an angry grimace.

I shrugged. I'd just achieved something important. I'd not only undercut Faulk, but I'd furthered my approval rating with the people. Richard would love that. And if I wanted to get closer to him, I'd need to get Faulk out of the way.

"You do not get to make the rules," she spat. "You do not get to flex any kind of power. You are here to look pretty and smile and *that is it.*"

I blinked innocently. "Whatever you say, boss."

She huffed and stormed away, a brigade of wannabes hot on her heels. I caught Dad's knowing expression and winked.

"That's my girl," he whispered under his breath. I slung my arm through his and leaned in. Maybe we were going to be okay, after all.

▼

The room was dark and cool, the air-conditioning causing a chill to spread over my exposed arms and legs. I shifted in my too-short dress. The flashing of the photographers' lights momentarily brought the room into illumination, followed by blinding darkness.

I sat in the front row, lines of chairs behind me filled all the way back to the end of the huge room. It was even bigger than the largest ballroom back at the palace, and whenever I turned around to look, the overwhelming amount of people staring back shocked me.

Such a long trip over, and so far, we'd never even left the hotel. The exhibition was being hosted in the same location as our rooms. At least when I'd been ushered down here, Dad got to sit right behind me. His nearness was the only comfort I had at the moment. But since Richard and Lucas were on either side of me, and all around us were Royal Officers and Color Guardians, that comfort wasn't enough.

I shivered as I watched the guards and soldiers lining the walls.

"Don't worry," Lucas leaned in and whispered into my ear. His closeness brought a mix of warmth and worry careening through me. I still didn't know how to settle on one emotion when it came to him. "You're not going to have to do anything but watch."

I already knew that. Faulk had been very clear that the alchemists performing in the exhibition had trained for it and if I intervened in anything, she'd kill me.

"Okay," I replied anyway. He shifted closer and kissed me gently on the cheek. I stiffened.

"For the cameras, remember?" he whispered, a trace of hurt in his voice. I reached out and laced his fingers through my own. My ring pressed against my finger. It was weird wearing an engagement ring. Earlier, Richard had handed it to me like it was nothing. Maybe it was. But when I'd slid it onto my finger, it had felt like everything.

Lucas frowned and glanced down at our hands, his face paling. "Where did you get that?"

I laughed quietly, but laughed all the same. Where did he think I got it? "Your father gave it to me this morning. Who do you think?"

His eyes darkened and flickered over to his father. Richard was busy talking to Faulk on his other side. "He should have had the decency to let me give it to you myself," Lucas said bitterly.

"It's okay," I said, sighing and turning once more to look at the guests assembling in their seats behind us. Big mistake. I caught the eye of Celia. She sat with her family, just a few rows back and glared at me haughtily before looking away. Her mother said something and then all three of them turned toward me. A guilty pit formed in my stomach. I shouldn't feel bad. She barely knew Lucas when they got engaged. Besides, I'd been coerced into our engagement.

"It was my mother's," Lucas said.

"What?" I turned back to him.

His expression became even darker. "The ring."

"Oh–yeah, well, it's beautiful," I stammered. I'd had no idea it was Queen Natasha's ring. Geez, Richard really was heartless.

Lucas released his hand from mine.

I studied the ring, admiring its beauty. It was silver, featuring a large circle diamond in the center with two rectangular green emeralds on either side. It sparkled like it had been dipped in glitter. It was perfect for someone like Queen Natasha. But on me, I wondered if it looked silly. Wasn't seventeen too young to be engaged? Apparently, nobody else thought so. I caught a cameraman nodding at me, and I smiled proudly and flashed the ring.

"Time to get started," Richard said and stood from his chair. Sitting so close to the King had me in fits of nerves, but as he left, I found those nerves multiplied. Within seconds, he climbed the stairs to the long rectangle stage in front of us. It had been assembled just for this event. A podium and attached microphone stood off to one side. With a few sweeping steps, he took his place behind it and smiled out toward the crowd. Dressed once again in his royal regalia, he was a sight to see. A sight I was entirely sick of. *Better get used to it.*

"Ladies and gentlemen," his voice boomed over the microphone. "My beloved citizens across our prosperous kingdom, welcome."

Applause rang out.

I clapped along but bit my lip in worry. When Richard held an audience, nothing good ever came from it. What would he do next?

"This exhibition will feature the incredible magic of color alchemy. Today, specifically, we'll be showing you the power of yellow and green. These are two colors that our alchemists often use together in combat."

With that, four of the alchemists surrounded the corners of the stage. All teenage boys. I recognized Dax immediately. His black, greasy hair that normally hung in his face was tied back. He grinned at his competitors, ready to pounce.

"Oh brother," I mumbled.

"What?" Lucas asked.

I shook my head. "It's nothing."

I snuck a look behind me to catch Dad's eye. He rolled them, the silent exchange between us calming me for a moment. I chuckled and turned around. Lucas wasn't looking at me anymore, his eyes were trained on the scene in front of him, his body tense.

The boys jumped at each other, engaging in combat without holding back. The yellow alchemy flowed around them, tendrils of strength. The crowd ate it up. Every time one of the alchemists pulled color from their stones, the energy in the crowd heightened. The alchemists were enhancing the magic as they continued hand-to-hand combat. They sent the magic out into the air, displaying it, before calling on it.

This was a show, after all.

The excitement that coursed through the crowd was palpable, like a collective pulse that rose and rose with each blow. Soon, two of the guys were knocked out. Officers swept in to drag them off the stage, leaving Dax and one of his friends to finish the exhibition. Dax grinned, another blast of magic surging through him when he landed the final blow. His opponent's body smashed against the stage with a dull thud, splitting the wood. He stood, staggered against the unevenness, and then crumbled in on himself.

Blood ran down Dax's arm as he raised it into the air, victorious.

Richard had long since removed himself, beaming with heady satisfaction from the sidelines. The stage was destroyed. Dax jumped off the edge onto the floor, coming to stand in the center of the room. I could smell the salty sweat and hear his labored breath as he stood only feet from me.

His friends were now laid out on the carpet. They weren't dead, but the slick blood and swollen bruises that covered them was enough to make bile rise to the back of my throat.

"That's enough fighting," Richard's voice rang out. He stood at the side of the room, the microphone tight in his grip, as he strode to join Dax. I sunk further into my seat. "Now please, show them how green is done."

An officer hauled a potted plant over to us.

"Now, this is something to watch closely," Richard said and nodded to Dax.

Dax smirked at the closest camera as he grabbed a large palm frond. The crowd of people stood, everyone vying for a better look. But now that there wasn't much of a stage, they didn't have a good view anymore. Someone must have thought of that because even though I had a perfect view, nearly every other head in the audience turned toward a ten-foot screen that was off to one side of the room. It displayed the alchemists in a clear view, zooming in close on Dax's hand as he manipulated the green leaf. The green color wafted out in strings of iridescent magic, spinning in the air above his bloodied hands. With the quick flick of his wrist, he sent the magic to his friends. It soaked into their skin like water, gone.

Broken bones straightened into place. Oozing blood stopped. Pale faces returned to normal. One-by-one, they blinked and sat up.

"It's a miracle," someone called from the back. And that was it; the room was swamped in the chaos of applause. People talked over each other, the noise rising, as the realization of green alchemy stoked what was already an excited fire.

"There you have it," Richard said, his voice booming over the crowd. "That is yellow and green alchemy. That is the reason our soldiers will survive and thrive on the warfront. They have magic at their aid, to make them stronger and keep them healthy."

How much of that was actually true? There were a lot of alchemists out at war right now, but how many of them were helping everyday soldiers?

"For those of you looking for adventure, for a noble cause, this is it," Richard continued. The gold buttons on his jacket gleamed as he leaned toward the camera. His salty black hair, his steel gray eyes, his square jaw, trusting smile, tailored royal clothing, everything about him seemed perfect. "Join our war, avenge our queen, spread the truth, and do something you can be proud of."

Again, the crowd burst into applause.

"Thank you, and goodnight!" Richard boomed once more through the microphone. I startled, letting the gravity of it sink me deeper into my chair. I glanced at Lucas from the corner of my eye. He was expressionless. Unreadable.

Did he agree with his father? Did he want this, too?

It was over. Just in time, too, as I was beginning to shake, the frenzied kind I couldn't control. *Get back to the room, get away from all these people, and you'll be fine.*

They had no idea of the costs of magic, not when it was controlled by a man like Richard. I shook the thoughts away and focused on Faulk. She'd taken Richard's microphone. "Everyone, please rise and stay in your places so that the royal family can be escorted from the room first."

I stood, but Lucas's warm arm quickly threaded through mine.

That's me. I'm the royal family now.

Richard led us down the center aisle. We smiled and strode to the back of the room. Hundreds of eyes followed. A camera, too. My cheeks burned. My jaw ached. My dress felt even tighter than I remembered, and I ran my hand down the black sequins, finding the roughness somehow soothing.

"Can you use that green magic on more than just people?" a voice bellowed.

Richard stopped, his shoulders tensing under his jacket. A wave of panic rushed through me. We turned to the man who dared speak. He stood tall, a tense look about him. It was the same bearded man from yesterday, his wife and children sitting next to him. They were gaping as they stared up at him, as if speaking out wasn't something they expected of their father. From the way his eyes shifted, I thought maybe he was just as surprised as they were.

Oh please. Please be careful what you say to Richard.

"Do not address your King like that," Faulk said, striding

to stand next to Richard. She glared at the man, one hand resting on the gun at her hip. "I'm so sorry, Your Majesty." She swung back to Richard. "I thought we properly vetted everyone and coached them on what was and wasn't allowed here tonight. Well, we did, but then Jessa invited this family and—"

"Hush." Richard put up a hand. She shrunk and stepped back, silenced, her glare shooting to me. How was I to know the man would do that?

"Yes," Richard said to him, "to answer your question, we can use it on any living thing, depending on the severity of the wound. We can't heal disease or bring back the dead."

"But crops? Can you heal crops?" He raised his chin.

The crowd had completely quieted.

"We can, and we have."

"My entire crop died earlier this year. Not just mine, but the whole area was hit with early frost. Thousands of acres were lost, and our pay was cut. Where were your alchemists then?"

The room stirred uncomfortably.

A couple of the cameramen who'd come up behind us, filming the whole exchange, turned away. Richard was completely still. "We didn't arrive in time, unfortunately. But rest assured, we would have helped if we could have."

The man blinked, as if suddenly coming to realization as to where he was and whom he was addressing. He'd been brave, but now he bowed quickly, muttered a thank you, and sat down. As we filed from the room, I was certain he wasn't the only farmer in there.

I couldn't smile about it. But I wanted to. I wanted to champion those families and challenge the King myself.

"Find out who that man is," Richard said to Faulk once we were alone, "and punish him accordingly."

"Father!" Lucas chastised, stepping forward. In the brightness of the lobby, he looked even more like his father. The two were dressed almost identically but that was only where it started. "Punishment is hardly necessary. First of all, you had to expect there to be questions after the exhibition. Secondly, he was right! We didn't come to their aid. Or did you forget about that already?"

Richard and his son stared each other down.

"It doesn't matter," Richard finally replied. "He can't talk to me that way. Nobody can."

Lucas shook his head.

"No, it's my fault this happened," I said. "I invited that family here. Faulk didn't vet him, didn't coach him. He just saw the green alchemy and like Lucas said, he had questions. Please don't punish him. That will only make it worse. You're doing this to get the people to like alchemy, right?"

There was a long pause as Richard turned silvered eyes on me. A chill ran down my spine, but I held his gaze. "I'll consider it," he finally replied.

I nodded. "Please, do, Your Royal Highness." I sunk low into a curtsy, something I rarely did for Richard. But I was playing a game, and part of that was appealing to his arrogance.

"We leave first thing in the morning," Richard said to his son. "I'm tired of this place already. The rest of them can follow on the train in our wake."

We began to move toward the bank of gleaming elevators.

"Sir." Faulk cleared her throat. "I have something I have to tell you. I'm afraid you're not going to like it."

Richard's already angry face turned beet-red. "Out with it, Faulk!"

The elevator dinged, and the door opened. We all stepped inside, the four of us and two other officers who I recognized as Richard's personal bodyguards. We were crammed inside. Richard's growing irritation made the space even smaller.

"I think I'd better wait until Jessa is back in her room." Faulk sneered at me.

Something burned deep inside my chest.

"I think Jessa might have more logic in her pretty little head than you do in your entire department, lately," Richard snapped.

Faulk paled. "We lost Sasha," she said bluntly. "Or Frankie."

The doors closed, and we began to rise. Nobody said a word. Mirrors surrounded us on all sides, so nothing was hidden. Only Richard and myself had any measure of surprise on our faces, as if the rest of the party already knew this information. I studied Lucas, biting my lip.

"What are you talking about?" Richard finally asked. Lucas grabbed my hand and pulled me behind him.

"She escaped," Faulk said.

There was a long pause. "How?" Richard asked darkly, his hands forming into tight fists at his side.

"We still haven't figured it out, but we have to assume with magic."

"When?"

"The night I left to come here."

The door opened and chimed. We'd reached our floor. One of the guards placed his hand over the elevator door so it wouldn't close, but still, nobody made a move to leave.

Finally, Richard spun on me.

"Did you do this?" he growled.

My jaw dropped. I hadn't seen Sasha in days.

"How could she?" Lucas questioned. His sturdy frame blocked me from the rest of the group. "She was traveling to get here. So was her father."

Faulk and Richard both glared at me.

"We'll figure out what happened," Richard said, eyes bulging out of his head, "and when we do, I can promise you someone will pay for this." He turned on Faulk. "And you, I'm beginning to wonder just how incompetent you truly are."

Then he stormed out of the elevator and down the hall. Lucas walked me to my room, gripping my hand tightly in his. For once, I let myself lean into him. As we approached my door, Faulk blocked us.

"I'm watching you, Loxely. Don't think I'll ever let another one of your family members slip from my grasp again. Because I won't. You will live the rest of your days under my watch and you will learn to behave, or else those days will be numbered." Her eyes were ice blue daggers directed right at me. She meant every word. It wasn't a threat. It was a promise.

▼

My body relaxed as I danced, trying to let anxious thoughts go. My feet pressed against the hardwood floor; my toes crammed against the points of my shoes. I felt the emotions in the movements, felt it all with each step, with each jump, each turn. The fear of my situation came crashing down on me as heavy as iron. I fell to the floor and sobbed, giving in. Finally, giving in. Gasping, awful sounds that I could hardly recognize as my own echoed through the empty room. Still, I didn't care, I just let it all out, an unstoppable catharsis.

The door squeaked open. "Jessa, what's wrong?" Madame Silver rushed into the room, draping her petite frame over mine in a hug. "Darling, it's okay. It's going to be okay."

I stilled. "You're early," I stated, my voice croaking. "I'm sorry. I wasn't expecting you for our lesson for another twenty minutes."

"Oh darling, no. I'm right on time."

"Oh," I sighed, wiping the mess of tears from my face. They stung against my raw cheeks. She sat back, and I looked up to meet her kind eyes. "I was practicing. I must have lost track of time."

"You do that often," she teased with a wink, and I laughed softly. It was true. There had been a time in my life where ballet had carried me away on a daily basis.

"I think I've cried enough for one day. You must think I'm so weak."

"Actually no," she said, standing and reaching out to help me up. "You're one of the strongest people I know."

"It's just this place," I confessed. "It's not as glamorous as it looks."

She paused, studying me. We stood close together in the empty dance studio, with its wood floors, white walls, mirrors and ballet barre on the far end. The light filtered in through the windows just the same as it had in my old studio, soft and muted. It had immediately become my favorite room here, and the only place I could fully be myself. Madame Silver's lessons were my saving grace, but after the exhibition and Faulk's threats, I was beginning to think grace didn't exist.

And hope. Don't forget hope.

"Darling, I believe you," Madame Silver said, stepping closer. Her rose scent filled me, stirring old memories. "I know you didn't ask for this. I know what your dream was, and this wasn't it."

I looked around the room and fought the urge to burst into tears again. I wanted to spill it all, to open up and tell her *everything*. She was one of the people I trusted most in the world. But how many more people would get hurt because they cared about me? I was dangerous to love.

"Can I help you?" she asked. "I mean it, Jessa. What can I do?"

This wasn't safe.

"Maybe there's something," I whispered. I was still weak, weaker than ever. A strong person wouldn't bring her into this. I knew better, but still, the words grew from my tongue like thorned weeds. "I think you might be able to help me."

SEVEN
LUCAS

The landscape stretched out, as dead as the horizon. I turned around and surveyed the farm from a different angle.

"Still dead," the farmer said, and I nodded, though it gave me no satisfaction.

When everyone had loaded on the train, Richard taking to the air, I'd stayed back. It had been easy to talk him into the idea. He'd been distracted. I said that I wanted to get a better feel for the issues facing the rural farming communities, see if I could brainstorm ways to help them. He left me with an army of bodyguards and plans to send the family jet back for me in a couple days.

"When we can't produce crops," the man continued, his tone gruff, "we get our wages docked. Trouble is, this is all we've got. There's no other job for us. Farmer's kids are almost always assigned to take over the trade. My old man passed away years ago and I've had this land in my care ever since."

We ambled along the dirt path, right through the center of

empty fields. The back of my neck itched as the sun pressed down through the cool breeze.

"What do you grow out here?" I watched the farmer as he talked, noticed the way he thought over his words, as if tasting them first.

Taysom Green was the same man that had challenged my father at the exhibition. I'd instantly liked him and wanted to learn more. I also suspected he might be Resistance, or would be if given the opportunity. It was the way he'd first approached Jessa, as Faulk had described it, and the sureness in his voice when he'd challenged my father. This was a man who wasn't afraid of standing up for the little guy.

I hoped so, anyway. If I was going to get his help...

"In this part of the kingdom, we can grow all sorts of food. My farm is mostly wheat, though we *usually* have a nice tomato crop as well," he said forlornly. There was no trace of a smile now. It had struck me as sincere when I'd come out here. It glowed against his dark skin, magnetic. "It's been a rough year. Everything keeps dying. You name the problem and we've probably had it. Too much rain. Not enough rain. Frost. Wind storms." He rubbed his hand through his curls and faced me. "I'm okay. It's my wife and kids I worry about. We keep getting our pay docked but we're not allowed to find other means for work. Now you tell me, how am I supposed to take care of them? Feed them? How are any of the farmers out here going to make it until next harvest?"

My face burned at his questions, ashamed. What use was a prince in this kingdom? I examined the churned-up fields. "You're right," I said. "We need to be doing more. We should have a few full-time alchemists living out here to help with the crops. I know it's something we used to do, though my father has kept all his alchemists busy with other things lately."

"I've never seen an alchemist on my farm, but I believe it," he said. "There's been a few times where someone's crops were close to dying and miraculously, those same dying crops returned to full health overnight."

I nodded. It was what magic was meant for, if you asked me.

"Now that how it's done is no longer some big secret," I said, "I can work on convincing my father to help you. He should agree since this food helps to feed the kingdom."

"You're a good man." Taysom smiled, "You'll make a good king someday. Much better than your father."

I glanced back to the bodyguards trailing us, hoping none of them had heard that. Any one of them could be a spy for Faulk or Richard. But they didn't seem to care either way. Maybe they agreed.

What would Mom think of all this? Of me? I wondered suddenly.

We'd come down near this part of the kingdom to go to the beach, but never to the farms. Mom had loved the beach when I was a kid. I could picture her there, sitting on the sand, the morning sun hitting her red hair in just the right way, lighting it up like fire. I shook my head, momentarily erasing the memory so I could focus.

I cleared my throat.

"I'm so sorry." Taysom stepped back, looking ashen. He gulped and raised his hands carefully. "I shouldn't have said that."

I must have looked pretty bent up over the thoughts of Mom and he'd interpreted that to be offense over Richard.

"Oh, it's okay." I hesitated, peering at the guards several yards away. "I often think the same thing."

He raised a curious eyebrow and I shrugged. "Come on, show me more."

The next few hours were spent walking the length of the farm, answering each other's questions. I liked the guy. There was something so organic about him, so honest.

"And what of this war?" Taysom asked. "Do you support it?"

I swallowed.

"We were attacked at my mother's funeral and innocent people died," I said simply, as if that answered it. He nodded, seeming to accept the simple answer.

Truth was, I didn't know. There wasn't definitive proof that West America had anything to do with that attack. And the war certainly was an opportunity for my father to be greedy with other people's lives. Growing up in the palace, I'd learned the politics of greed with the best of them.

I looked out again at the land before me, stretching in endless fields of emptiness. "If we leave the dead crops, it will rot," Taysom said, standing next to me. "It's painful to do it, but we have to get it out, roots and all."

Richard wanted to expand his territory. And he also created the shadow lands, used alchemy to destroy entire expanses of terrain in a vain attempt to garner more control. He was an oxymoron, a walking contradiction, and my biggest fear was that we were the same, and maybe my roots were rotting, too.

"Come eat dinner with us. My wife has been preparing a meal all day."

Ahead stood his family's white, two-story farmhouse. It had dormer windows, a wraparound porch, and a grassy lawn with a towering willow tree. It looked centuries old, but well cared for over the years. How many wars had this farm home endured? And how many more before it was lost to the violence of humankind?

"I couldn't possibly eat your food," I said, "not after

everything you just told me. But thank you for the offer."

"Nonsense! Samantha will never let me live it down if I had *the* prince here and we didn't dine with him. Trust me, she'll be the talk of the town after tonight." He laughed heartily, his tall frame towering over my own 6 feet 2 inches. I followed him inside.

▼

After enjoying tender roasted chicken and butternut squash that could rival any meal at the palace, Taysom led me down to his cellar to show off where he brewed his own beer. Samantha climbed in the other direction; two floors up to put the twins to bed. The bodyguards were left to their own devices. Some waited at the top of the stairs. Some crowded the kitchen, finishing off the leftovers that Samantha had offered. And others cased the perimeters of the house, at the ready to defend me in the event of an attack. But none had come down to the cellar, and with that, I'd found my moment.

"If I asked for your secrecy, for your trust, and most importantly, your help, would you offer it to me?" I asked.

Taysom didn't even hesitate. "Yes."

▼

I stepped out of the black executive car, legs aching from walking for hours yesterday with Taysom. The sight of the familiar sleek jet calmed me. At least I'd get to rest today.

It sat centered on the tarmac, large, pearl white, and with the royal family insignia of three red stars, painted across the side. I climbed the stairs, wind whipping through my hair. I hurried to one of the white chairs, relaxing into the heated leather seat. I was only going north into more cold, but I'd get to see Jessa again soon—that made it worth it.

I hoped she would be happy to see me, too. The likelihood, or rather the lack thereof, left me feeling raw.

I glanced out the window. A man struggled with a bulky suitcase. He had a limp, and was dragging the case across the ground with a strangled expression. I glanced over to the bodyguards huddled together outside talking. They'd be inspecting everything before we took off if they hadn't already done it. That was their job. But to make this poor man, whoever he was, battle with loading the cases all on his own? Not okay.

I sighed and stood, making my way out of the plane.

"Here, let me help you with that," I called out, climbing down the stairs and approaching the man. I grabbed the handle of the case. The suitcase was made from black fabric, bulging at the seams. It probably belonged to one of the guards flying back with me.

"No, Your Highness," the man spluttered. "You couldn't possibly."

I lifted it to the cargo hold and winced. "I *could* possibly," I said. "Really, I'm happy to help out. You don't have to treat me like my father, you know? I don't like to be waited on hand and foot."

"Well, okay, thank you," the man replied with a weathered smile. He looked pretty old, but that could have been from his manual labor job outside. He wore a black coat and a reflective orange vest that flashed in the sunlight as he moved. "I pulled a muscle this morning, but a job's a job. Gotta work."

I opened my mouth to ask if he could get the day off, but then decided better of it. Most likely, that answer was no. People worked in New Colony. They had what they needed, but they worked hard. It was what we believed in: give a man work and give him a roof over his head.

"Hey." A guard trotted over. "Your Highness, what are you doing? You're supposed to be inside the plane. This isn't your job."

I eyed the guard and caught the patronizing look he sent to the injured man, like it was his fault I was out here. If anything, those guards should have seen a man in need and stepped in to help. Getting mad at me for doing the right thing and taking it out on this innocent guy was not okay. "I can do as I please," I said coolly to the guard. "It's no concern of yours if I decide to lift a suitcase."

"Yes, but," the guard went on, shaking his head, "you need to get back on the plane. It's cold out here and we can't have you catching your death."

I rolled my eyes. These guys? Seriously? They thought I was made from feathers or something. "I think I can handle it."

"Are there more bags?" I turned back to the lone worker. "Can I help you finish up?"

"Sure." The man shrugged and waddled away, still limping.

We walked to a car parked ten yards away from the plane, piled high with luggage.

"That was the first one in the pile," the man said. "I still got all of these to load up."

Well, at least I can call this my workout for the day.

"Your Highness, I really must insist that you board the plane and relax." The bodyguard had followed us to the car but did he offer to help load bags? Certainly not. I shook my head and hefted another bag into my arms.

Boom!

It pulsed through the air, pushing me to my back. Hard. I gasped for breath, pain and heat shuddering through me.

What the—?

Adrenaline raced through my veins. Sweat bubbled on my skin. A strange crunch echoed through the air. I stared, mouth agape, at what was left of the jet.

"Get away from there!"

The remaining bodyguards swarmed me, pulling me away from the scorching flames as they grew wild into the sky. Still, the heat pressed down. The inferno was maddening, overcoming the jet in seconds. I blinked rapidly, trying to take it all in. As the faces of my bodyguards leaned over me, realization sunk in deep. Where was the man that had been so insistent I stay on the plane?

"Where is he?" I demanded of the guards. They'd now surrounded me, aiming their guns outward.

"Where's who?" The guard closest barely looked at me as he surveyed the area.

I shook my head and focused past the ringing in my ears.

"The bodyguard who just tried to kill me!" I yelled.

They all exchanged worried glances as they looked around. "He's gone."

▼

After returning home and debriefing with my father, Jessa was the only person I wanted to see. I knocked on her door.

"Are you okay?" Jessa asked as she swung the door open. Her eyes filled with tears, blue oceans of worry. "I heard about what happened. That's insane. I can't believe it."

I nodded, even though I wasn't sure if okay was the right way to describe how I felt. The attack on my life had come way too close to ending it. The danger of it still pulsed through my veins. My mind couldn't stop replaying the scene over and over again, nor could my body relax. I kept catching myself shaking, my pulse climbing.

I'm so lucky to be alive.

She laced her arms around me in a hug and I held her tight, lingering in her familiar scent. I finally relaxed. After a long moment, she led me into her room and closed the door. Staring up at me, she frowned. "I know things between us aren't what they used to be, but I would never wish you dead. I'm really sorry you had to go through that. I'm still shaken up about it, but I can't imagine what you're going through."

My heart ripped in two at her words, part of me relishing in her closeness and gratitude that I was still alive; but the other caught up on her words. *Things between us aren't what they used to be.* Would they ever be normal again? Did she even want them to be? The more time I spent with her, the more I realized it was hopeless.

"Can I help with anything?" she asked.

"You can." I nodded and moved toward her couch, sinking into it.

After the attack, our plane was nothing but a heap of ash and metal. I'd taken a train home, traveling all day. It was getting late and I needed sleep, but there was something I wanted to do first.

"Did they find out who did it?" she asked.

"Oh, I know who planted the bomb," I said. "It was one of the bodyguards. But I'm not sure who they were working for or where they are now."

Faulk and a few of her best people had gone in to clean up the pieces and run a full investigation. Richard had been livid when I'd returned home. I could only imagine how he must have reacted when he'd first received the news. I wondered how much longer Faulk had here. If it was me, she'd be fired.

"So the bodyguard got away?" Jessa sat down next to me.

I nodded.

"The easiest explanation is that West America had planted him—," I shrugged. And that was the interpretation my father had taken. But I had questions. Up until the war, West America had left us alone. We'd been the one to initiate the war. Not them. Maybe it was the Resistance behind these attacks; maybe it was someone else entirely. What happens next time?

I peered over at Jessa. She sat inadvertently close now, her face twisted in fear, a faraway look in her eyes. I knew she hated this place, but I loved having her here. Once we were married, we'd have the option to move into my bedroom or takeover a different suite. We'd move, of course. I'd let her decorate it however she wanted, and we'd only have to see Richard when necessary.

You really think that's going to happen? Get real...

"What do you believe happened?" she asked.

"Something isn't adding up," I finally said. "I don't know if West America is truly behind these attacks."

"Maybe you could go question that couple?" She shrugged, pulling the elastic from her hair and letting the locks loose. Curls tumbled around her shoulders, and when she ran her fingers through them, I had to look away. My gaze inadvertently flickered to the bed beyond her and I closed my eyes, pushing my emotions down. "You know the ones Faulk brought in a few weeks ago? They might know something," she continued.

I racked my brain, annoyed with my lack of focus. "Remind me?"

"The ones that Faulk used for one of my alchemy tests, remember? Did you ever know about them? It was a man and woman that had something to do with the attack at your Mom's funeral. Well, at least, I think they were closely related to the gunman. And they definitely had something to hide because the orange alchemy amplified that tenfold. I'm pretty sure Faulk has them locked up somewhere."

How has nobody told me about this? This could be the key.

"Help me," I said, grimacing at what I was about to ask. "Use your red alchemy and come interrogate them with me."

She leaned back, her brow furrowed.

"No way." She stood and lifted up her hands in protest. "The second I start doing something like that, it's over. Richard is going to be using my red alchemy left and right."

"That logic makes no sense. You already did it on Sasha before she broke out. Plus, you know it's only a matter of time before he makes you use it again. At least this could help save my life. And who's to say you won't be interrogating them tomorrow anyway. At least this way we can learn what we need to know together."

She bit her lip. "It'll become an endless cycle. That's my *logic*. Once I start doing it, I won't be able to say no. I'll just keep doing it." She turned away and walked to the window, quiet for a moment. Then she looked at me, shame pulling at her lips. "Part of me likes doing it and I don't want to feed into that."

The guilt tore at me. I strode toward her, stopping inches away.

"Please, Jessa," I pleaded. "I really need your help. My life is at stake here. I know you're angry with me. I know you don't want to be with me anymore. But please, at least help me find out who's trying to kill me."

She looked into my eyes, her resolve softening. I reached out and grabbed her hand, placing it on my heart so she could feel what I felt. It raced underneath my skin. For fear of death. And for her closeness.

"Fine," she relented, sighing and biting her lip again. She

did that all the time and I *always* noticed. My heart raced faster, and I dropped her hand. "But let's go now while Faulk is gone and before I chicken out."

"Deal," I said. "We'll go down to the prison and I'll get the guards to tell me where they are. Once we're in there, we'll make it quick, in and out. I just have to know if that gunman was really working for West America or if it was someone else."

She was pale now and looked like she was about ready to be sick, but she nodded, heading for the door. "Okay, Lucas," she said. "I really hope we don't regret this."

▼

We descended the stairs to the prison quickly. The palace was crawling with guards and officers tonight. Since Sasha's escape and my own near-assassination, they seemed to have multiplied again. With that in mind, I expected the prison guards to put up some kind of fight. I tucked Jessa's arm through mine when we entered the dim corridor.

"Where is the married couple located?" I asked the nearest guard. He stared at me, mouth hanging open.

"What? Do I have food in my teeth or something?" I joked.

"Oh, sorry." He bowed. I didn't recognize him and wondered if he was one of the new guys.

"Your father said to let you do whatever you want," he said, then shrugged and pointed toward a steel door.

Interesting. Whatever I want and report back to him, most likely.

"There's only one couple here. They're in there."

With the rustling of keys, he opened the door and stepped aside.

The couple sat close together on a cot that was pushed

against the far wall of the cell. Beat down and tired, they didn't seem the least bit fazed by me, but a flash of interest lit in the woman's eyes when they ran across Jessa.

The man glared up with a sullen expression. "What do you want?"

"We don't have anything left to say," the woman added and leaned against her husband, exhaustion stretched across her face. Their hair was ratty, and their limbs looked skinny in their prison garb.

"Let's be quick about this." Jessa and I walked closer to the couple. I couldn't help noting the bruises along their arms. I inspected them for the best place to poke them with the needle that was hidden in my hand. We didn't need much. Jessa could use a drop of blood and it could be enough to use her alchemy.

I rolled the needle between my thumb and forefinger. It glistened in the dim light as I stepped forward and poked the man first, right in his upper-arm.

"What was that?" He balked and jumped up, crazed eyes leveled with mine.

Jessa pressed her palm to his bicep, covering the bubble of blood that had formed there. "Sit down and relax," she said. Immediately, his countenance changed and he sat on the floor.

I moved in for the woman. She slid back against the wall, thin hands in front of her face. "Stay away. I'm so sick of you crazy people and your magic. Please," she begged. "Just leave us out of it."

But I was much bigger than her, and I swiped the needle at her arm before I could change my mind, the needle striking the skin. There was a small prick of blood and she grimaced.

Again, Jessa was quick. She reached out her arm, connected with the magic, and told the woman to sit down and relax next to her husband.

They looked up at us with pliable, vacant expressions, relaxed and open for anything. I fought the urge to feel guilty. *But they know something. They could have been involved in the attack during Mom's funeral, and maybe even the one yesterday. Don't feel bad, just do what you need to do and get out of here.*

"Stay relaxed. Don't get up. You two are going to answer our questions with complete honesty and zero reluctance." Jessa knelt in front of them.

"What do you know about the attack during the Queen's funeral?" I asked, squatting to study their expressions carefully. I watched for any break in the magic, but they were as lost to it as anyone had ever been.

"My brother was the gunman," the woman said softly and slowly, but with no hesitation. "We hadn't expected him to kill so many people. That wasn't what he was trying to do."

"Who was he trying to kill?"

"You and your father."

I figured. "So why kill all those other people?"

"We don't know," the man cut in. "Maybe he had a problem with his gun or maybe he lost his mind or something? We don't know."

I shared a glance with Jessa, and she nodded slightly, urging me to dig deeper.

"Was he working alone?"

"No," the woman said. "He wanted us to help but we refused."

"Do you know who he was working with?" I pressed.

She shook her head adamantly. "We don't know. Some woman. He kept referring to his contact as a 'she' but we never learned more."

"Did they call themselves the Resistance?" Jessa swung her

head to look at me when I asked the question, frustration in the tilt of her mouth. But I had to ask it. I had to know.

The woman shrugged. "I never heard him say anything like that."

"Was it someone from West America?" I continued, desperate for something more than this.

"We don't know," the man said. "We've told you everything."

"Who gave him the gun?" I remembered the sickening ping-ping-ping of the semiautomatic rifle's gunfire.

"We've never seen him with one before," he said. "We don't think he was very well-trained. I mean, why would he be? Maybe that's why he ended up killing so many people."

Such recklessness. Who would be stupid enough to do that?

And this only confirmed what we'd assumed anyway, that someone put him up to it. Supplied him with the weapons and told him where to go and when. A she? It could have been Jasmine or someone else in the Resistance. It could have been someone connected to West America. Their president *was* a she, after all. But she wasn't our enemy until recently, as far as I knew. Dad had started the war, not her. I doubted she was somehow secretly interacting with someone all the way out here. Then again, there was no way to know for sure.

"Do you know how she, whoever she was, got in contact with your brother?"

"We don't."

I growled and stalked to the back of the small cell. The lights were soft, casting long shadows over everything. "Do you have any other information about your brother, that attack, the woman, anything you can tell me?"

They sat in silence.

"I give up," I sighed, exasperated. "These people shouldn't be here."

"But they *were* hiding something," Jessa pressed, talking to me but pointing to the couple. "I'm certain they were."

I turned back on them and stalked in close. "That night you first met Jessa and you got so nervous that Faulk decided to throw you in here, what were you hiding?"

"We don't support the monarchy," the woman said simply. "We haven't for a long time. My brother knew that, which was why he tried to get us to help him execute the royal family. But we never signed up for something like that. We're not killers." A tear slid down her cheek. She still appeared completely relaxed, but I wondered if Jessa's magic was starting to wear off, or if she was so upset about her brother's ultimate demise that the tear had leaked through.

"They don't know anything," I sighed. "Let's go."

"After we leave, you won't remember ever seeing or talking to us today. Got it?" Jessa's voice cracked as she gave her last command.

They nodded, and we left them there. The guard quickly locked the door. I was tired, the weight of it all suffocating me. I usually took the stairs, but not tonight. I glanced back to four men who stood along the wall. They'd been my tail ever since I'd gotten home, my bodyguards. I'd ignored them because they had kept their distance. I wondered if they could be trusted. Who among them was a spy, or worse, an assassin sent to kill me?

I shot them a distrustful look and turned back to Jessa.

"Well that was a bust." I sighed. We made our way to the elevator, stairs be damned.

"They're not that different from me, you know?" She shook her head. "Do they really deserve to be locked up in here? They don't support the monarchy, sure, but they didn't do anything. They didn't take action against anyone."

She had a point.

"I am not in control around here," I replied. "And it isn't fair for you to always get mad at me for someone else's actions."

She sighed. "Fine." She ran a hand through her hair and looked up at the ceiling, I think just to avoid eye contact with me. We strode into the elevator, my bodyguards filling in any empty space. We rose to our stop, and we stepped out onto the marble-tiled floor, never uttering a word.

"I'm going back to my room. I need to get to bed. I'll see you tomorrow, Lucas," Jessa said. She stood looking at me for a moment, then turned and walked off without a backwards glance.

There was nothing else to say. She didn't get it. She was never going to get it because she wasn't me, and didn't know the constant pressure I was under. And maybe she didn't care.

I ground my teeth and strode toward the royal apartment, in search of Richard. As much as I hated it, I needed to tell him about the failed interrogation. He might be convinced of West America's hand in this, but I believed there was someone else trying to kill us. We needed to take it seriously before it was too late.

When I found him in his private office, he motioned me in with a cunning grin. "I was wondering when you'd come to me," he said.

I shut the door behind us.

It's not like I'm on the same side as him. It was easy to tell myself things like that, but part of me was beginning to wonder if it was just another lie.

EIGHT

SASHA

"It's a good thing we learned to pilot a helicopter, or we wouldn't be here," Tristan said, shaking his head once again in disbelief. We'd come so close to death, but those lessons years ago had paid off with our lives once again. I kept replaying what had happened over in my mind, how just a few more seconds falling or a few more inches in the wrong direction and we'd be dead and gone.

But I'd gotten ahold of the controls, and our backup had escorted us to our destination. Tristan and I had followed, shockwaves of adrenaline slow to wear off.

"We're so lucky," I mumbled and met Tristan's familiar gaze. *So lucky.*

"Well, you're here now," Mastin said as he stood across from us.

That we were. The airport below had looked enormous when we'd flown into a private runway. As we'd deplaned, soldiers surrounding us, Mastin had instantly locked gazes with me.

Something flicked through his mossy eyes as he studied

Tristan and I. Jealousy, perhaps? Tristan was mine just as much as I was his. We'd simply been through too much together. We were used to jealousy. But something about the look in Mastin's eyes made me lose my train of thought.

"How did the debriefing go?" Mastin asked.

"The usual," Tristan said. "We were placed in holding for a couple of days to corroborate our stories and go over details."

Nobody had protested. Of course they'd want to make sure we could be trusted before letting us into their country. I understood that. With everything going on, with death and war, it only made sense. Tristan seemed annoyed that Mastin still hadn't showed up to help. In his opinion, Mastin should have gotten us through this process immediately. But Mastin was only one soldier. How much pull did he *really* have? This wasn't some outpost of Resistance hiding up in Canada. This was West America.

America. It's just called America here, I reminded myself for the millionth time.

In the end, our stories had checked out and we'd been transferred by plane to the capitol city of Los Angeles.

"This is crazy," I said, looking around at the terminal. It was gorgeous, all white surfaces and shining steel. "I can't believe I'm here."

Outside, palm trees swayed in the wind. Sunshine shone through the window, warming my shaking limbs. My eyes kept returning to the trees. I'd never seen palms in person before, but I'd learned about them. Even though I wasn't officially in school, Hank had made me study. Geography was important to him.

"Believe it." Mastin nudged me and pointed toward a group of people gathered outside. "Because it's about to get a lot more apparent that we're not in New Colony anymore."

I lifted my eyebrows, my curiosity piqued at his statement.

We followed him out the sliding doors. A team of security surrounded us as we walked into the pleasant sun and made our way across the sidewalk. A soft breeze brushed against my face, and I smiled. I could get used to this weather.

The chanting tumbled through the air and I nearly stumbled.

"No magic allowed!" they screamed, holding up signs with things written across them like "GO HOME OR DIE" and "GOD HATES ALCHEMY" and "MURDERERS ARE NOT WELCOME." But that wasn't all; there were also those chanting, "Alchemy is Progress" together with signs reading "WELCOME HOME FRIEND" and "MAGIC IS AMAZING" and "WE LOVE YOU JUST AS GOD MADE YOU."

Tristan tugged me close, his arm around my hunched shoulders, as he and the security cleared a path through the crowd. Mastin ushered us into a waiting car and slid in after us, shutting the door with a thud. It left only muffled sounds of the frenzied crowd. They swarmed the car and the driver took off before I had a chance to put on my seatbelt. My hands shook so wildly I couldn't get the belt secured. Mastin reached over to help, his cool hand brushing against mine. I didn't move.

"What was that?" Tristan asked, twisting around to watch the crowd disappear. "Who are those people?"

"Alchemy is a very politically charged issue here," Mastin said.

"But why were they doing that?" I asked. It wasn't anything I'd ever seen before. There was no such thing as that kind of crowd in New Colony. Sure, there were crowds, but they showed support. That was it.

"They're just protestors," Mastin said.

"Protestors?" Tristan raised an eyebrow.

"It's a normal thing here. People assemble to yell about their rights or opinions. It doesn't really do much most of the time. People are pretty set in their ideas. Not everyone would agree, but protesting is a waste of time, if you ask me. People have to vote."

I'd never voted, and I wondered if it made anything better. *What happens when you vote, and you don't get what you want?*

I turned to look back out the window, looking for more protestors. Maybe that's what you did.

"Your president?" I flipped back around and watched Mastin carefully. "You told me she was in favor of alchemy. Is that true?"

"Yes," he said, "she is. As are about half of the country." His eyes fixed on me, so intense and sure. "And me too, after meeting you."

My face burned, and I looked forward, watching the road in front of us. I couldn't face either of the men.

"You better be," Tristan snapped. "This girl has been through hell and back."

They both shifted toward me, sandwiching me between them, and the backseat grew infinitely smaller.

"What happened to you at the palace?" Mastin asked.

I decided to be blunt. I'd told the story so many times over the last couple of days; it wasn't like there was anything left to hide. "They tortured me. Used my sister's red alchemy against me so I gave them info about our camp, but they were too late getting there. Lucas was the one who broke me out."

"Lucas?" Mastin replied, surprised. "As in, Prince Lucas?"

"The one and only," I muttered. "But *that* part isn't public knowledge, okay?"

He nodded. "What's his endgame?"

"How should I know? He's not like his father, never has been. He's not evil. But he is self-serving. He's the reason we were ambushed that night. He thought he was protecting Jessa by giving us away. But now he's back to helping the Resistance. I think he's trying to play both sides of the fence to keep her happy. I'm not really sure where he stands."

"That's not going to work." Tristan chuckled, but I could tell he didn't think it was funny. Nobody did.

"No kidding." I leaned back against the seat and watched as palm trees passed outside the window. Loads of green waxy-looking shrubs, and buildings of all shapes, colors, and sizes flashed by. It wasn't as urban as I'd been expecting. Everything was close together, but small. Actually, Los Angeles wasn't anything like what I'd seen of New Colony and was certainly a world away from Canada.

And the people. Some strode along the streets as if they didn't have somewhere to be. Didn't they work? And others, they were dressed in rags, sitting under trees or walking slowly down cracked sidewalks. New Colony had plenty of diversity, but for the most part, everyone was fed and clothed in similar fashion, they all worked, and always had things to do.

What was better? Guaranteed mediocrity but nobody was left behind? Or a free life, with the guarantee that some people wouldn't make it out of poverty? I didn't know. And now I was here, too, stuck between two lives. Two choices.

I peeked at the men on either side of me, my feelings conflicted.

They were so similar in certain ways, but so different in others. One had been my friend for years, and I loved him more than words. There had been times when I'd been sure we'd end up together. But now there was this other man. He'd come marching into my life against my will, but had taught me to see things differently, forced me to grow. To fight even harder than I already was.

Mastin caught me looking, his eyes narrowing, so I quickly changed the subject.

"So, where to next?"

I figured I'd be joining the others from camp. I hated to admit it, but I wanted to see my mom. And I wanted to see Hank and Lacey, too. I missed them all, a feeling I had kept hidden away while I was in the prison. But now that I was here, so close to them, the longing hit me with an unexpected force.

"That's the thing I wanted to talk to you about." Mastin shifted uncomfortably.

"Are they okay?" I sat up straighter, glaring at him.

He raised his hands. "They're fine. They're great." Then lowered his voice, "But nobody knows Lacey is an alchemist. We've chosen to keep that a secret for now. She's with your mother."

"Okay?" What was his point?

"It's *your* identity that we weren't able to keep secret."

Obviously, considering the protestors, that was true.

"What are you getting at?" Tristan pulled my hand into his lap, holding it tight.

There was a long pause as Mastin leaned back against his window and studied us. "Okay, so Cole might have taken some creative liberties back at camp."

"What are you talking about?" I glared at him, my heart about to beat out of my chest. I had a sinking feeling I knew where this was going. Cole, the general who'd died, had said if the alchemists would help him then we would get to come to West America and be free. I'd seen the paperwork signed by their president herself. If that wasn't the case, what was?

"You don't exactly get amnesty here, though you're not

about to be thrown into prison," he said, his expression shifting to shame.

Good! He ought to be ashamed!

Tristan's tall body tensed next to me as he squeezed my hand, like he was about to fly out of his seat and over me to beat the crap out of Mastin.

"How bad is it?" I asked.

"When those men died getting you out, your identity was compromised. There are a lot of people here who hate alchemy. It broke as a huge story. You're not safe here. The others have been given temporary living arrangements but you need to be kept in a more secure location."

"So, put her with me. I'll protect her," Tristan said.

"You've noticed all the security everywhere, haven't you?" Mastin interjected.

"I sure have." I rolled my eyes and leaned back against my seat. The air conditioning was starting to add to the chill and I shivered. "So where am I staying? Out with it, Mastin, you're driving me crazy."

"My father is a general. We've been stationed at a base here and you're going to be our guest."

"No, she is not," Tristan spat. He leaned over me and glared at Mastin. "I got her out of there, she stays with me."

"It was the best I could do. Either that, or another prison. She'll be safe with me on base."

"How convenient for you," Tristan growled.

"As far as America is concerned, she's enemy number one. They hate New Colony and this war. They want someone to take it out on and Sasha is it."

"Can't Tristan come stay with us?" I felt his body slightly relax against my side.

"He'll go stay with the others." Mastin shrugged. "My father doesn't know him well enough to trust him."

I laughed. "And he trusts me?"

"No," Mastin said simply. "But he's curious, so that's enough."

"Did you forget the fact I was the one who went back for her while you saved yourself?" Tristan yelled.

"I have other duties," Mastin snapped back. "I'm a soldier!"

"Stop!" I shouted over their rising voices. They turned on me, hurt, each wanting me to take their side. "Seriously, you two are like kids fighting over their favorite ball on the playground."

I spun toward Tristan, touching his face gently with my fingers. "It makes sense. We'll figure out a way to spend time together, and to bring my sister to see me."

"You need to continue her training. Hiding her alchemy or not, she needs to learn before she accidentally hurts someone."

"I agree," I said. "And thank you for coming back for me. Nobody else would have done what you did for me."

He quieted and studied me with thunderous frustration in his eyes, but he nodded.

Then I turned on Mastin. "And you, give Tristan some credit, will you? He crossed the shadow lands to get to me. He's amazing and if you have as much pull as you seem to think you do, you'll find a way to get Tristan some sort of security clearance so he can help with this war." Then I added, "Hank too, for that matter."

Mastin's mouth had thinned into one long line. I took that as his way of appearing chastised and I held back a bitter laugh. Had he already forgotten what I was like? Of course I was going to stand up for my guy. He was my best friend, almost like a human security blanket. He centered me like nothing else. And Hank, he was like a father to me. The fact he'd gotten out of that palace alive in the first place was a miracle. I wasn't about to let him sit around and do nothing; the man was useful. Mastin was a fool to overlook these men.

"Fine," Mastin relented, relaxing back against his seat. "I'll talk to my father."

"Fine," I said, grinning. I turned to Tristan and winked.

"Fine," Tristan said, studying my face. I willed him to be happy, and he must have sensed that because he winked and smiled, returning to his happy-go-lucky self. I had to admit, it was an impressive ability. And one the always-grumpy Mastin should've adopted. A pang of longing ached in my chest. I rested my head against Tristan's shoulder and tried to relax as the car drove us onward toward our uncertain future. Would I fit in on an American military base?

I considered the magic that flowed through my veins and laughed.

▼

"This is your room." Mastin opened the door and revealed a simple bedroom. It was nicely decorated in sage greens and cotton fabrics. A queen-sized bed sat in the middle, with wooden nightstands on either side, and a wicker chair in the corner by a large window overlooking the yard. A closet was open, empty hangers on the rod. "Mom is kind of the ultimate hostess," he continued, "so she's going to go shopping for you once she gets your sizes."

"She doesn't have to do that."

"Believe me," he replied, "She'll love it. You'll be like the daughter she never had."

The house was the largest on the base, which made sense considering Mastin's dad was some kind of general. It was bigger than most of the homes I'd seen on our drive in, red-brick, with white columns and green shrubs lining the sidewalk. I had immediately teased Mastin about it, delighted when he turned bright red.

The second we'd walked in the door, I'd been met by Mastin's mother, Melissa, who was the older female version of her son, all pale skin, white-blonde hair, and sea foam eyes. She'd immediately fed me, talked my ear off, and treated me like we were old friends. She was quick to inform me that though Mastin was an only child, his father would be there that evening and we'd all have a proper family dinner.

I'd caught Mastin staring at me as she'd told me about their family, about *him*.

And now we stood together in this bedroom, a tangle of emotions between us. We used to hate each other, and that had been easy. Trying to be friends was hard. Weary, I rubbed the back of my neck and yawned.

"Would you mind if I took a little nap and met you for dinner later?"

He nodded. "Sure, and don't worry about the dress or anything, we're pretty casual around here."

I looked down at the simple jeans and black t-shirt I'd been supplied with and shrugged. "Your mom will be playing dress up with me soon enough."

"I'm sorry about that."

"Why? Are you jealous? Need a little shopping time with Mom?" I teased.

He shook his head, laughing. "You really are a brat, you know that?"

"I know." I smiled.

"Alright, get some rest," he said, knocking on the doorframe once and closing it as he left. I sat on the bed, taking everything in. I still couldn't believe I was staying with Mastin's family. It only made me want to see my own. I didn't know when my icy opinion of them had melted, but it had. After everything we'd been through the last few weeks, I was ready for a fresh start with them.

I noticed a slim slatebook charging on the nightstand and powered it on. It was a different style than the ones I'd grown up with, but I figured out the differences quickly and began to scroll through the newsfeeds. It was filled with stories, with countless sides of the issues. The main ones being about alchemy and about the war, all sorts of sources gave their varying opinions. There were comment sections where people waged verbal battles on each other. Some of the things they said to each other made my skin crawl.

Was this what it was like to be free?

In New Colony, the palace controlled what news was released. They controlled the story. And there wasn't a comment section. But here? There were no restrictions. Some of the headlines seemed completely bogus, and others drew me in like a moth to the flame, especially the ones about me. I read through story after story. I quickly found one thing they all agreed on. King Richard Heart was an evil dictator, controlling both his people and their magic, with greedy intentions to take over their America and control them, as well. They weren't generally a country who supported war, from what I read, but this was different. This was personal and they were going to win, no matter the costs.

Wow. I sighed and laid back. There was no chance of napping now. I'd read the afternoon away and I needed to get freshened up for dinner. I went to the bathroom, and before I knew it, someone came knocking.

"You ready?" Mastin asked, his steady voice muffled through the door.

"Yup," I replied as I swung open the door and stepped into the hallway. I was still in the same clothes as before, but the shower had helped. He raised his eyebrows and I was suddenly annoyed. Why did he affect me so much? He was just a stupid boy, and I'd reserved my heart for Tristan long ago!

I followed him down the stairs to the dining room, with its table set with blue and white patterned china and its scent of seasoned meat and fresh baked bread. Mastin's parents were already seated. This was so weird, like I was meeting my boyfriend's parents or something. But I was *not* with Mastin, nor did I want to be. *I don't think. Maybe. I don't know.*

"There she is." Melissa beamed from the table and stood. "Honey, this is Sasha." Then she said with a conspiratorial smile, "The alchemist girl."

Her *honey* glared at me, looking me up and down with a sneer on his lips. "Oh yes, Sasha? Or Frankie? Which is it?"

I gulped. As if I knew anymore.

"Dad, we've been through this," Mastin clipped. Apparently, they had. They seemed to know all of my business.

"Sasha works fine," I added with a weak smile. My eyes shot to Mastin, bulging. *Hello, introduce me?* He squinted before getting it.

"Sasha, I'd like you to meet General Nathan Scott."

"Pleased to meet you," I replied smoothly. It was at that moment that I realized I didn't even know Mastin's last name. We'd shared a few conversations, a few almost-kisses, and battled together, but we didn't really know each other.

Nathan harrumphed at me, folding his large arms, and turned to his son, "Mastin, would you bless the food, please?"

We sat, and I followed along as they clasped hands and Mastin asked God to bless their family and their meal. I watched the family, thoroughly confused as to why God would bless us. Mastin's Dad caught me staring and I blushed, quickly closing my eyes and bowing my head.

I've never heard a prayer before, so what?

It wasn't something people did in New Colony. It wasn't illegal, but it was customary to keep religion private within the family. And there certainly had been none of that at the palace or in the camp with Tristan and Hank. I nearly laughed at the image of Hank praying. He wouldn't know what to do.

But this family treated God as if He were in the room with us.

"Amen," I said when the rest of the family did.

"In this family, we pray over every meal, attend church each Sunday, and read the Bible," Melissa said gently. "You'll learn."

That's probably why you hate alchemists, I thought. Maybe that wasn't fair. Melissa didn't seem fazed by my magic. But as we ate, General Scott certainly glared at me like I was the devil come to dine with his precious family.

"So, how long have you been in this home?" I asked politely, pushing the food around my plate and trying not to look as uncomfortable as I felt.

"Oh, not too long," Melissa said. "We've moved every few years, depending on our assignment but I hope we'll stay here for a while now that the war's broken out."

"I don't expect Mastin and myself will be here long," Nathan said with a grunt. He cut into his steak with a knife, his movements brisk. "I'm needed elsewhere, for obvious reasons."

"Just waiting for the right timing," Melissa chirped.

Mastin smiled. "It's killing him," he said. "Me too. We're made to fight."

The general nodded.

I chewed my food slowly and tried to ignore Melissa's worried expression. Unfortunately, I related with the men in the room, eager to fight. "Me too," I said. "I want to help."

Nathan laughed. "I wouldn't count on it."

"Dad—" Mastin interjected.

"And why not?" I asked, urging myself not to glare back at the man. He looked nothing like his son, except for his tall muscular build and his buzzed cut. He was all dark hair and olive skin and black calculating eyes.

"You're here, in my home, because my son has vouched for you *and* because I am going to be watching you carefully to make sure you are who he says you are. But let's just make one thing clear," Nathan replied, jabbing his finger at me, knife still in hand. "I don't know you and I don't trust alchemists, so I don't trust you. Men died to get you here. If you turn out to be as useful and as trustworthy as Mastin says you are, you *might* one day get off this base and be allowed to help with the war. But until then, until I say so, you will behave yourself as any self-respecting guest would."

Wow. Someone is used to getting his way! No wonder Mastin had been such a jerk when he'd first met me. I pinched my leg under the table, pushing the anger down deep, and smiled sweetly, nodding. "Of course, sir. I wouldn't dream of crossing you."

He was lucky I knew how to control my alchemy. He was on the receiving end of a hailstorm of dangerous emotion.

"Dad, I know you don't trust her, but you also don't know her. Don't be so quick to judge," Mastin cut in.

I smiled, despite myself. I had befriended Mastin, hadn't I? Pretty sure to the point that the man wanted more than friendship. I could get his father to trust me and take me with him to the warfront. I just needed to play my cards right.

"Thank you so much for this delicious meal, Mrs. Scott," I said, sending a practiced smile to the woman. "Please, I would like to help out wherever I can while I'm here.

Whatever you need, just let me know."

I turned to Nathan Scott: man of this house, a man who strategized for a living. He had no idea who'd he just invited into his home. "That goes for you as well, General Scott. I'm here to help."

"We'll see about that," he replied.

I smiled. "Yes, you will."

▼

My feet echoed a familiar rhythm on the pavement as I ran along the path. My stone necklace thumped against my chest, reassuring. The sunrise was just beginning to peek over the mountains, a small bit of warmth tickling my face. I brushed away the beads of sweat dotting my forehead and pushed on, running faster. An ache twisted deep into my side, but I ignored it for as long as I could. Eventually, I stopped to catch my breath. My throat burned, and my heartbeat raced. I wasn't in the same shape as before being in the palace prison, but I would get it back. I was determined to come out stronger than ever.

Nathan had assured me I would be safe on the military base, so when I'd woken extra early, my body clock messed up, I'd decided to do the one thing I always did when things got weird, when I needed to think: run. But that early trust had started to wear off as I stood catching my breath and took in my surroundings.

The base was huge, expanding much wider than the tidy neighborhood where the Scott family lived. Nondescript buildings littered the area, with sprawling green lawns and several apartment buildings. I'd stopped on a bluff. On one side the glorious blue of the Pacific Ocean stretched out far below, and the mountains loomed on the other. The base was nestled in between. There were far more people out at this hour than I'd expected. Men and women were doing their morning exercises, some alone, others in units. I watched them move, their routines practiced. It was every time I crossed paths with one that my senses fired. They stared like they *knew* I didn't belong, expressions a mix of curiosity and mistrust.

I shook it off, ready to head back to the house.

A group of four men jogged toward me. I glanced around. The path had cleared out except for these men with cruel eyes trained on me. Worry crept up my chest. I turned, ready to flee, and ran right into the chest of another runner. His chest was akin to a brick wall, and I fell back onto my butt. I cursed.

"Sorry," I mumbled.

"Watch where you're going," he yelled, his voice harsh and scolding. His cheeks flushed, as his muscles bulged out of his khaki shirt.

"Yeah, my fault. Sorry." I brushed myself off and stood, wincing at the pain in my hip. If I were alone I would just use some of the grass to heal myself. But five men, much larger than me, all glared in a way that told me I'd better keep my magic to myself. But so what? Should I hide who I am? They would never understand alchemy if it was always kept hidden away like something shameful.

"You don't belong here," the same man said, stepping close and towering over me. "We ought to just take you out right now and get it over with." The other four surrounded me and nodded, like it was the best idea they'd ever heard.

Not today, buddy!

I straightened and met his gaze head on. "That would be a very bad idea."

"Nobody will know it was us. Sun's barely out," he said.

"I knew those men who died for you, you know that?" the youngest of the men sneered, moving in closer as he looked me up and down. He pummeled his fist into his palm. "Wasn't worth it."

Guilt burned, a twisting knife. The death of those men had been added to the memories that haunted me. It wasn't my fault, I knew that. Nobody made West America come pick us up. If these guys had a problem, they should take it up with Mastin and his father; but no, they'd rather pick on the girl practically half their size. If only they knew...

"Have you ever seen an alchemist in action?" I lifted my chin in challenge. One thing I'd learned about bullies, they liked to prey on the weak.

He spat on the ground. "Of course not."

Interesting. So, he hadn't been to the front line yet. If he had, he'd have seen the Guardians, would have first hand knowledge of how powerful magic could be.

I lifted the necklace out from under my shirt. I knew a rainbow of stones were visible even in the dim light. "I could use yellow to beat the crap out of all five of you, by myself. Hmm, or maybe I should use purple and spy on your thoughts, tell all your friends here your deepest, darkest secret. Oh, the possibilities." I smirked.

He rested his hand on his holster. They all had guns here. It was the first thing I'd noticed about the soldiers on base. They could kill me with a single bullet to the head. But that would make noise, and bullets could be traced.

"Who's first?" I asked. I wasn't bluffing anymore. If I needed to take these guys out, I would.

"Watch your back, little girl," the guy said, pointing at me, before backing off. His buzzed hair glistened in the sun as he and his gang jogged away. I sucked in a breath before sprinting back to the house. My limbs shook, and my hip throbbed the whole way, but I pushed past the pain. Mastin stood on the front porch, hands on his hips, his glare visible from across the street.

"Why on earth would you go running alone?" He snapped, his eyes running up and down my body as I caught my breath. "And you're limping. What happened?"

"It was nothing. I fell." I wasn't about to tell him the truth and prove his point. Mastin wasn't someone who needed any more validation. I leaned down to stretch out my legs, making sure to point my butt away from him. Because, let's be honest, that's embarrassing.

"Just because my father says you're safe here doesn't mean you are," he said, running his hand along the back of his neck. "If you want to go running, you go with me. In fact, if you want to leave this house at all, you don't do it alone. Understood?"

My, my, aren't we bossy in the morning?

"I was fine," I said. "I can handle myself."

His expression darkened, and I relented. "Fine," I huffed, exasperated.

"Good," he replied, his body relaxing. If you could call it relaxing. Mastin probably didn't have the word "relaxation" in his vocabulary. "Because you and I are going on a little excursion tomorrow and I need to get you there in one piece."

"Where?" I asked.

"You'll find out tomorrow." He glowered and then walked back into the house. Wait; did he seriously think I would be patient about this? I pushed through the door. "Where?" I pressed.

He turned on me then, eyes flickering across my face. I was lucky my cheeks were already red from running. The sudden urge to kiss him slammed through me, a reaction I hated and loved all at the same time. I bit my lip, weighing the possibility in my mind. How much would change between us? And what would it mean for my relationship with Tristan? I tried to think through it logically, but Mastin was too close for that. I leaned in a fraction of an inch, my lips parting.

"You need to learn some patience," he said, eyes flicking up and down my face. Then he turned and walked away. I stood awkwardly in the dark entryway, wondering if he was talking about our trip tomorrow or about our almost-kiss.

NINE
JESSA

The problem with red alchemy was the blood. There was no other red that came to me, no matter how many times I tried. Stones, synthetics, plants—none of it worked. Only blood. Purple, however, wasn't too difficult and didn't require such a high cost as blood. It got me into this mess, maybe it could get me out.

Madame Silver and I finished our dance lesson early today, just as we had planned for the foreseeable future. We were going to do a little more than dance with the rest of our time.

"Are you ready?"

She smiled wisely, coming to stand in front of me. She put her cold hands on my shoulders, still warm from dancing, and nodded. "Whatever you need."

"Let's start with this." I skipped to my jacket and found the stone that I'd put in the pocket earlier. I ran my thumb along the smooth purple and flashed it to her, so she could get a better look. "Alchemy is typically a magic where we have to touch the recipient of the magic to do anything to them, but with purple, that isn't always the case. And I'm wondering,"

I trailed off.

Madame Silver smiled tentatively and nodded for me to continue. She didn't fully know what she was getting into, and for that I loved her even more. Our eyes met, and her bravery steeled me. The tingle of magic found its way inside and filled me. I reached out to her first with my hand, and then with my mind.

Can you hear me? I asked.

Her hand jumped to cover her mouth, eyes wide as she nodded.

I continued, speaking to her in my mind. *Try talking back to me. It's like thinking a thought but directing that thought at me instead of just to yourself.* I wasn't sure if a non-magical person could reply but since the connection was strong, it might be possible.

This is so strange, she said. *Can you hear me, Jessa?*

I nodded, excitement bursting out. "Okay," I said, breaking the magic. It washed away like sand swirling under an ocean wave. "I want to try again but this time let's go to opposite sides of the room and turn the music on really loud."

She flipped a switch on the stereo-system. The classical melody I'd been practicing to just minutes before blared through the room like thunder. I yelled out, "Can you hear me?"

She scrunched up her face and cupped her ear. I gave her two thumbs up and reconnected with the purple stone warming the hollow of my neck. It was an odd alchemy, like lightning as it made contact. When I directed it at Madame Silver, the magic seemed to both zap through me and settle on her at the same time.

Can you hear me? I asked the question again, this time with the telepathy weaving its path between us. I couldn't see it, but I could feel it, could sense the way it wound around its two hosts.

She burst into spontaneous laughter, once again pressing her palms to her cheeks. When she replied, it came straight through to my mind. *This is amazing. I can hear you as clearly as if I were thinking the words myself. You can hear me too, even with all this music?*

Sure can.

She jumped and clapped, then steadied herself. I'd known the woman for years, but I didn't think I'd ever seen her so excited. She was one of those people who took a while to read because she was usually so demure and classic. But not today!

I smiled and shook my head, our grins mirroring each other as she danced over to the stereo and shut off the music.

"So what's next?" She placed one hand on her hip.

"Hmm, that's a good question," I said. "I don't want to try anything that might hurt you, so red alchemy is out. I'm terrible with blue, so we could try that, though I bet it will be pointless. Yellow isn't really something I need to work on. Orange…well, we won't even go there."

"What does orange do?" she asked, her eyebrows rising.

"Ha, well, it just enhances emotion," I said. "An angry person becomes more angry, happy becomes happier, that kind of thing."

"What about white? Black? Do those do anything?"

I bit my lip. "No." The lie came out before I had a chance to consider the different angles. She was helping me, trusting me, so shouldn't I trust her too? But the amount of people who knew about white alchemy I could count on one hand and I wasn't sure she needed to know about it anyway.

Madame Silver ran her hand along her chin, her signature inquisitive pose. She always did it when solving a problem in her brilliant mind. I fought the pang of guilt knowing I'd lied to her.

Well, half-lied, as I didn't know if black did anything.

I think we should keep working on purple together and I'll work on the other colors alone, I said through our telepathy. *I want to set a time where we can connect again, but this time you'd be outside the palace and I would be here.*

She nodded and smiled wickedly. *Do you think that would work?*

It's worth a shot, I continued our telepathic conversation. *I've done it long distance before, just not that far.* The memory of the purple test and the young girl I'd "saved" flashed through my mind.

Well then, let's do it tomorrow and we can report our findings on Friday if we don't know right away.

I pulled her into a hug, sinking into her small frame. *Thank you.*

As I left our lesson, a sense of hope stirred in my heart. It was the first time in weeks that emotion had found its way to that broken place. Could I trust it? Probably not, but just for today, I desperately wanted to try.

▼

I pulled the coat around my shoulders, shivering in the cold.

"What are we doing, Lucas?"

"There's something I want to show you," he said.

"Do I have a choice?" I asked, attempting to rub the exhaustion from my drooping eyes. It didn't work. My vision blurred when I opened them to find Lucas's hurt expression staring back at me. His breath fogged as he thought of what to say. Regret crawled up me, but I squashed it before it took root. *Can't let that in.*

We'd spent the morning finalizing things with the wedding

planner, and I'd agreed with everything Lucas had said. I'd figured that was better than voicing my true opinions on this wedding, a wedding that was only a few short weeks away.

"Please," He tried again, concern etched in his brow. "I promise you'll like it."

"All right." I nodded. He wasn't going to back down. "Let's go."

"Oh, we're not going for a walk out here," he said with a boyish grin. "We're leaving the palace."

I squealed in delight, the idea of getting out of the palace instantly perking me up. He led me to the drive and soon we were climbing into one of the royal armored cars. A heavy security detail joined us both in the car and in three others. Ever since the attacks on him and his father, his security had tripled. With things so dangerous for him lately, Lucas must have gotten permission from the King for this outing. The idea set me both on edge and gave me chills.

We drove for over an hour until we had left the city and its suburbs. We took a winding road out into the surrounding forest. The snow had melted into murky piles of slush in the capitol and around the palace, losing its fresh scent and becoming ashy and putrid. But out here where it was still mostly untouched, the snow had hardened into shining sheets of white ice under the December sun.

I watched the scenery both in interest and as an excuse to ignore Lucas. I was still angry with him. Our relationship was so far beyond repair that I was doubly frustrated with his persistent efforts to mend things between us. The ballet studio, Madame Silver, my father's close proximity, they were all bridges he was trying to build to reach me. And while they were appreciated, they didn't matter. Not really. How could I *ever* forget what he'd done? I couldn't. I wouldn't be so naïve again. Taking him back would be the mistake of a lovesick girl, something I refused to ever be again.

After a long ride, we pulled up to a large maroon brick estate. I decided it was called an estate because the main house was enormous and had smaller outbuildings around its perimeter. It had "grounds" similar to the palace with a sprawling lawn, pastures filled with horses, and a neat garden, all frozen under the winter tundra.

"What is this place?" I asked, finally turning to Lucas in the seat next to me.

"It's one of our royal residences," he replied. "We have the main palace, a beach house in the southern province, and this place up here."

"It's beautiful," I said, stating the obvious. It really was gorgeous. But did he think he'd win me back by flaunting his wealth? By showing me what kind of life we'd be sharing together? My stomach dropped, and I sank back into the leather seat.

"It *is* beautiful," he said with a knowing smile. "That's why I convinced my parents that we didn't need to keep it to ourselves. We rarely came up here and it has a fulltime staff, seemed such a shame to let all that beauty go to waste."

So what is it used for now and what does it have to do with me?

We stepped out of the car, our boots crunching on the mix of gravel and ice. The cold wrapped around me like a wet blanket, and I shivered deep, pulling my coat around me. Lucas took that as an invitation to wrap his arm around me and while his warmth was nice, I took no comfort in it.

He didn't ring the doorbell, just pushed open the huge black door and called out, "Knock, knock, we're here!" We stepped inside.

"Prince Lucas!" a young boy squealed and came running, socks sliding on the hardwood floor as he dashed to Lucas.

Although he only had socks on his feet, he was dressed in a blue school uniform. He smiled wide, revealing gapped teeth. Lucas reached down to rub his mess of blonde curls.

"Hey there, Joey." Lucas laughed, hugging the boy. "How's it going, man?"

"We've been decorating for Christmas. Do you celebrate that at the palace? I know most people don't anymore. You probably don't. But Ms. Franklin does, and she said we could decorate this year. We actually got to cut down a tree. Did you know they do that at Christmas? It was so fun! I helped, I did. It's huge. It's in the main room. And we made strings of popcorn to wrap around it and—" The boy prattled as he led us to the sitting room. The home was old, but it was gorgeous. It reminded me of how Queen Natasha had decorated her parts of the palace, only this was the real thing; the original style.

I could easily see why she found inspiration in it. It felt safe. Welcoming.

"Prince Lucas, how have you been, dear?" An older woman padded in, her eyes shining with affection for Lucas as she pulled him into a tight embrace. "We've missed you around here. I know you've been so busy with this ghastly war business and of course, your exciting engagement, but do come visit us more often or I'll have to travel out there and drag you back myself. You know how the children adore your visits."

He laughed and apologized for his unusually long absence. And then he introduced me to the woman, the little boy, and a myriad of other people, a handful of adults and dozens of other children who crowded the sitting room. At first, I sat in stunned silence, realizing this was an orphanage. But it wasn't long before I loosened up and began chatting with some of the children.

"Would you like to help out here for a few hours?" Lucas leaned in and asked conspiratorially in my ear.

"I would love to," I replied.

We started by reading to the younger ones and then helping a few of the older ones with math homework. That didn't last long for me because I hated math.

"Are you hungry?" the older lady, who I'd learned was called Mistress Grace, asked. My stomach pinched at the mere mention of food.

The large dining hall had been set with plates for the forty-three children and eight adults who lived here full-time. We dined with the kids, laughing at all their childish jokes.

"Are you two getting married?" Joey's little voice rose in disgust. "Do you kiss and stuff?"

My cheeks burned.

"I'll let you handle this," I whispered to Lucas who'd turned on me with a wicked grin.

"Yes." He leaned toward Joey. "We are getting married."

"So do you love her?"

My chest throbbed when Lucas nodded and said, "Yes. I do."

The conversation changed as dessert was served, but I felt Lucas's eyes heavy on me for the rest of the meal.

Soon it was time for us to go. The sun had set hours ago and I couldn't fight the tiredness any longer. Maybe I could sleep on the drive back. I hugged the children tightly and had to pinky-swear promise most of them that I would return after the wedding. It was a promise that came with a stab of regret, because if I had it my way, I wouldn't be keeping it.

We walked quickly back to the car, huffing in freezing air, and climbed inside. The heater was a welcomed friend, and my body softened against my seat. Exhaustion overtook me, and my eyes fluttered closed.

Lucas sat beside me, and even with my eyes closed, I could feel him watching and waiting.

"Okay, you win," I said softly. "That was worth it. Thank you for taking me here. Those kids are wonderful."

We were alone in the car this time. One of the security team had climbed up front but the partition window was up so it was just the two of us. Was that Lucas's doing?

I peeked open my eyes to see his turned on me, two shining orbs in the darkness. A hint of light cut an outline against his cheekbone and forehead. He was so unbearably handsome that I had to hold my breath. "Those kids used to live somewhere that wasn't very nice," he said. "Let's just leave it at that."

"And you convinced your father to let them take over one of *his* residences?" I asked, though I already knew the answer. "Wow."

He nodded. "Mom loved the idea," he said in a choked voice. "Really, she was the one to convince Dad. This was about four years ago. We hadn't been up here in a while and after a trip to the old orphanage for a charity thing, I brought up that this place was probably collecting cobwebs."

"Good for you, Lucas. You did a good thing," I said earnestly. I shifted away to watch the world rush by outside the window. My breath created a circle of fog on the glass, and I resisted the urge to reach up and doodle in it. As a kid I wouldn't have thought twice.

"I didn't bring you here to boast about something good I did years ago. I brought you here so that you could see the kind of thing we can do once we're King and Queen. We can do so much good, Jessa. We can fix things."

And how long will it take? Richard wasn't going anywhere, certainly not anytime soon.

My hand rested against the seat, and Lucas placed his on top. His thumb ran the length of my hand, and my chest burned. His touch warmed my frozen fingers, which only served to anger me.

"I don't want to talk about this," I snapped, pulling it free.

"When will you talk about it? Because like it or not, the wedding is only three weeks away."

"Don't you think I know that? I don't need a reminder."

He stiffened as he replied in an icy tone, "I'm sorry. I'm sorry about how this all played out. I'm sorry about Jasmine—you have no idea how sorry. I can keep saying it and it will still be true. But we're here now, we're engaged, we love each other, so why can't we just find a way to be happy?"

I gaped at him. "You think it's that easy? You broke my trust, Lucas. And not in some small, insignificant way, either, in case you forgot. You got my mentor killed. Because of you, my father and sister were locked up. My dad still is. And my mom and sister are who knows where."

"But Sasha got out." He leaned close, his jaw popping.

Seriously? Had he not heard anything else I said? "No. Just no. I'm not talking about this again. I'll marry you because I must, because your father has commanded it and I have no choice. But that's it, Lucas. Don't fool yourself into thinking it's real."

"But it is real," he sighed. "I know you love me as much as I love you."

"My love was destroyed. You destroyed it!" I yelled. There was a long pause as the air between us crackled. "I will play house with you in public, but I won't pretend behind closed doors. I won't open my heart to you *ever* again. You would be better off to end our engagement and find someone who will give you what you want."

His expression hardened as he shook his head, and turned

away. My heart ached, beating a steady rhythm of *liar, liar, liar,* as it pushed my angry blood through my veins. I did love him. The second I'd said I didn't, the lie nearly choked me. But I refused to take it back. It was time I grew up. I was finding a way back to the Resistance and a way out of this palace. It was either that, or I had to turn on the royals and use my magic against them. Jasmine would have loved that. That's what she'd wanted all along, wasn't it?

Either way, it would be what was best for me. Not for Lucas. Not for *us.*

I shifted away as well, pressing my body against the door and staring through blurry vision out into the deadened night. I imagined doodling in that fogged up window once again. As a child I loved to draw hearts. Much like the children at the orphanage, I'd only seen the good in people, the light in the world. The love. But tonight, that drawing would no longer be a whole heart, but one left in pieces. One broken and battered and looking for revenge.

I wasn't trying to be cruel. I wanted him just as much as he wanted me. It killed me to be so cold, colder even than the frozen tundra outside. But I had to do what needed to be done. I had to step up, even if it meant giving up my first love.

▼

At the agreed upon time, I retreated to my room and used purple alchemy to reach out to Madame Silver. Nothing happened.

Either she didn't hear me, or I couldn't hear her reply, but the attempt proved fruitless. Frustrated, I tried it again and again. Fifteen more minutes ticked by before I gave up, deciding to wait until our next appointment to see if she heard anything. And then, if she agreed, we'd keep trying.

In the meantime, I had another class to teach.

I quickly found myself standing in the corner, bored, counting down the minutes until we could be done with this. I observed the students, each having zero success with red alchemy. Faulk had started the class by trying other red sources, to no avail. Now the students were attempting again with blood. It was a waste; the sight of it made my stomach churn.

"You could at least pretend to try," Faulk said with a sneer, her boots clipped the floor as she walked over.

"What's the point?" I asked. "Seriously, it's not working. Nothing is working. Maybe we should just give it up and focus on a color that actually matters."

"Red matters. Or haven't you figured that out yet?"

I gulped. Oh, I had.

"Fine," I muttered, scooting from the wall. I strolled around the room, giving encouragement and tips to the students. They weren't very receptive. They ignored me or rolled their eyes, some even made sarcastic remarks.

"Hey, don't worry about it." Callie was working with her two best friends, Tessa and Sam—the trio was normally together. I could tell Callie wanted me to be part of their pack, but Sam seemed indifferent either way, and Tessa hated me. "It's not like anyone actually expects this to work," Callie continued. "It's just one of those things, I guess." She shrugged and returned to her red flower, which didn't have a speck of color missing.

The trio had pushed their desks together and were chatting before I'd interrupted. Sam watched me with equal parts expectancy and curiosity, waiting for me to add something to the conversation. And Tessa ignored me, healing a small cut on her hand, her face twisted in disgust.

"I'm sorry," I said. "I wish there was more I could do to help." Another lie. I wished red alchemy didn't exist; my opinion was probably obvious.

Tessa huffed. "Whatever. I'm going to the bathroom." She rolled her eyes and left. Sam watched her go and then turned back to me.

"Is there any other way?" he asked. "Maybe something we haven't tried yet."

"If there is," I said, "then I haven't thought of it, yet."

He nodded pensively and went back to twisting the petals of the poor flower. The room was full of plants. A bushel of colors sat atop each desk, the large red exotic flower blooming in the center of each.

Are you still with us? a male's voice echoed through my mind.

I blinked, peering around the room. The voice sounded familiar, but also muddled somehow. And it was most definitely coming through with telepathy. My eyes shot to Dax, the boy who'd already revealed his talent for this kind of alchemy. But he was joking around with his friends, not even paying attention to me. And his voice sounded nothing like the one I'd just heard. I turned around in a full circle, looking for something out of place, someone staring at me, perhaps.

After Jasmine, you can understand how I've decided to keep my identity from you a secret, the voice said.

I bit my lip, attempting not to look startled. If this person was using purple alchemy to talk to me, I should be able to respond.

Who is this? I asked, pushing the question through the bond.

Like I said, it's best for you not to know my identity. But I was a friend of Jasmine's before she died.

You're Resistance?

I am, the deep voice said. *And I wanted to know if you're still part of our mission.*

I paused, considering my options.

At this point, my only mission is to get out of this palace before I'm married off.

That's a shame. You're closer now then you ever were before.

Jasmine had urged me to turn my red alchemy against the King, to bring him into their control. But it was too dangerous. Wasn't it?

You want me to control the royals? I asked.

Who better than the red alchemist engaged to the prince?

My heart raced and my fingers tingled. He was right. Who better?

I'll think about it, I finally replied, *but I can't make any promises.*

I continued to search the room, trying to catch the eye of someone who could be communicating with me, but nobody seemed fazed, let alone like they were in the middle of using powerful telepathy magic.

Who are you if you can't follow through? Jasmine died to save you, died so you could do this.

It felt as if a bucket of ice was being poured down my back. I surged for the door, ready to face whoever this man was. I whipped my head back and forth, looking up and down the hallway, but there wasn't a soul.

How can I find you again? I asked desperately. *We should meet.*

The voice didn't respond.

TEN

SASHA

I met Mastin at the door, hand on my hip, my head cocked casually to the side, but a fire burned low in my belly, one I refused to extinguish. "Let me go with you."

It was the third morning in a row that I was being forced to stay back in the house while the men went off to trainings and meetings, and I was beyond sick of it.

"I've said it to you the last three days and I'll say it to you again," he replied with the same flash of annoyance I'd learned to ignore. "No." He wasn't dressed in his typical khaki. He looked sharp in a military suit, and it seemed to me he was meeting important people today.

"You won't even give me a chance," I huffed.

"Only because the entire reason you're here in my home instead of somewhere else is to protect you." He eyed me wearily. "Did you forget that people hate you in this country?"

I laughed. "Right? Like you think that ever stopped me before?"

He shook his head and squared his wide shoulders. The

sunlight hit his eyes, turning them emerald. Honestly, he looked better than ever, and it was starting to get on my nerves. I wanted to train, to fight, and to help with the cause, not to crush on this idiot. *If Mastin doesn't see my value, well, that's his problem, not mine.*

"Fine, I gave you a chance, but you leave me no choice." I brushed past him. I strode into the kitchen where I knew his father would be finishing breakfast before leaving for the day. We ate dinners in the elegant dining room, but the rest of the food was shared in here.

"Hello dear," Melissa said with a warm smile. "Are you still hungry? Would you like some more?" She held up a heaping bowl of scrambled eggs in one hand and a plate of bacon in the other.

She placed them on the table and patted her husband on the back.

"No, thank you," I replied, pulling out the chair next to Nathan and sliding in.

His gaze flicked to me, guarded, and he gave me the rise of thick eyebrows. Although they didn't look alike, the action reminded me so much of his son that it almost slowed me down. Almost.

But then again, I've never had any trouble giving Mastin hell before, have I?

"I want to help," I said, leaning forward and meeting his glower with one of my own. "I'm used to being on the inside. I've worked with the Resistance, hand in hand, since I was ten years old. I went undercover for them when I was seventeen and spent two years at an outpost before making my way into the palace." My heart raced as I continued, "I know more about New Colony than most of your operatives, even your spies. There's no point in having me here, in your home, on this military base, no less, right where you could use me, only to lock me up in a *guest room*."

He stared at me, considering. I took a deep breath and continued, "I have friends and family back in New Colony, so I have more on the line than most. I'm an alchemist, yes, but you should use that to your advantage instead of ignoring the opportunity you have right in front of you."

He leaned back in his chair, folding his arms across his bulky chest. Mastin had come to stand behind him, glaring down at me. I shook my head, not quite finished.

"You think King Richard won't use alchemy to destroy you? Because he will, he is, and there's a lot you who need to learn about alchemy if you're going to fight it."

"Sasha," Mastin cut in, "that's enough."

"I'm not talking to you," I spat, turning back to General Nathan Scott.

"Did you know you gave King Richard *your* alchemists? Yup, that's right, he recruited all the people you'd sent to the slaughter in some foolhardy attempt to assassinate him. They are being wined and dined, trained, and turned into weapons."

"And what would you have me do about that?" Nathan finally said, his jaw tensing.

I laughed. "I think it's about time you invite me to come along to whatever it is you have planned and put me to good use. He recruited your alchemists? So, you recruit his."

"Father, I'm sorry," Mastin said. "She's not used to civilian life."

Nathan held up a hand to shush him and studied me for a long moment. His face had slowly darkened to a deep red as I'd gone off at him. He was either going to agree with me, or punish me.

"Anything else you'd like to add?" he asked darkly.

"You will have no idea what I'm capable of if you don't try

me," I replied.

There was another long, stretched-out pause, and the color drained from his face. *Yup, I'm right, old man. Deal with it.*

"She does have a point," Melissa said, strolling over and placing her hands gently on her husband's shoulders. She began to rub his tense muscles. "If you want to win this war, you should know everything you can about your enemy and Sasha could be the answer you've been searching for."

"Mel," Nathan replied, shutting his eyes. "You really think this is a good idea?"

"No!" Mastin interjected. "It's not a good idea. It's too dangerous for her."

I shot him a glare, annoyed and also a little hurt. Hadn't I proven myself to him by now?

"I think it's a great idea," Melissa replied, then she patted him on the back, picked up his empty plate, and began cleaning up the kitchen as if everything we were dealing with wasn't as important as keeping her house clean. But I liked her for it; she had a happy nurturing quality that I certainly didn't have myself. I didn't envy it. I liked who I was.

Nathan stared at the table for a while before he finally nodded. A surge of triumph rushed through me. "Fine, Sasha, you win. We'll start today."

I wanted to turn to Mastin, stick out my tongue, and yell *I told you so*. But I was twenty, I reminded myself. Be cool. Instead I smiled at his father and leaned back in my chair. "Trust me, sir, you won't regret this."

He shook his head and stood from the table. "Trust is a mighty big word for such a little girl," he said. I froze, ignoring the impulse to jump up and smack him. Oh, I'd show him what this *little girl* was capable of, with or without his support.

▼

"Okay, you wanted your chance," Nathan said. "Let's see what you can do."

The morning sun beat through the clear blue sky. Several long rows of soldiers were lined up on one of the vast lawns. No kidding, probably three or four hundred soldiers stared at me like I was an alien, an evil demon, or something. Each stood at attention, camo-style green-brown pants and tops like a second skin over taut muscles. They eyed me warily, but stood at attention for their General.

I peeked at Mastin, wondering again why he'd kept his father's position a secret from me for so long. Was it a trust issue? A pride issue? Mastin stood with a stick-straight back, his mouth set in a firm line, arms behind his back and eyes ahead.

Nathan Scott turned on me. "Well, are you all talk or are you going to do something."

I shook away my nerves as his comment seeped into my bones, the realization settling deep. "What do you mean?" My heart sped up with the questions. "You want me to do alchemy here? Right now?"

"You tell me," Nathan grumbled. "You were adamant that your alchemy is so useful, so show me. Do something."

"Fine." I smiled despite myself. "Hand to hand combat with one of your men." That could be fun.

"We use guns and bombs," Mastin spoke up. He didn't bother to move to offer his opinion. Not that anyone asked him!

"Not always." I'd seen men practicing their fighting and it looked much the same as it was back home. "Besides, I can use green alchemy to heal any wounds that don't immediately kill me." I walked nonchalantly to stand in front of Mastin.

I winked. His mouth quirked ever so slightly as he stood at attention like all the other soldiers. *Ha! Got you!*

I used to wonder how he stayed so aloof most of the time, even if he did have a temper, it was nothing compared to mine. But seeing him here in his element, and meeting his powerful father, I understood.

"My son has a good point. How would you use an alchemist to fight against bullets and bombs?" Nathan asked. I turned to meet his smirk, shaking my head. He had no idea.

A bead of sweat formed on my temple, but I didn't wipe it away. "The alchemists working with Richard have trained military with them, it's not as if they're defenseless in that area. Alchemists aren't the soldiers, they're the weapons."

His eyes were hard black slits as he leaned in. "Interesting choice of words."

I shrugged.

"I don't think a little *healing magic* is going to save them from real weapons," Nathan quipped loudly, his voice carrying over the lawn. He put the words healing magic into air quotes. The group of men close enough to hear our conversation laughed at his joke. I didn't find it funny.

"Maybe not," I shot back, hands fisted at my sides, holding my temper at bay. Scott was the General after all, and I was keenly aware that I was probably the only person on this base without a gun. "But I've seen alchemy do more than just heal wounds, even life-threatening wounds. I've seen it turn people mad with emotion. I've seen it convince whole crowds that obvious lies are the truth." My voice roared, echoing across the lawn for everyone to hear— the blue resting against my chest aiding me. "I've seen it used for telepathy, to read the future, to eavesdrop on conversations happening miles away. Some can use it to control people's minds, make them do things they never would otherwise.

It gives people super human strength. I've even seen it turn an entire helicopter invisible, completely invisible, *even* on radar."

The snickering had long since dissipated now, and I stared out into the crowd of naysayers. "So yeah, any one of your men can shoot a gun, and believe me, New Colony has those too, but not just anyone can do what an alchemist can do, and as far as I can tell, I'm the only willing alchemist *you've* got."

It was my second tirade of the day and it left the people around me more speechless than the first. I steeled myself for the fallout, not at all regretful of what I'd said. It had all been the truth. And these people needed to hear the truth. Everyone did. I was so sick of the lies, and wasn't going to let my time here be used to create more.

I studied the faces of the men in front of me and was instantly hit with a wall of hatred and fear—hardened eyes, clenched jaws, and fisted hands. Here I was, what they saw as a *little girl*, someone who clearly didn't belong, and I was holding my own with their General. Not only that, I'd revealed to them things about color alchemy that they didn't know, things that should terrify them.

Mastin broke protocol and stepped up next to me, muttering under his breath. "Are you trying to get yourself killed? I swear to God, Sasha, you're going to give me an ulcer."

I elbowed him in the side. "Don't swear."

"Let's start with your super human strength," Nathan cut in, loud enough that it also echoed across the lawn. His body language wasn't defensive anymore. Dare I say, it was proud? "Show us."

I nodded. "I can't do all those things I mentioned, no alchemist can. But I can do that one."

"What else can you do?" He turned, his eyes narrowed slits, along with hundreds of others. I quivered under the pressure, swallowing hard.

"The healing, the super human strength, the enhancing emotions," I said, "pretty much all alchemists can do that. But I can also block people from hearing me if I need."

"But not the rest of the...powers...you mentioned?" He studied me.

"That's all."

Liar.

If I told them about red alchemy they'd probably kill me on the spot. Or maybe just lock me up for safekeeping. And besides, I hadn't done it in years. I wasn't even sure if I could still do it if I wanted to.

"The invisibility? The telepathy? Mind control?"

"Super rare." I gulped. "But King Richard has alchemists at the palace who *can* do all of those things."

He stilled, then nodded and flicked his wrist toward the space of lawn between the three of us and the rest of his men. "Like I said, show us this super human strength."

I took five long strides forward until I was between Mastin and his father, and the rest of the men. My rainbow rock necklace rested under my clothes, flush against my skin. They didn't need to see the color. It was safer for me if they didn't know quite exactly how I accessed my magic, better if most of these men thought I could do it at any time. Though I figured Nathan and Mastin knew well enough that wasn't the case, that I actually needed access to the organic colors.

I reached out to the yellow with my mind and it met me like an eager puppy, excited by the attention. The magic shot through me with a jolt, a tickling burning sensation rolling through my body. I used the momentum to start running. I ran between one of the rows of men. Startled, they had no issue getting out of my way. I was fast, zipping down the row, blood pumping. To everyone else, I was a blur of blonde hair, white skin, and black clothes.

Getting closer to my target, I jumped, easily clearing thirty feet, before landing with a thud in the sidewalk with such force that it cracked the pavement. A huge army tank was parked just in front of me. I hunkered down and placed my hands under one of the rubber tires. It was taller than me! Taking a deep breath, filling the magic through my entire being, I lifted the tire off the ground, the tank tilting as I stood tall. I strained against the insane weight, the ridges from the tire digging into my arms like rubber knives. After a few seconds I couldn't take it much longer, so I dropped the tank and stepped back, brushing myself off.

Swinging back toward the crowd, I issued a bow. Admittedly, it was not my brightest move. Tristan would have laughed.

"She's unnatural."

"A witch!"

"Get her out of here!"

Mastin and Nathan jogged toward me. I didn't miss the fire raging in Mastin's usually mossy eyes. I couldn't look away.

"That was amazing," another voice boomed over the crowd.

"I wouldn't mind some of that magic on the battlefield."

A few snickered.

"Show us more, little witch!"

"I really don't appreciate being called a witch, thank you very much!" I yelled back.

Mastin stopped in front of me, putting both hands on my arms. He pulled me away from the soldiers, moving his body to block me like a human shield. "Let's get you out of here," he growled low.

"No," Nathan said, his voice soft enough that only we could hear. "You don't want to appear to be too friendly with her, Mastin. Step away."

The crowd was stirring, growing louder.

Mastin froze for a second but did as his father asked.

"Squadron, attention!" Nathan called out sharply. The men immediately stood at attention, their bodies tall, feet at 45-degree angles, their fists balled at their sides, and their mouths? Oh, they shut those real fast. It made me wish I was a General. Nathan had earned the kind of power that came from respect, not magic, and it was a sight to behold.

"You will treat Sasha as if she were one of our own," he said, his voice clear. "This is a direct order not only from me but from our Madame President. Sasha is here to help us, and she will be shown utmost respect at all times. Not only that, but you will protect her as if she is our biggest asset in this war, because quite frankly, she might be."

There was a long pause and then he finished with a single nod. "Please continue on with the rest of your scheduled activities for the day. As you were!"

The men disbanded. I watched them go with the kind of curiosity that lifted my spirit ever so slightly. I could relate to these people and maybe I would be one of them soon. True, most of them ignored me, others nodded their approval, and even more eyed me with suspicion, fear, or hatred. But I didn't let it get to me. These people had just seen their first bit of color alchemy, and whether positive or negative, it had made a lasting impact on each and every one of them.

They wouldn't forget me, and maybe that's how change would start.

▼

Nathan brought me along to all his meetings that day. It was like getting a bucket of cold water dropped over the head.

A wake-up call.

That night as we sat around the dining table, I didn't have anything to add to the conversation. I stirred the food around my plate, lost in thought.

First, the war was not going so well for West America.

Richard's troops were gaining ground every day. And if the American citizens didn't go along with whatever he wanted, they faced some nasty consequences. Torture and death in most cases. Color alchemy destroying land in others, but it seemed that particular problem had started to let up the more ground New Colony gained.

In the last two weeks, West America had tried several times to bomb the New Colony troops, but nobody got through. People were starting to wonder if the bombers should just go and bomb the palace. Never mind the fact that there were plenty of innocent people living there, many of them children. The very idea of it made me ill, and I hated Richard. But it wasn't right to send others to an early grave because of him.

The President had felt that way too, apparently.

That had been why they'd started with the original plan they'd involved me in, the one that had failed miserably, delivering a boat-load of alchemists right into Richard's hands.

And now everything was a mess.

War was a mess.

I sighed and leaned back in my chair, watching the family on either side of me. They seemed to have it all, the perfect home, perfect careers, love and respect. Would all of that become a casualty of this war as well?

The very idea officially ruined my appetite. I dropped my

fork down with a clatter.

"May I be excused, please?" I turned on General Scott.

He studied me for a moment and nodded.

I took the stairs two at a time, retreating to my bedroom. I didn't want to watch that family downstairs anymore. Not with what I knew was coming. It wouldn't be long before Mastin and his father were out on the frontline, leaving Melissa to worry.

I plopped down on my bed and rolled onto my stomach, groaning into the squishy pillow. Would they let me come with them? I had to go! I needed to save who I could. Get Christopher and Jessa out somehow. Help those innocent West American alchemists I'd let down. Plus the many others who were Resistance, or who simply didn't deserve to die.

And it wasn't going to happen sitting on this military base.

Someone knocked on the door.

"Come in," I muttered.

Mastin walked in, rubbing his hand along the back of his buzzed hair and watching me with trepidation.

"I'm fine," I said, sitting up. "Really, it's all good."

He nodded once.

"Are you up for a surprise?"

I rolled my eyes. "Is it a good surprise?"

"It is. We get to leave base. It's already been cleared for approval."

Adrenaline shot through my veins as I jumped up.

"Are we going to the war?"

He stared at me, his mouth turning down in a frown. "No," he replied. "We're going to the beach."

Oh. Well, fine then.

I followed him out to a black, shiny SUV that turned out to be his. As we drove out of the base and into the city, down winding roads that led to the ocean, I was plagued with guilt. I shouldn't be here, shouldn't be going to the beach. People needed me. I rested my forehead on the window, telling myself it was okay to enjoy this moment. Having a good life when others suffered, that didn't mean I should suffer too. Right?

I closed my eyes against the setting sun and drove the thoughts from my mind. *Just breathe.*

We turned into a parking lot. The view unfolded before us, a spectacular horizon. The sun was setting over the ocean, transforming the sky into a vibrant mix of oranges, pinks, and purples. The second he parked, I was out of the car. I sprinted, kicking off my shoes as I reached the sand.

"The water is super cold this time of year," Mastin called after me. "Don't go in there!"

But I didn't care what he said, and besides, I was hardly listening. I planned to dive into the water and lose my worries to the thrashing waves. The salty air whipped past me as my feet buried deep with each heavy stride. The crashing sound drew me to it like a relief I didn't know I needed, but now that it was here I *had* to be a part of it.

"Well it's nice to see you, too!" a voice called out and I jerked from my run and spun, sand flying, to see Tristan coming down the beach. He walked toward me, Mom and Lacey on either side of him. I cried out, abandoned the water, and darted toward the group. I tackled Tristan as I jumped on him, my body wrapping around his in a full-body hug.

"Whoa, hold on there!" He laughed. "It's only been a week."

"Shut it," I said, nuzzling into his warmth and squeezing tighter for a second longer. Then I released him and hugged Lacey, and a surprise to us both, I hugged my mother.

"I've missed all of you," I said, putting special emphasis on the all. "This has been a crazy couple of weeks and I'm just so glad to see you're safe and healthy."

"We agree," Mom replied, though I could see lines on her face that weren't there the night I'd left her behind. The very same night Christopher had insisted on coming on that foolhardy mission and gotten himself captured.

"He's all right," I said, answering the question I knew was on the tip of her tongue. "Last I saw of him they'd moved him up into the palace, in a room right next to Jessa. They're treating him good, as leverage on her, I think. But he's all right. And so is she." *For now.*

She breathed out a sigh of relief and nodded.

I kneeled down to Lacey and wrapped her in a second hug. "I missed you." Her little body melded against me and I breathed in her sweet scent. A pulse of love went through me, so strong, I nearly cried out.

"Mom says you're my sister, too," Lacey said when I'd finally released her from my grip. "I'm so happy to have another sister *and* I'm so happy that it's you!"

She grinned up at me, her blonde hair wild in the wind. The sun reflected off of her blue eyes, mirrors of Jessa's, and the longing for all my family burned deep.

"I'm glad I'm your sister, too," I replied, the words a catharsis on my lips. "You have no idea how much I've missed my family."

We all sat down on the sand and talked, watching the sun set, the colors fading from bright, to pastel, and then to nothing at all. When the darkness overtook us, the chill set in.

"I'm so cold." Lacey started to whine as kids do and it was clearly time to go.

"It's okay." We stood, and I hugged Mom and Lacey goodbye. As they walked up the beach, a heaviness weighed me down. Tristan leaned into me and I rested my head against him, drawing on his strength.

A few military men stood in the parking lot. They helped Mom and Lacey into the car, then nodded toward Tristan. My gaze drifted toward Mastin who waited patiently, leaning against the side of his car. He gave me a quick wave, but that was all. I bit my lip, pondering.

"I'll walk you back," Tristan said, tucking his arm around me. I realized that I'd begun to shiver, and only now could I feel it.

We ambled toward the parking lot, moving slowly. We weren't ready for our time together to end. I didn't think I was ever ready for my time with Tristan to end. He was home to me. He was comfort. Some people have comfort items or blankets or animals, I had him.

"Where's Hank?" I asked.

"He couldn't come. He's been in so many meetings," Tristan replied. "He's working with lots of high-ranking people these days. But I'm sure you'll see him soon. I know he misses you."

I nodded. "I miss him. And I've missed you," I added, rubbing my forehead against him. We stopped and pulled each other in for another hug. He rested his chin on the top of my head and relaxed into me. I lingered against the hard plains of his body. They did something to my insides, something that caused the opposite of relaxation. I buzzed.

"I missed you, too," he whispered. "How's it staying with Mastin's family? Do you feel safe there?"

"Safe enough," I said, careful to keep my mouth shut about how there were just as many people who hated alchemists inside the base as there were off of it. But I didn't want to worry him.

I looked up to meet his pained expression. "What is it? What's wrong?"

He shook his head once, the wind flipping his black hair to one side. It blended in with the sky above him.

"Just tell me."

"It's selfish," he muttered.

"I don't care." And I didn't. I would do anything for Tristan.

"Can I ask you to do something for me?" He stepped back, only slightly, so we were inches apart. My gaze flicked to his lips and then back to his eyes. They were dark pools. Unreadable. Dangerous.

"You can ask me to do anything and I'll do it."

He cleared his throat, like he was afraid to ask. And that was weird because Tristan wasn't afraid of anything. "Don't date Mastin," he said. "I know there's something between you, but I also know there's something between us."

I stilled, my chest icy hot.

His thumb trailed up the side of my arm until his palm cradled my face. "I want my chance. I know it's not the right time, and I might not get to see you for a while. It's not your fault that you're spending every day with him." He had started to ramble and a smile tugged at my lips. He let out a shuddering breath. "I don't want to lose you, Frankie. Please, wait for me."

I blinked rapidly, trying to process everything. Was Tristan confessing feelings for me? For *years*, I'd dreamed of this moment, fantasized about it, wanting nothing more than to hear those words come from that perfect mouth, directed at me. And now it was here—I didn't know what to do or say.

And I hated it. I hated that my heart was unsettled. But I couldn't turn him down. I just couldn't, because I did love Tristan. And I wanted him, too. I just wasn't one hundred percent sure in what way. To lose our friendship would destroy me.

When I looked him in the eye and nodded, he smiled.

Then he tugged my hand into his. We wrapped our fingers together and everything felt good again.

ELEVEN
LUCAS

A crashing thud slammed through my sleep, followed by a sickening roar. The very foundation of the palace rattled, shaking my bed and waking me with a start. I ran to my window, threw open the curtains, and peered out into the inky darkness. A billowing cloud of fire raged just off the horizon, glowing so wildly it was almost mesmerizing.

Two guards rushed in, shouting orders. They pulled me from the window and ushered me to the entrance to our family's safe room. It was hidden behind a nondescript paneled door off our main living area. I stumbled into the tight space, my shoulders brushing either side. It had been years since I'd been down here, and then, only for drills.

"Lock it from the inside," one of the guards said, throwing the door shut in my face.

Hands shaking, I gripped the metal bar that clicked into place, securing me inside. A few steps and I began to descend the narrow, winding staircase. With each step, the adrenaline only rose in me.

Below, I heard Richard muttering to someone. They were already heading down the stairs that led into the underground bunker. I hurried to follow close behind, trying to ignore the cold air. At the bottom was a concrete room, no more than fifteen feet by fifteen feet, fortified with food cans, water jugs, and three sets of bunk beds. Along one of the walls gleamed black guns, rested on several racks. The sight was unsettling and reassuring at the same time. I knew how to use one if it came down to it, but I'd rather not. At the far end of the crammed space was another door. It was solid metal, the huge lever locked in place. Behind it was an underground tunnel. It led out of the palace to a secret exit almost a mile away. I'd never used it before. Never had to. War was new for me.

And yet one thing I can count on is everything changes, and this has, too. I'm not safe as long as this war continues.

I shook out the nerves and then sat on one of the bunks. The adrenaline that was coursing through my body threatened to make me sick. I glanced at the only other door down here, knowing it led to a bathroom. Resting my head against my hands, I breathed slowly. Someone sat next to me and I glanced up at my father. I stiffened. Did he think I was weak?

"Where's Jessa?" I asked. "She should be down here."

Richard rubbed at his temples, ruffling his messy sleep-rumpled hair. It always caught me off guard to see him out of his normal formal dress, instead donning black silk pajamas. He was clearly out of his element.

"Well?" I prodded.

He shrugged. "I don't know. But I am guessing she's fine. They didn't make it to the palace."

I frowned, unsatisfied.

"Look, son," he continued. "When you're married, she'll

be with you, so this won't happen."

I huffed. He tugged at his hair, trying to straighten it out. It was one more thing changing lately. He'd lost so much color in the last few months. It used to be lightly streaked with gray, but now it was succumbing to the color. The lines that marked his face were carved especially deep in the dim light. When he exhaled, I could feel the exhaustion. But all this was his own doing. He hadn't protected Mom. He'd started the war. Lied about so many things. No wonder he was exhausted.

"How did they get through our men?" Richard asked, looking up at the three men who'd somehow been prioritized over Jessa because they were with us in this stupid hidey-hole. And where, exactly, was she?

"Only one of their bombers made it past our fighters but we were able to stop him before he made his target," the man replied, an officer, one of Faulk's best.

"I'm guessing the palace was his target?" I interjected.

Everyone looked at me, like I'd said something obvious, before continuing on with their conversation. Okay fine, the palace had been their target—it didn't take a genius to realize that. They wanted to murder me in my sleep. Me, and so many others, so many innocents, would have died with me. Nerves rolled through my body again, uncoiling like a snake.

I locked eyes with one of the other men who'd been granted access down here. Mark, Celia's father, and the man who I'd suspected was up to something for a while. Clearly, he was working for my father in more than just some kind of agricultural capacity. He was a war advisor, or he wouldn't be in this room.

The man regarded me as if I were of little consequence, focusing on my father.

"We were coming to wake both of you and move you down here when the plane crashed," Mark said. My eyes adjusted as I took in the frustrated set of his shoulders and the hard line of his jaw. "But our bomber was able to drop them before they got to the palace," he continued.

"They got too close," I huffed, thinking about how large that ball of fire had been, and probably still was.

"We should have been woken at the instant our territory was breached!" Richard yelled, standing up and breaking out of his exhaustion in a moment of fury. The group of men staggered back and cowered, but the challenge in Mark's eyes stayed put. He wasn't openly defiant, but it was there, just the same. Was he Resistance? Was it something else? My curious mind buzzed.

"We had it all under control," Mark said slowly. "Your Royal Highness." He bowed to Richard. "We didn't want to wake you with these trivial details."

"I don't think a West American bomber crashing into our capitol city qualifies as having it under control," Richard snapped.

I have to agree with that!

I thought back to what I'd heard and seen, and it clicked. It wasn't a bomb exploding but a plane being taken down. Which neighborhood had been hit? How many were now dead, injured, or without a home because of this?

"We have patrols on it and Faulk is already on her way," Mark continued. "They'll clean up and get a body count within a few hours. The bomber crashed in a field, so we don't expect the casualty count to be too high. Still, some of the neighboring homes caught fire pretty quickly, unfortunately. We're waiting to get word about the damage done there."

"Faulk," Richard huffed. "She and I are going to have to have a little chat. I have a feeling she's not going to like it."

A long pause followed; Richard's anger settled in. I noticed Mark's small smile. Was he gunning for Faulk's job? I wouldn't be surprised if he had it by the end of the day.

Dad stood and marched from one side of the bunker to the other.

"All right, we'll have to use this for our own benefit," he said, continuing to pace. His eyes filled with his trademark spark of excitement and my heart sank. What was he up to now? "We will let the people know what kind of savages we're dealing with, targeting innocent homes like that. I'll make a statement about it to the press first thing in the morning," Richard said. "Is it safe for us to go upstairs?"

I clenched my hands into fists and fought the urge to roll my eyes at his immediate plan to spin yet another problem toward his own favor. But nobody seemed to notice me, nor care. Did it not matter that the plane had been taken down by us? That they hadn't been targeting random people but the leaders of this kingdom? Of course it didn't matter. This was politics.

Mark slid a slatebook from his suit jacket and called one of his men on the outside. After a moment, he nodded the go ahead to leave the bunker.

"And one more thing," Richard said as we made for the stairs. "We're not postponing or canceling the exhibition. We're leaving this afternoon."

"Wise choice," Mark replied.

"Wait, what?" I sputtered on the question as I followed the men up the staircase. "Am I going? Is Jessa? Why didn't anyone tell me about this? It's *today*?"

"Always so full of questions, Lucas, but it's not my fault you missed the meeting on this," Richard said, not turning back to look at me. "You need to pay attention, and show up. If you had, you'd know we decided to keep this one quiet. We'll *all* go, do the alchemy exhibition for a few hand-selected families, and then air the segment after we've returned home. It will be a quick trip. Less than twenty-four hours."

"Why so secretive?"

"I'm not risking any more chances for someone to catch wind of our absence from the palace," he replied. "The less people who know, the better. The palace is the safest place for us, and being away puts us at risk."

I wasn't sure that was true, considering the circumstances, but I bit back the remark. He never listened to me anyway, not when he'd already made up his mind.

"Well then," I said sarcastically. "Sign me up."

"Don't worry, Lucas. I already did."

▼

The hunting lodge loomed ahead as we shuffled from the cars. Immediately, we were assaulted by freezing wind, the kind that clawed angrily at any exposed skin. I tucked my scarf tighter around my face and neck, wrapped my arm around Jessa, and hurried us toward the building. It was a massive log cabin, with wide gleaming windows and several wraparound porches. I'd been here a number of times; this was one of Dad's favorite places to schmooze his court. Still, the initial sight always sent a shiver of anticipation up my spine. I loved this place.

Tall pine trees surrounded the lodge on all sides, except for the front where we'd driven in our procession of armored cars. Now the cars were quickly emptied, hordes of wide-eyed alchemists, officers, guards, media crew, and even military men ambling around the drive.

The northern province wasn't very populated, and besides the lodge and forest, there wasn't much to see up here. But still, the crew filmed it all because Richard said it was a great opportunity to show off different parts of the kingdom. All of this was meant to build popularity among the people. Popularity was the lifeblood of the royal family, and now, the alchemists needed it as well. I hoped it didn't backfire but I could easily count a million ways why and how it eventually would—starting with the fact that these alchemists being televised used to have families. What would happen when parents recognized their stolen children from long ago?

I shook my head. *Not my problem.*

I tugged Jessa in closer as we stumbled into the entrance of the lodge, a tail of security close behind us. The warmth of the space was welcoming, and I relaxed into it. Jessa stepped away, rubbing at her ears and jaw, her cheeks and nose bright red. Her smile faltered when she saw me watching her, but then she wrapped her hand in mine and smiled, dropping a small kiss on my cheek. I ignored the cameras in our faces, documenting the royal love story. I also ignored the cool doubt that was chillier than the air outside.

Seeing the way she fought against me with every passing day was killing me. Betrayal and anger clawed at my confidence like puncturing wounds.

Her hand was icy cold in mine. She peered up at me with a coy smile. "Show me around? You said you know this place pretty well, didn't you?" Her eyes flicked to the camera as it zoomed in closer.

I froze, anger burning me up. I wanted this to be *real.*

An overwhelming need overtook me to either warm her small hand against my lips or push it away. Instead, I left it tucked in mine and led her out of the crowded foyer.

▼

I gave her a quick tour, starting with the game room, then on to the various living rooms stacked with comfortable chairs, leather couches, and pillows. We passed the dining area briefly—we'd be eating in there soon enough. We finished in what would be her room for the night. A burly cameraman, who'd kept his equipment trained on us up until this point, stepped back and saluted me.

I smiled conspiratorially as I closed the door.

"I'll just go out here for a few minutes to give the illusion that we're as happy as ever and then I'll get out of your way," I said. I dropped her hand and pointed to the balcony off the back of the bedroom. Nobody would see me up there since it was at the top of the lodge and tucked back against the tall pines.

"Are you sure?" Jessa asked. "It's really cold outside and your coat is still downstairs."

"I'll be fine. We only have to put on this show at dinner tonight and at the exhibition tomorrow. The rest of your time here is all yours. Don't worry about me."

"Okay," she said softly, her lip pouting. Did she actually have the nerve to be hurt by this?

"You can't have it both ways," I snapped, stepping through the balcony door and closing it behind me before she could respond.

She'd made it aggressively clear that she had no interest in forgiving me, let alone actually trying to make our relationship work. And I was done. With the camera following us around, the fact that she was *acting* had become excruciatingly clear. I had to let her go. It killed me, but it hurt worse to force it with her. My feelings were real, which only made her fake ones stand out in contrast.

I need to get her out of New Colony. That's what you want for her now, I told myself, forcing myself to believe it.

I breathed in the cold air, no longer affected by it. My body had settled into the bitterness. The pine scent washed over me, giving me a moment of tainted joy. I leaned against the wooden railing. This place only proved to bring back memories of Mom. This was another one of our vacation spots when I was a kid. I always knew I'd have this lodge to visit. It would be mine, too. And someday, I planned to bring my own wife and kids here to enjoy the stillness of the forest.

The way things were going, my future looked a lot like my parents' past. I closed my eyes and tried to picture it being any other way.

Tired of self-loathing, I pushed off the railing and let myself back through the bedroom door. Jessa startled, sitting on the bed with a slatebook in her lap. I didn't even look at her. Didn't say a word. I continued out into the hallway and down two sets of stairs. I found my coat on the rack, and bursting through the main doors, I let myself outside. I didn't mind the wind smacking my cheeks or the bright sun glaring in my eyes. I just needed to get away. When my bodyguards followed, I turned on them.

"Give me five minutes," I barked, and they faltered.

I strode into the thick set of trees, my feet carrying me down a hidden path I knew like the lines on my own palm. Dad had always said it was a deer path since it wasn't made by humans. Instead, it was barely visible to the eye, just a line of dirt to follow between the trees. As a kid I'd spent many summer afternoons walking it until I'd get scared and turn back. Then I'd go again the next day, always pushing a little further each time I ventured out.

In the winter, however, it was much harder to follow. That didn't surprise me. Even though it was more overgrown than I'd remembered and there weren't any leaves to block the way, there was snow. Mostly it was pines, and hibernating bushes and trees lined the path. The snow was muddied from where the deer and other animals had come through, so I found it and followed as best as I could, driving deeper into the forest.

Think. It's time to think.

I need a better plan. So far, all I have are a couple of addresses. Those won't be enough, will they?

A twig snapped. Boots crunched against the icy snow. Stillness descended upon the forest like a blanket.

I crouched against a tree and waited. It was most likely a bodyguard. I'd snapped at them, but this was their job. They probably followed anyway. But what if it wasn't a guard? The image of fire flashed through my mind. The planes. First the family jet. Then the bomber plane. Not to mention the gunman at Mom's funeral, the way the bullets had pinged off the pavement.

Coming out here alone was reckless. What was I thinking?

"Lucas? Is that you?" a soft, feminine voice called out.

The crimson red of Celia's hair appeared between a couple of trees, and I exhaled my breath.

I relaxed, and I slid out from behind the tree.

"Yeah, it's me," I said, approaching Celia. "You shouldn't be out here. You could get lost. It's going to be dark soon."

"I could say the same thing to you," she said. "Anyway, I was just heading back. You want to walk with me?"

"No," I replied.

Her mouth clenched. Was she surprised? Offended? Not that I blamed the girl. I was surprised with myself, but I was tired of the games, and Celia was certainly one to play puppet-master whenever she could. I wasn't dealing with that today.

"Well, then," she huffed, "so much for chivalry."

I shrugged. "I'm not ready to go back," I said. "I just came out here. But I'll see you at dinner."

There was a heavy pause. A gush of wind weaved through the trees, rattling the pine, a few dropping needles around us to rest on the white snow.

"Was it worth it?" She stepped close and peered up at me with intense curiosity.

"Was what worth it?"

"Choosing love over the logic?" She smirked, tugging the hood on her white fur coat over her hair.

"I assume you're talking about my engagement to Jessa."

"Of course." She cocked her head and smiled demurely, her bright red lips a contrast to the snow.

I wasn't going to talk to her about this, not right now. "Go home, Celia," I said, brushing her off and turning to head further up the barely-there path.

"I see the way she looks at you," Celia said. "I don't know what you did, but you certainly have an angry fiancé on your hands. What *did* you do, Lucas?"

I walked away. She didn't follow me, and I didn't care.

That family was trouble.

They were nosy, attention seeking, and lately, they were everywhere. Was I going to confide in Celia about my betrayal of Jessa only to betray Jessa's secrets even more? *Not likely.*

A few minutes later the scraping sound of boots on snow returned.

"I told you to go back," I said, turning to look for Celia. There wasn't a reply, only a sharp stillness. I paused and listened, then froze when I heard the sound once again. This time it was slower, softer, like whoever it was, was trying to be quieter.

"Who's there?" I called out.

Silence.

The sensation of being watched spread through me.

If it was a guard or someone meant to protect me, they'd have replied. Celia would have replied, and anyway, now that I thought about it, the sound of her boots had been different. These were heavier somehow, but also, quicker.

They sounded again, closer this time.

I took off at a run, ducking through low-hanging branches and working my way up the path. My breath was hot in my ears as I worked out where to go next. I probably knew this forest better than anyone. Would that matter?

I stopped abruptly, stilling to listen. The distinct sound of boots on snow crunched through the air once again. I jumped behind the biggest and closest pine, hoping I was hidden. I ripped off my glove, grabbed some snow in my hand, and turned myself invisible.

Please don't let them have seen that!

Then, I waited.

I waited for whoever was looking for me to pass so I could know without a doubt who they were. Maybe if I caught a glimpse, I would discover who wanted me dead. Could they be one and the same? It seemed a likely scenario as I stood motionless and invisible in the cold winter landscape.

Realization sank deep. Whoever they were, they were in the inner circle. They had to be if they were here, at such a private event, an event that only those invited knew about in advance.

I waited eagerly, wondering if I'd see Faulk stumbling through the trees. Or maybe Mark or Sabine. Maybe an officer, one of the alchemists or teachers. Maybe someone I'd never expect.

But the sound of boots was gone.

The forest once again fell silent. They must have retreated. No longer able to bear the cold, I slowly maneuvered back to the lodge. I didn't take the same path, in case someone was waiting for me. I stayed invisible as long as I dared, despite leaving incriminating footprints in the snow.

Visible or not, every step I took these days was a step in a dangerous direction. The trouble was, I didn't know how to course-correct. People wanted me out of the picture, many of them, and all I could do was continue on a path that might one day lead to my death.

TWELVE

JESSA

Jessa, are you there? Can we trust you? The smooth voice filtered through my mind, familiar and deep. I fought to hold onto sleep, my body cocooned by the fluffy comforter and my emotions exhausted. The nap came without much thought, but I wasn't ready to wake up quite yet.

Jessa, are you in there? The voice jerked at me once again.

Jessa…

I sat up, realizing what was happening. My heart sped, and my hand swept to clutch the rainbow stone necklace that hung around my neck.

I'm here. I reached out with my mind. *What do you want?*

Are you still with the Resistance? they asked boldly.

I stilled, weighing the decision on whether or not to tell the truth. What if the person on the other end of this conversation was a spy for Faulk?

If you're really with the Resistance, I said, *tell me something to prove it.*

There was brief silence. *Your sister was never really with the prince; it was a deal they made together to get her closer to the King and Queen.*

Relief washed over me.

I could accept that. As far as everyone else knew, Sasha had played Lucas. They didn't know about his brief interlude with the Resistance.

I got up from the bed and paced the room, my feet padding softly against the hardwood floor. I peeked outside the main door and into the hallway, hoping maybe I'd see someone acting suspicious, but there were only guards. All the bedrooms were on the top two floors, so whoever was talking to me could easily be in their own room, hidden.

There had been about twenty alchemists and officers, plus a few higher-ranking families loaded into those cars this morning. And guards. Lots of guards. And I couldn't forget the camera crew.

Whoever it was, I was just going to have to trust them if I wanted answers.

If there's still a Resistance, then I'm still with them, I replied.

We thought so, but we had to make sure. Why did you tell the royals about the attack?

We? I bit my lip and sighed. *I told Lucas because I thought I could trust him. I wanted to save him from getting hurt, but he betrayed me.*

We've already received word about that. But it looks like Lucas may be on our side again. We're being cautious about it.

Why would they think he was on their side again?

Doesn't matter, I replied. *I'll never tell him my secrets again.*

There was another long pause. The wind howled against the windowpane, rattling the frame. I shivered and sat back on the bed, pulling the comforter over my jean-clad legs. Even with the white sweater I'd thrown on that morning for good measure, I was freezing, the cold wind relentless.

Are you going to use your blood alchemy against King Richard? the voice asked. *If you can get him close enough, get him alone, you could end this all right now. End him and end the problem.*

But wasn't the issue deeper than just one man? What about the officers? Faulk? What about the alchemists who willingly participated in hurting innocent people in the name of New Colony? If Lucas took over, he might turn out to be the same. After everything, I just didn't know anymore.

I'm not a murderer. Jasmine never mentioned murder and I won't agree to it.

You say that now, but you might change your mind.

I mean it.

Okay, so what's your plan then?

I laughed. *Plan? I just want to get out of here before I end up married to a Heart. I don't want to end up like Queen Natasha.* Guilt ripped me at the statement. Lucas might be misguided, but he wasn't Richard. And I wasn't Natasha.

Maybe things would be different?

But still, my chest burned at the idea of a loveless marriage. I thought about what my parents had, how they treated each other, and the trust between them. That was what I wanted. A love that came before politics and circumstance.

Who are you? If you want me to help you, I deserve to know who you are.

There was another break in time, and I waited as patiently as I could. It was as if the person talking with me wasn't alone, like they were conversing with someone else. He had said "we", hadn't he?

I know there's at least two of you, I said, trying to see if I was right. *I know one of you must be a purple alchemist. I'll figure it out eventually, so you might as well reveal yourselves.*

And have us end up dead like Jasmine? the voice shot back. *How do we know you won't go to your fiancé about us?*

Prickly tears burned at the back of my eyes. Not because I was upset with him but because he was right. People had died because I'd told Lucas too much.

I already explained how I feel about what happened with Lucas. I won't say a word to anyone about you. I swear it.

More silence. I waited once again, but my nerves were beginning to get the best of me.

Besides, you need me, I added, *or else you wouldn't have reached out.* I jumped up from the bed again and paced the length of the bedroom. The longing to get back in with the Resistance, to not be alone in this, pulsed through my veins.

Come out on the balcony, the voice said.

I grabbed the fuzzy throw-blanket from the end of bed and wrapped it around me. I opened the door and stepped out onto the small wooden balcony. There was an overhang from the roof so no snow had reached the porch, thankfully, but the planks froze my bare feet. I ignored the cold and surveyed the back of the lodge with its identical balconies, searching for another alchemist. A few guards were posted along the edge of the forest, but nobody else was on their back balcony as far as I could tell.

Where are you? I asked again, getting annoyed. *I'm not standing out here all day. I'll freeze.*

A door opened a few rooms over, and Lily Mason slipped out. Her white-blonde hair whipped in the wind. After a long pause, she turned to smile at me.

"Hi, Jessa. How are you?" she called out, her voice nearly lost on the wind.

"Hi," I yelled back, narrowing my eyes.

I know I'm talking to a man, I said back to the voice in my mind. *Does Lily have anything to do with you?*

The pause this time was short.

We had to be extra careful with you, so Lily shared her magic with me.

Then another person swung open Lily's door, joining her. An officer. Not just any officer, either, but one of the men who worked directly with Faulk. I didn't know his name, but I knew him to be an enforcer. Brute strength. And worst of all, one of the men who'd beaten up my sister and father right in front of me.

I stilled at the sight of him, bile rising in my throat. How was I supposed to trust a Royal Officer, let along *this* one?

He turned his cunning smile on me, his dark eyes flashing, and ran a hand through his curly black hair. *As you can see, I need to be extra careful about anyone knowing I'm Resistance.*

I pushed my suspicion down and focused on the matter at hand.

I don't get it. Can Lily give you her purple magic?

He reached out and placed his hand on her shoulder. She leaned into him, her cheeks pink. *Yes. Most alchemists could share their magic if they really worked at it. It takes practice but it's possible. She can transfer yellow to me, purple, green. I can administer the magic, though it fades quickly. I have to keep getting hits from her every minute or so.*

I stumbled back and leaned against the railing as this revelation sunk in.

Why doesn't the King do this? Wouldn't he want that kind of power?

And would he want me to give him my red magic? What would happen if I refused him?

The man met my eyes across the space. *He does.*

My breath caught.

He's very sparing about it because he doesn't want anyone else to know about this kind of power.

Why not?

For the same reason he polices the alchemists with us officers in the first place. So nobody will get strong enough to rise up against him.

A bitter gust of wind flung my hair into a million different directions, but I ignored it as I studied the man with Lily. They weren't quite touching but I could *tell* they wanted to. There was something there. A familiarity that went beyond friendship. The way they stood near each other, looked at each other, revealed it all. They were lovers.

So you're both Resistance, I asked for the confirmation again. The link between us was strong despite the howling wind. I could hear every word as if I were the one thinking them.

We are. And as far as I know I'm the only Royal Officer in the Resistance. I've been in and out of the palace on assignment, but I've been called in for the time being. I'll probably be back to the war front soon.

And you're with Lily? Are you a couple?

He stiffened and paused, then whispered something in her ear. She shifted to meet my gaze and nodded ever so slightly. For anyone watching us, perhaps the guards below, we'd look like people standing on balconies, having nothing to do with each other. And except for the initial hello between Lily and me, we hadn't spoken another word.

You can trust me, Lily's ethereal voice drifted into my mind. *Things aren't always as they seem, and your path has been laden with misfortune. It's not over yet, but stay strong and you'll find your way. You're the key to everything.*

What does that even mean? Why do you have to be so cryptic all the time?

She smiled one more time in my direction before going inside, the officer following. They shut the door with a slam, that I wasn't sure was from the wind or some sort of anger at me. And still, they'd never answered my question about being together.

What's your name? I called out, hoping to connect with the man again. He was so much easier to understand than Lily.

Jose, he replied, his voice calm through the link.

Okay, Jose, what's the plan here? I asked. *What am I supposed to do?*

We know you want to leave New Colony, to run away from this engagement, he said with certainty. *Don't. Stay. Stay and fight.*

Shaking my head, I glared into the white forest and then rushed back into my bedroom. That wasn't a plan. That wasn't anything! Don't run away? Stay and fight?

What did they expect? I needed to get Dad out. *I* needed to get out.

Jasmine was dead. Others would perish as well if I stayed here.

I thought I could help your Resistance. I was wrong.

Richard had used me to interrogate Sasha. He would do it again as soon as he needed to. The Resistance would have to complete their mission without me. I was a weapon in the hands of the wrong people, and the only way to stop more pain from happening was to remove myself from the equation as soon as possible.

Don't give up so soon, he replied. *Lily knows what she's talking about. You're the key to everything. You have to stay and marry Lucas.*

I'm sorry but I can't help you.

I broke the connection.

Lily and Jose would have to find someone else to lead their rebellion.

▼

"**Miss Loxely.**" **Faulk** smiled coolly. "What are you doing all the way back here? You're supposed to be going to be on camera with your fiancé." She pointed to the front of the room with a long bony finger and I groaned.

I wasn't ready for this! The exhibition had come *way* too quickly. We'd only just spent the night here and first thing the next morning, we were expected to perform. The largest of the living areas, called the "great room" had been mostly cleared out of furniture, and I waited like a stubborn mule in the corner, desperate to sneak away and hide. Chairs lined the back wall for the spectators. Up front, a few strategically placed couches and chairs waited for those who would be on the cameras, and unfortunately, that was where I was heading.

"I'm going there now," I replied. "It's nice to see you back, Faulk. I hear you've had your hands full with my sister's escape and the assassination attempts on the royal family. Your job certainly is important." I did little to keep the sarcasm from my tone.

"It is important," she agreed, eyes narrowing.

"I know," I replied, just to throw her off. "I would hate for you to lose it."

I pushed myself off the wall and strode toward Lucas.

When the makeup artist and hair stylist had woken me before the sun, they'd said it was because I'd be on camera longer than ever before. The result was hair that was perfectly curled in long waves framing my face and falling past my shoulders. My makeup had taken an hour, expertly applied to look like I wasn't wearing any at all. As if anyone would believe my lips were always this full and pouty, my cheeks this naturally blushed, skin this smooth, and eyes this big?

Yeah, right.

Lucas was already sitting on a loveseat off to one side of the set, and I joined him, trying not to blush at my perfect styling. "Hi Lucas," I said, sinking into the cushion and brushing my dress so it laid perfectly smooth.

I wore a cranberry sweater dress that fell just above my knees and sleek brown boots with white fur along the top. Natasha's ring caught the light and sparkled on my finger as I placed my hands on my shaking knees.

"Hi yourself," Lucas replied. He looked so good. I had to admit my heart was more than a little fluttery at the sight of him. He was styled in dark jeans and a white button-up shirt that fit him perfectly, showing off his muscular body underneath without trying too hard. His hair was done in that messy yet planned look that he pulled off so well. He noticed me checking him out and his charcoal eyes darkened. He didn't say anything, but he did reach out for my hand. I wrapped it in his and ignored the fluttering feelings inside.

"Don't worry," he commented after a few minutes of silence. "I made sure that we're not part of the exhibition. Dad wants us to tell our love story to the cameras when we start. Answer a few questions, that sort of thing. Just follow my lead and you'll be fine."

"Okay," I replied with a gulp, suddenly aware that the cameramen were turning on their equipment and pointing it right at us.

Callie sauntered into the room. I perked up, seeing my friend. She was equally made up with hair and makeup but dressed in the typical black guardian outfit. They'd tamed her normally wild hair into a smooth blonde sheet, and her cute glasses were missing.

"Contacts," she mouthed to me, rolling her eyes and giggling. She sat down gingerly on the other loveseat across from us, smiling brightly.

Lily Mason stepped into the room next, an energy of quiet power following in her wake. She didn't smile, but a knowing glint shined in her eyes as she joined Callie on the loveseat. She was in her early to mid-twenties, I couldn't remember which, but she was gorgeous. She too was dressed in her regular black guardian gear.

Finally, King Richard swept into the room, his energy bigger than anyone else's here. The buzzing conversation quieted instantly and the silence that hung in the air became thick and stifling. He sat in the big chair that was between the loveseats, the center of the action, brushed off his collar, and rolled his shoulders in his heavy navy sweater.

"Let's get started."

▼

"I can't believe I got so lucky," Lucas said, pulling me in close and leaning over to kiss my forehead. He lingered for a moment, and his scent filled me, making this pretense easier than it should have been. I grinned and snuggled closer.

"Yes," I said to the camera. "We're very lucky it all worked out."

I turned back to Richard who'd been conducting the interview. "Thank you again for accepting me into your family. I hope I can make your son happy."

"You already do," Richard replied, smiling at me for a long moment.

"Well, then," he continued, breaking the eye contact and returning his attention to the main camera. There were two more on either side, and spotlights behind those that reflected in our eyes. "As much as we all enjoy a good love story, I think it's time we get to what everyone is most excited about: color alchemy."

He shifted and focused on Callie and Lily who sat patiently on the other loveseat. The cameras followed.

"Our first exhibition featured some of our best male alchemists, of course the ones who aren't off winning the war." The spectators laughed accordingly. "In our second, I'd like to introduce you to some of our best female alchemists."

Callie blushed deeply at the compliment, her eyes lighting with the praise. As far as I knew, she'd always been treated like the others. And actually, she wasn't sent out to the war because she said she wasn't a good enough fighter. Maybe being chosen for the exhibition was a great honor to her. Or maybe there was something else going on.

I watched her carefully, looking for a break, but there was nothing. The way she smiled openly, the gleam in her eyes, her upright position on the couch, they all indicated that she was genuinely excited to be here. And that made me question again why she'd sought me out before to inquire about joining the Resistance. I wanted her to be my real friend. But was she just a stand in for Reed? Another lackey sent by Faulk to spy on me?

"This is Lily," Richard said, motioning to the women. "And this is Callie."

They nodded at the camera.

"Now Lily, let's start with you. Will you tell us what color you specialize in?"

"Purple. Or some may call it lavender. Violet. Lilac. Plum. Amethyst." Her voice tapered off as she thought. "Periwinkle," she added.

Richard laughed. "Well, I'm sure our viewers at home get the picture. Will you show us what you can do with it?"

"Of course," she said. "Whose future would you like me to read?"

"Why don't you read mine," he said.

She nodded, reaching for the purple stone that hung around her neck. A second later the color floated in the air, a cloud of sparkling hues, and then drifted into the top of the King's head and then her own.

"There will be more assassination attempts on you in the coming weeks," she said, her voice darker now. "But you will survive them all. You will be the victor."

Richard nodded, eyes heavy on her. "Thank you. Anything else you feel would be beneficial for us to know right now?"

I suspected that she was holding back. Or possibly, she was lying.

It was the look in her eyes. They didn't have that same faraway gaze she'd had when she'd done my reading. Not to mention, she was much more direct with her words and not as confusing. And this kind of magic had a way of twisting words, leaving too much to the imagination.

"You will make more progress in the war," she said. "But it won't end quite as soon as you have been planning."

"Thank you," Richard replied.

He raised his eyebrows at the camera. "Lily doesn't always get her predictions correct as the future is fluid and not set in stone, but she's been right about a lot of things." His voice became deep, certain. "It's been helpful for our planning. Now, I know it sounds like this war is going to get more dangerous than we expected, but in the end, we will prevail."

Everyone nodded encouragingly, even me. Not that I agreed or knew Lily to be telling the truth, but because of the watchful eyes of the cameras.

Are they going to show telepathy with purple? But my question was answered for me when Richard turned on Callie next.

"And Callie. Tell us, what is your magic?"

She faltered for a moment. "Um–orange, yellow, green, and a little bit of blue."

"We saw green and yellow at last exhibition," he said. "Why don't you show us some blue and orange?"

"Okay," she said. "Which one first?"

She blinked rapidly, like she was fighting back an avalanche of nerves. Her eyes flicked around and she briefly made eye contact with me. I nodded my approval. *You can do this, Callie.* I knew she couldn't hear me as I wasn't using magic, but I hoped our friendship connection would be enough. *Just relax.* She nodded back before beaming a bright smile on the King.

"Let's start with blue."

He addressed the camera again. "Blue is very useful. One of its uses is for listening in from far away. Right now we have someone outside, about forty feet away from the lodge. There's a camera with them as well. They're going to say something at a normal volume, and Callie here is going to relay the message back to us, here, in this room." He paused to let the explanation sink in as his eyes traveled from one audience member to the next. "Callie, has anyone coached you on who that person is or what they're going to say?"

"Oh no!" Her eyes were as wide as saucers. "I would never cheat." Even if she was going to cheat, nobody would suspect it with the innocent look on her face. Maybe that's why Richard had chosen her? She was just so sweet, opposite of the ruthless Dax of the first exhibition.

"Of course you wouldn't cheat." Richard laughed. "Let's get started, shall we?"

She nodded, and an officer quickly handed her a blue flower, stepping off-camera. She held it in her hands, and the magic twirled out of the petals in a tiny blue stream. It bounced around her and then formed a cone shape before entering her ears.

I bit my lip, wondering what this meant for our friendship. She'd never told me that she was a blue alchemist. Reed was, and look how that had turned out?

There was a moment of silence while she closed her eyes in concentration. "They're repeating two words: progress and order." Her eyes popped open. "Is that right?"

Richard smiled. "That is right. Good job, Callie. The camera outside will now confirm it for us."

The spectators applauded lightly, just the right amount for this intimate gathering. They sat in three neat rows of chairs along the back wall, a mix of alchemists, officers, and Richard's favored family. As I watched them, I knew that although Callie might not have been coached, they had been. I scratched my lip, trying hide the smirk.

"Progress and order," Richard said, "that's exactly why we're doing these exhibitions and showing the world what we're made of here in New Colony."

More applause.

"Now let's move on to orange," Richard said. "It's a much more common color for our alchemists to be able to perform."

"It enhances emotions," Callie said, shifting excitedly in her seat. Next to her, Lily almost looked bored. "But only if they're already feeling it. It's great at parties! We have a lot of those at the palace." She giggled, appearing again as the perfect picture of sweet youth and wide-eyed innocence.

I studied the way the crowd looked at her. They were enamored. No wonder Richard had chosen Callie for this job. It was a brilliant move by an expert strategist.

"Would you say you're treated well as an alchemist?" Richard asked. "Are you happy at the palace?"

"Oh, *very* well," she gushed, her cheeks turning rosy. "We

all love it at the palace. We get our own bedrooms and plenty to eat. We get to learn about our magic, help other people, and have a great time together. We're a family. I wouldn't change it for the world."

And there it was. If anyone at home was wondering if their long-lost children were happy, they had their answer, straight out of Callie's pretty mouth.

Okay. Callie *had* been coached. She was a happy girl, sure, but I'd never seen her quite this excited about anything. And I *did* think she missed her real family, it was the same vibe I got from a lot of the alchemists.

I shifted uncomfortably in my seat, waiting for whatever was coming next. Lucas gently squeezed my hand. I met his eyes, and he stared back, his expression guarded. Something lifted for a moment, and I saw a vulnerable pain there I'd only seen when talking about his mother's death. I wanted to reach out and bottle it up, hide it away so he'd never have to feel it again. But then his eyes darkened, and he looked away.

"I'm pleased to hear you're happy here," Richard continued.

"Thank you, Your Royal Highness," Callie replied. "It's an honor to be part of it all."

He chuckled. "Well, all right, let's get on with the orange alchemy, shall we?"

She stood eagerly as an orange orchid was passed into her hands. She lifted it to her nose and smelled it, then leaned back with a wide grin and looked out to the small crowd of observers. "I need a couple volunteers, please," she said. She shifted toward me and Lucas. "Unless you two would like to volunteer?"

Lucas stiffened. My eyes probably looked like they were about ready to pop out of my head. If our feelings got enhanced, we might not be able to put on this charade any longer. After his behavior last night, I knew he was mad at me. And I was still angry with him. There would always be something between us, but it didn't feel like love anymore. It was tainted.

Richard laughed, swooping in to save us from the embarrassment. "Oh, I don't think we need to guess what those two are feeling, nor should we enhance it. There's been enough public displays of affection from those two lately."

The crowd snickered.

"Don't be shy." He flicked a wrist toward the audience. A few brave souls raised their hands to volunteer.

"How about you?" He pointed to a young woman who had most definitely *not* raised her hand: Celia. Her face flooded with color as she shook her head and sank deeper into her chair.

"Don't be scared, we don't bite," he teased. After another moment of hesitation, and a nudge from her mother, she stood and strode toward us.

"As you can see," Richard said, "this is Celia Addington, my son's first fiancé. I already admitted my mistake in pushing two young people together who, it turned out, didn't have romantic feelings for each other. Luckily for everyone involved, we're all still friends, aren't we, Celia?"

By now he was standing next to Celia, draping one arm laboriously over her petite shoulders. Her mouth twisted ever so slightly, skin turning paler than usual. Her ill expression cleared quickly, however, as she turned to the camera with a demure smile. "Of course," she purred. "My family is happy to serve in whatever capacity is best for New Colony."

"Considering who your parents are, The Duke and Duchess Addington, I'm not surprised by your loyalty. Though, I am grateful." He squeezed her shoulders once and stepped away, sweeping his arm wide. "Callie will give you a little boost with this orange and I'm going to ask you a few questions. Whatever emotions you're feeling will be clear to the audience. Should be easy enough."

I gripped Lucas's hand. This was bad. And cruel. I wasn't her biggest fan, but even I wouldn't subject her to this. How was she supposed to save face with orange magic working against her?

Callie made quick work of the orange alchemy as she teased it from the beautiful orchid. It flowed elegantly from the flower and into Celia, seeping into her skin before disappearing. Immediately, her body tensed, becoming much more guarded than she was before. Gone was her cool exterior and in its place was an insecure woman with shifting eyes. She wrung out her hands nervously as she waited for Richard's questions.

"How do you really feel about Lucas's and Jessa's engagement?"

I stilled, holding my breath.

Orange magic didn't make her say anything, but it did make her feel it, and enough would have her talking.

"I feel good about it," Celia hissed. Her expression darkened considerably, mouth turning down and eyes thinning into angry slits.

"Again, I'm sorry for my haste in setting up the match," Richard said, acting the part of the admonished and regretful man. "Did you get hurt by what happened?"

Still standing, her knees began to wobble as she looked at the floor.

"It's okay," he pushed.

Tears fell down her face as she turned to look at Lucas. I stood, wanting to end this, but Lucas tugged at my hand, holding me back. "Don't," he whispered in my ear. "Don't interfere with Richard. You'll only make it worse."

"More," Richard motioned to Callie.

Celia's parents were no longer sitting either. They glowered from the back row of spectators, eyes wide with undeniable fury. Mine would be too if it was my daughter made to cry on a national broadcast! But trained guards and Royal Officers surrounded them. I watched as Mark eyed the people around him, tense. He knew, as well as anybody, that he'd have to wait and see how this played out.

Callie hadn't moved. The magic swirled around her, ready, but she held it at bay, her mouth open in a small pout.

"More!" Richard barked, no longer caring to appear polite. Callie's hesitation vanished. The orange magic twirled through the air. It fell upon Celia quickly, like a drop of food coloring seeping into the exposed skin of her arm. She broke down into sobs.

"Tell us," Richard said, resting a hand on her back in feigned comfort. "Let it out. I promise, nobody will judge you."

"It's not what you think," Celia gasped between sobs. "It wasn't as if we loved each other. I'm just so…embarrassed."

Her cries continued.

"And whose fault is that?" Richard asked.

Celia looked at me again. "It's Jessa's fault. She took him. I offered to share but she wanted him all to herself," she sobbed. "And Lucas. He didn't even try to care about me. He never gave me a chance."

Lucas and I grasped onto each other, motionless and chastised.

Slowly, Celia's sobs relaxed and her demeanor became filled with something else: anger. She whipped her head around, hair flying in an arc, and glared at me.

"More." Richard motioned to Callie. When she didn't move, he said it again, louder, and she jumped into action. The magic once again went to Celia.

I stepped closer, wanting to stop this. It was wrong. Celia didn't deserve this. Whatever she was feeling, it wasn't right to enhance it this much and embarrass her further.

"Whose fault is it, did you say?" Richard asked again.

"Jessa's fault," Celia growled. She glared at me, hatred seething in her eyes. Her face contorted as she watched Lucas pull me closer against him.

"I'm so sorry," I replied, my voice cracking. Guilt ripped at me. "Nobody ever meant for you to get hurt. It wasn't your fault, just bad timing."

"More," Richard said.

The magic shot through the air. The moment it hit Celia, she pounced.

One second, she was across the room, and the next on top of me. My head bounced against the floor with a sickening crack and she clawed into me, screaming profanities. Lucas grabbed at her waist, pulling her off.

"Stop!" I gasped. She had a fist locked onto my hair and wasn't letting go. Pain ripped through my scalp. I yelped, my vision blurring. Instinct kicked in, and I fought back, grabbing at her wrists.

She was up now, in Lucas's arms, and guards were swarming, but she wouldn't let go of my hair. I was half up and half on the ground, trying to get free. The pain burned, shocking me, as she yanked and yanked.

"You're a monster. A home wrecker!"

Reaching up, my nails dug into her wrists. I recognized the wet slick of her blood. I called to my magic. It only took a second. The red danced between us and then it was exactly where I needed it.

"Stop," I yelled. "Get off me!"

She did. She stepped back, all the emotion clearing from her face. It was a complete 180, one second she'd wanted to hurt me, the next she barely even cared about me or about anyone else. She slumped against Lucas and stared at the floor.

"Go to your room and clean yourself up, forget this ever happened," I ordered. I turned from her and assessed the damage she'd inflicted on me. There were a few small cuts on my arms but overall, I looked okay. It was my scalp that hurt. I needed something green…

When I looked up to make sure Celia was long gone, my heart raced in my chest. The room was silent. Everyone watched me, their faces confused and shocked. A few shook their heads. A few smiled knowingly. And that stupid camera was right in my face!

I closed my eyes for a second, counting down from five. Then I spun on Richard. "What did you just do?" I was careful to keep my voice down.

"That got out of hand." He raised his hands in protest. "I'm so sorry. Are you okay, Jessa?"

"I'm fine." I gritted my teeth. Then I took a deep breath. "I just feel bad for Celia. She didn't deserve that."

"But she attacked you," Richard pressed.

"Only because of the orange alchemy." I sighed and found my place back on the couch. Lucas joined, looking for wounds while I canvased the room.

What just happened?

"Well, it's a good thing you're a red alchemist," Richard said. He turned to the camera. "As you just witnessed, red alchemy, when used on blood, can be very useful." He paused for dramatic effect and my blood burned hot. "It can be used to control the mind." More silence. "Jessa is very special. She is our only red alchemist and that makes her our most powerful alchemist. Can you think of anyone better suited for the throne? To not only protect Lucas, but to aid him in leading this kingdom one day? I certainly can't. We are all very blessed to have Jessa as our future princess and one day, our queen."

The group applauded, the cameras zoomed, the lights just above them burned my eyes but I stared into them anyway. I couldn't bring myself to smile. I finally looked past the lights to the audience. A mix of trepidation and fascination had filled the expressions of any spectators who didn't know about my magic before today. The alchemists and officers, however, glowered at me in the way they always did, like I was the odd one out.

"That's all for today," Richard said. "Be sure to tune into our next exhibition. It will be broadcasted live from the palace in one week's time. We have a *very* special surprise for you that I am positive you won't want to miss. Goodnight all."

I waited until the cameras powered down, then I whirled on Richard. "What was that?"

"Explain yourself, Father!" Lucas said at the same time.

Richard held up his hands in surrender, but his eyes were awash in power. He walked over, squatted down, and smiled. His eyes flicked back and forth between us. His face shifted to the same threatening expression I knew well. "Jessa, my dear girl, you couldn't have handled that better if I had told you what to do. You see, there was a lot of sympathy for Celia still, which didn't look good for us, so I needed to squash that. And at the same time, I needed the people to see you use your red alchemy, but in self-defense. That would be considered proper, and well"—he paused—"justified."

He straightened up and patted Lucas on the head. "Good job picking this one, son. You were right. She's perfect."

Rage poured over me like boiling water. This man was crazy! And way too smart for his own good. He would never stop manipulating people, never stop hurting whomever he needed to get what he wanted. The worst part was, there was nothing I could do about him. My chest rose and fell with my angry breaths as the thoughts circled through me.

I caught Lily's "I told you so" expression. She was still sitting in her spot. Never once had she moved. She raised an eyebrow and cast me a knowing look. I nodded. I understood now.

Do you have something to say to me? Lily asked. The telepathic link between us pulled like a tight string.

I smiled, and for the first time that day, I actually meant it.

Tell your boyfriend I'm not going anywhere. I'll help you. I'm in.

THIRTEEN
SASHA

I knocked on Mastin's door for the tenth time that day. Okay, I pounded on it. But I was *not* very happy and wanted…no, I needed, an explanation.

"Not right now," he called out.

"No!" I knocked harder. "I need to talk to you right now, Mastin."

"Hold on."

"You've been avoiding me all day and I'm sick of it. Let me in!"

No response. I wiggled the handle but it was still locked.

"That's it," I muttered, employing a dash of yellow magic and breaking the lock with a quick snap of my wrist.

I flung open the door. "You better have a good explanation for what you did last night," I said, bounding into his room. He stood by his closet, a towel wrapped around his waist, and from the looks of it, nothing else. I swallowed, fighting the blush that blossomed on my cheeks.

He glared, but I barely noticed, too busy staring at his six-pack. Sometimes I annoyed myself. Why was I looking at his abs? It wasn't like they were all that special. They were amazing, but so were about a million other guys. Whatever. I huffed and crossed my arms over my chest, tapping my foot.

"Did you break my lock?" he asked, incredulous.

"Get dressed." I turned around so he could have a bit of privacy. And because I needed to get a grip. His room was perfectly tidy, as expected. I blew out a breath.

"You did, didn't you? You broke my lock with your magic. This is what I'm talking about, Sasha! You're going to do something at the wrong time in front of the wrong person and get yourself killed."

I glowered at the white wall, listening to him rifle through his clothes. "Serves you right for locking me out all day."

"It's Saturday," he said. "I'm off work. I don't have to talk to you if I don't want to."

Oh, excuse me!

I flipped around. "Am I work to you?"

He chuckled low but didn't reply. Apparently, he was far too busy buttoning his jeans and pulling a t-shirt over his stupid head to be a grown up and have a conversation.

I stomped over and shoved him against the wall. That got his attention. His eyes flared. "I don't want to fight you," he growled, staring down at me, "but I will if I have to."

"And how did that work out for you the last time?" I scoffed, referring to our first meeting where I'd beat him with my magic. We both knew he couldn't fight me. I'd always have the upper hand and I didn't care what kind of guns he had—I had yellow alchemy.

I took a half step back, the proximity beginning to cause me to lose my train of thought.

You're mad at him. That's why you're here, nothing else. Focus.

"Why did you sell me out last night?" I peered up into his green eyes, hoping to find a suitable answer in their depths. But they were masked and shrouded in secrecy, like they always were.

His jaw ticked as his eyes narrowed.

For the last week I'd been invited to shadow Nathan everywhere and give my input in meetings. *I loved it!* I was proving myself to be invaluable. And when it came to training, I was showing everyone on base that I could hold my own and then some. And the best part was that my magic was stronger than ever. Each time I used it, it grew. It felt so good to be myself in an environment where I could actually make a difference. It was only a matter of time before I'd be allowed to fight in the war.

But last night, during a fighting session, Mastin had downright refused to spar with me. When nobody else would either, I'd found out he'd threatened anyone who would. No one wanted to cross Mastin, not only because he was talented, but because he was the General's son. I'd been left without a partner.

"It's simple. You shouldn't be training with us." He shrugged.

"Says you."

"Not just me. Says most of those guys. Do you keep forgetting that alchemy isn't very well accepted here?"

"I'm trying to change that!"

"No, you're trying to convince my dad to let you play soldier so you can run off to the war. This is serious, Sasha. You're here to be safe, not to get yourself into more trouble."

I folded my arms, the black active clothes that Melissa had found for me stretching with the movement.

"Oh, so that's what this is about? You're afraid I'll get hurt? Guess what, Mastin? I never asked for your opinion. I can make my own decisions."

He fisted his hands and stepped close, leaning his face closer so it was only a couple inches from mine. "Just because you *can* fight doesn't mean you *should* fight."

"Why do you even care?"

"Because you're going to get yourself killed!" he yelled.

Silence stretched between us, the room growing hotter by the second.

He moved back to lean against the wall, his chest rising and falling in heavy breaths. Then he squeezed his eyes shut for a few moments. "I just don't want to see another one of my friends die, okay?"

I could understand that. I could even respect it. But it didn't change the reality of our situation. I shook my head.

"This is bigger than your fear. Your country needs me right now and, quite frankly, so does mine. You're just going to have to trust me. I know my limits."

"Don't you get it?" he said in a strained voice. "War isn't a training drill. It's not a situation where you can choose whether or not you'll be the one to get shot. Nobody wants to die, but thousands do. What happens if you're one of them?"

My anger began to dissipate. I turned around, really checking out his bedroom. I'd been so hyped up, I hadn't had a chance to take it in. But the room was similar to mine. Nondescript. Neatly decorated. No personal effects.

This wasn't his childhood home.

Or maybe he'd never stayed in one place very long. Something about it tugged at me, a lingering sadness. Even I could think back fondly on the Resistance camp and consider it as home. And that too was gone. But maybe it was okay. Maybe home wasn't a place. It could be a person. Tristan.

I still had Tristan.

"I'm sorry," I said, turning back to Mastin and talking as calmly as I could manage. This wasn't some passing fancy. I was serious about everything, just as much as any one of those soldiers out there, and he needed to understand. "Nothing you say or do is going to stop me. I'm going to continue to work with your dad and as soon as I get the chance, I will be first in line to get out there and fight. It's who I am. I'm a fighter."

The energy between us softened. He nodded once and then strode toward me, pulling me into a tight hug. The animosity dissolved like ice in sunshine. "I don't think you know how much you matter to me," he muttered, his voice a tender vibration against my body.

But I did know.

Heat radiated off his entire body, drawing me in. He smelled like the clean shower intermixed with his own spicy scent. The mood in the room shifted, like a cloud passing over the sun. I tensed. My stomach dropped. Heartbeats sounded in my ears, picking up speed. He leaned back to peer into my eyes, searching for something. He must have found what he was looking for because the next thing I knew, his warm lips covered mine.

I couldn't allow myself to react, to give in. I pushed him off and took several steps back, wiping my mouth and staring at the hardwood floor.

"What's the matter?" he winced.

"I can't." The image of Tristan on the beach was all I could see. And my promise to him. Because as much as I was attracted to Mastin, it was Tristan who felt like home. That had to mean something.

Promise me you'll wait for me.

"You want to, though, don't you?" Mastin stepped closer,

his eyes studying me for cracks.

But I couldn't answer. I didn't want to hurt him. I didn't want to hurt Tristan. And most of all, I didn't want to lose myself in something that would only end in heartache. I'd had enough of that in my life.

I was here to fight. That was all. Maybe one day, when all this was over, I'd be able to find it in my heart to love.

"We need to stay focused on what matters most." I strode toward the door. Swinging it open, I walked through, leaving him behind.

He called after me, "That's what I was doing."

▼

"Do we send out a call for more alchemists?" The man's wrinkly red face lit up with the idea. "We could offer to pay if they come forward. Then we'll train them, of course." He motioned across the table toward me. "Sasha can do it."

Thanks for offering my services. I rolled my eyes.

"Like that would ever work," Mastin replied.

"It's worth trying," the man shot back. Lip curled, he glared darkly at Mastin like he was the ultimate traitor to America.

"Mastin is right," Nathan said from his spot at the head of the conference room table. "This country hasn't been very kind to alchemists."

That was the understatement of the year.

"It's going to take some time before anyone willingly gives themselves over to us, especially if they know it's to fight in the war."

We sat around a long table, windows on one side that overlooked the base, stark white walls on the others. We'd been brainstorming ideas to combat New Colony's alchemists for the better part of an hour. So far, nobody knew how to stop the havoc they were wreaking on the frontline. The only logical explanation was to fight fire with fire. But how, when I was the only willing alchemist they had at the moment?

"What about the kids?" the man asked. "King Richard uses kids, doesn't he?"

I turned on him, shocked at his horrible suggestion. Did he want to send children to war? He sat at the other end of the table, second in command to General Scott. He was a weathered man, with a red face and judgmental eyes. "King Richard trains the kids in his palace, and they stay there until they're initiated as a Guardian of Color, usually around age eighteen." I said. "Have you seen any children out on the frontline?"

There was a stilted pause as the man regarded me coolly. I'd forgotten his name, but now I wished I had it, just so I could put a name to this face I hated.

"No, you haven't," I answered for him. "I went through hell because of that King, but I can say even he wouldn't send children to the slaughter."

"It was just a suggestion." The man glared.

"And anyway, what do you mean, 'what about the kids?' What are you talking about?"

There was a heavy silence. "You don't have the high enough security clearance to be asking about it," Nathan finally said.

I looked him up and down, no longer believing what I was hearing.

"Screw security clearance. I think we're long past that." He'd been taking me to meetings with him all week. Now he wanted to shut me out?

I glanced around at the others in the room, but they also avoided my weighted stare. It also wasn't lost on me that I was the *only* woman in the room. Finally, it was Mastin who had the nerve to meet my gaze and when he did, he grimaced and shook his head.

"You have child alchemists locked up, don't you?" I snapped.

"It's not what it sounds like," Nathan Scott grumbled. He fiddled with some of the paperwork in front of him for a moment.

"It's not? It sounds like you had all the alchemists locked up and you sent the ones you deemed old enough to work with me, and the rest you left in some kind of prison. Young children, am I right? And probably some elderly alchemists, too. You only sent the most able-bodied up to Canada."

Silence.

"And you call King Richard the monster," I huffed, standing. The chair scraped across the concrete floor, echoing. "I'm not helping you until you give those people a real life. Locking them away just because they're different is wrong and you all know it."

I slammed my weight toward the door. I'd had enough of this too small room, filled with too big egos. They thought they could get together and somehow save the world with their idiotic backwards ideas? Not likely.

"Just hold on a second, Missy." The man who'd originally suggested that kids be used in war stood. His face had transformed from scarlet to plum as he met me at the door, slamming his palm against it before I could leave.

Oh, you do not want to try me, old man!

"It's only been very recently that some people in this country have become accepting of you alchemists," he said, spit building in the creases of his thin lips. "There's still plenty of us who find it unnatural and evil."

I scowled, my temper rising. "Oh, plenty of *you*, huh? Great to see you leading a military that's going to lose to a bunch of those evil alchemists. Now, get out of my way before I physically move you."

"Are you threatening me?" he snapped. "Are you hearing this?" He looked around the room. "She's threatening me. *Me*, a two star General!"

I laughed, beyond done. I didn't care how many stars were in this room. These people weren't going to get anywhere with such terrible attitudes toward alchemy. I pushed past the guy, shoved him hard, and reached for the door, but as I was about to go through it, it opened and a blast of air conditioning washed over me.

Hank strolled in, followed by Tristan. My mood lightened and I squealed. I didn't know which one to hug first. I froze, letting their presence settle over me, then I dove for Hank.

"You have no idea how much I've missed you, kid," he said, wrapping his arms around me. His scruffy facial hair rubbed against my cheek.

I breathed him in. "What are you two doing here?"

"About that…" He smiled, and stepped aside. "It seems you've been causing a bit of a stir on this base. Can't say I'm surprised."

Tristan chuckled.

"Well, we've also been in quite a few meetings lately," Hank's voice trailed off.

A barrage of security streamed in, and we shuffled to the side. Tristan sidled up to me, nudging me and smiling down. Our eyes connected, and any lingering effects of anger melted away. We turned back to the door and I watched, transfixed, as an elegant, older woman in a black pantsuit sauntered into the room. Everyone stood.

"Madame President," Nathan said, eyes wide. "It's an honor to have you here. I must say, we weren't expecting you. We can move to a bigger room if you'd prefer."

"Oh nonsense, this is fine." She shrugged and slid into the closest empty chair. "I know my trip to your base was unexpected. But my new friends Hank and Tristan here have been talking with me at length, and we decided it was high time we *all* got together and figured out how we're going to end this ridiculous war that New Colony has decided to launch on American soil."

Since cheering would probably be frowned upon, I shot the room a wicked smile as I followed Tristan and Hank to the last of the empty chairs.

I'd quickly learned to call this country America, not West America as I'd grown up doing in New Colony. As far as these people were concerned, New Colony had seceded from them, but they were still proud as ever of their heritage.

Studying the American president, I felt myself wanting to like her. She looked so put-together and smart in her black suit. A knowing twinkle filled her eye when she talked, her white hair cut into a professional long bob that bounced when she moved her head. Her presence commanded the room far better than anyone in here, and with attendees such as these, I was impressed.

When the room had finally settled, she asked her first question, her eyes sweeping from person to person. "So, any marvelous plans you'd like to pitch?"

The two-star general I'd been arguing with cleared his throat. "We were considering bringing the alchemists we do have onto the base so Sasha here can train them."

He motioned to me like we were old friends and I rolled my eyes. *Figures.*

"And what use would that be?" she replied. "We only have children and elderly left."

I straightened in my chair. "That's what I said. But I still think we should remove them from whatever prison they're in and give them a proper life."

She smiled and studied me. She wasn't annoyed by my input like so many of the men had been. It was quite the opposite. She looked at me like I had valuable opinions that deserved a chance. I perked up, confidence building.

"It's already done," she said. "We've moved them to a much better facility where they can live as normally as possible given their particular set of circumstances. Even their family can stay with them as often as they'd like."

"Oh, thank you so much!" I gushed. "If only I'd had that kind of treatment as a child, so much would have been better for me."

"Don't thank me," she replied. "Hank convinced me of it. It was his idea. He's even offered to train them."

I leaned into Hank and gave him my biggest megawatt smile. He wasn't an alchemist, true, but he knew more about the magic than anyone. And he was the most patient person I'd ever met. He would be perfect for the job.

"That's wonderful," I said.

"It is wonderful," she agreed.

Over the next hour they dived into the current status of everything war-related, factoring in the tumultuous political climate and what could be done about it.

In the end, it was decided that more troops would be leaving in two days' time to go shore up those already fighting against the New Colony soldiers and alchemists. The plan was to beat them with sheer numbers and weaponry.

I kept my mouth closed. Hank, Tristan, and Mastin would never support me going with those troops. But I was brimming with excitement. It didn't matter what anyone else's opinion was on the matter. I was done letting other people control my life.

One way or another, I would be joining those soldiers.

I'd be getting out to where the action was, making all those people who worked for King Richard see that they'd made a huge mistake. Going to the war would mean fighting my own kind. It caused my heart to pound so hard I could hear it in my ears. But I refused to be afraid.

I was ready. I'd been training for this my entire life.

I would fight those who'd stolen my childhood. I would reunite my family. And I would prove to all these closed-minded Americans that alchemy was a gift.

Mastin caught my eye over the table and his jaw tensed. Ever so slightly, he shook his head. It didn't matter. I didn't need his support.

I nodded once and then turned my attention back to the President. She was a woman who'd climbed her way to power, who wasn't afraid to do what needed to be done, even if the men around her hated her for it.

I smiled. She would understand.

FOURTEEN
JESSA

The music moved through me like my body was another instrument in a grand orchestra. I danced for everything I couldn't say, my arms and legs extensions of the feelings playing inside. The song ended, and I plopped down in the middle of the studio floor, flat on my back, looking up at the ceiling and catching my breath. While my chest rose and fell, the faint scent of floor polish wafted around me. The room was dim since the lights were off and the curtains drawn, only some of the afternoon sun peeked in around their edges. It relaxed me, dancing alone in the dark.

This studio was the perfect place to spend as much time as possible between alchemy classes and training in the gym, but it still wasn't enough to quiet the stress. It was building to something bigger, louder and louder.

My eyes fluttered closed, and I forced it down.

Madame Silver would arrive any minute. Surely, she'd seen the disastrous broadcast. Maybe she'd have some sage advice to offer about my situation. She always did have a level head about these kinds of things, even though ballet issues and life issues didn't always cross over.

Dad was livid when he found out what happened with Celia. He hadn't been invited to the exhibition, and now we knew why. He would have intervened in King Richard's publicity stunt! The broadcast aired around the same time we'd come home that night. I refused to watch, locking myself in my room. Dad had come knocking an hour later. When I'd opened the door, terrified at what he would think of me, he'd buried me into a comforting hug, letting me cry it out. Eventually, as my tears mellowed, his anger grew. He'd stormed from the room, demanding to speak with the King.

Needless to say, I didn't let that happen.

I'd been able to talk him down, and eventually he'd relented, not because Richard deserved the benefit of the doubt, but because his entire stay at the palace was precarious as it was. We *both* needed him to stay under the radar as much as possible, to get in line and behave like everyone else. The next day we'd had an interesting Sunday dinner with Richard and Lucas. It had been filled with awkward silences and three uncomfortable people trying desperately to avoid eye contact. Richard didn't seem to care.

I groaned. Why was this my life now?

And where was Madame Silver? She should be here by now. I sat up and rolled out my neck. A quick glance at the clock confirmed she was five minutes late, and that woman was never late. It was in her DNA to be early to everything.

The stray image of Celia attacking me flashed through my mind. I rubbed my scalp, wincing. It was all healed now, of course, but the memory lingered. Even though she'd been manipulated, the look on her face would haunt me to my grave. The girl *despised* me. Did I blame her? The way she saw it, I had taken the crown.

It had been two days since the incident. I couldn't shake the feeling that my confrontations with her weren't over. Lucas must have thought so too because he wanted her gone. He'd lobbied hard with his father for Celia's immediate removal from the palace. Richard didn't care. He had brushed his son's demands off with the flick of his wrist, citing the orange magic as the reason for leniency.

But wasn't Celia humiliated? She seemed like such a prideful person. If I were her, I would want to leave. Geez, I wasn't her and I wanted to leave.

But she didn't.

She was still a permanent guest and her parents, permanent fixtures. Lately, I'd seen them every day, always talking with Royal Officers or Faulk, even going into private meetings with the King.

The studio door opened, flashing a stream of light from the hallway. The overhead lights blazed and I covered my eyes. Madame Silver pranced in, a flurry of energy. "So sorry I'm late, Darling. We had an impromptu meeting at the company that I simply had to attend."

I smiled weakly up at her, unable to share her enthusiasm. That should have been *my* dance company. Recognition gleamed in her eyes and she rushed over to me.

"Jessa, what are you doing on the floor? Are you okay?" she gasped, kneeling down and gently placing a cold hand on my arm.

I raised my other hand to quiet her worry. "I'm fine," I said, trying and failing to make my voice sound happy. "It's nothing. I've just been dancing for hours and I was resting up before our lesson." Okay, it was more than that. It was *everything*.

"Don't you have an exquisitely decorated bedroom

somewhere for your beauty rest?"

I laughed bitterly, patting the hardwood. "Aw, but this is so much better."

She laughed along. Then she stood gracefully and reached down to help me up. Her eyes searched mine.

"Do you think it's safe to talk," she whispered, looking behind us at the closed door. On the other side were guards, of course, but there could just as easily be a spying alchemist around here as well. I'd thought Reed was the only blue alchemist who could listen in like that, but Callie had obviously proved me wrong.

I held up a finger. I skipped over to the corner of the room and snagged my stone necklace from where I'd left it, on top of my hooded sweatshirt, next to my stainless steel water bottle. I strung it around my neck, noticing all the colors individually. It amazed me that each could be manipulated in such different and incredible ways. The sheer magnitude of it hung heavy around my neck like another responsibility.

"Are you okay, dear?" Madame Silver asked.

"How is it, that out of all the people in the world, I was born with this ability?" My voice cracked on the question. "Sorry, I sound so ungrateful," I rushed to add.

Her gaze held mine for a moment. "I don't know, Jessa. I don't know why things happen the way they do. Sometimes it doesn't make sense, there's no explanation. But hear me." She reached out her hands and placed them on my shoulders. "You're this talented for a reason. Don't doubt yourself. Embrace who you are now so you can grow into the person you're meant to be."

"But how do I know who I'm meant to be?"

"That's the great thing about it. You get to choose."

I smiled softly and ran my hand along the stone necklace. Some were smooth, others jagged. The stones had been drilled with holes to allow for the black leather cord to pass through. It was mine to wear proudly, nothing to cower from.

And I was lucky. Not everyone could use stones as I could. My magic was strong enough that I didn't need to use plants, though I could. This necklace added a convenience, a security, to my already dangerous life.

"What color is your favorite?" Madame Silver carefully ran her fingers along the necklace. "Some of these are faded," she added.

"I need to replace a few of the stones soon. They're almost used up." I paused to consider her question. "I want to help people," I said. "All the colors can be used to help, so it's hard to choose a favorite. But for now…"

It was time to talk.

She stepped back and I placed my forefinger on the purple, knowing I still had plenty of color left for what was needed. My energy pulled at it purposefully, and I felt it sink in like ink.

What's going on, I asked Madame Silver, reaching out with the thought. I felt the magic working between us, an invisible string of energy. I walked over to the ballet barre and started the beginning exercises. We always started class the same way. Nobody would ever have to know that we were doing more than just dance in here.

The ballet company is going on tour, she said. *We had expected it to be delayed or canceled because of the war, but we just got word that it's been approved.*

My heart sank, and I faltered in my current set of stretches. *That will be fun.*

I paused. *So, does this mean you're leaving the capitol?*

She met my eye with a quick nod.

When? For how long?

She came to face me at the bar, going through the same stretches. She often did that, even though she wasn't a professional ballerina anymore, she still danced. I guess the same thing could be said about me.

Tomorrow night, she replied. *We'll be traveling, the whole company, to all the large cities in New Colony. We'll be gone for two months.*

I frowned for a brief moment, then pulled myself back together. This was her job, it was normal. *I shouldn't be surprised, as you do this every year. I just forgot about it with everything else going on. I'm really going to miss you.*

Her eyes caught mine. *I want you to come with us.*

What? Confusion settled deep. My heart raced even thinking about it, the pain a dull thud-thud-thud in my chest.

That's not possible, I said. *I'm getting married in a few weeks. And even if I wasn't, Richard would never let me leave the palace. He doesn't care about ballet. I'm a Guardian now.*

She kicked her leg up gracefully and bent at the waist. I followed, grateful for the momentary break in eye contact.

What I mean is, I've met with a few of the other staff and we want to sneak you out with us, she replied, her voice confident as it filtered through my mind. *Our first stop is all the way down south and then we're working our way back up. You know how many trucks of scenery we have for these kinds of things. And I get my very own trailer, as I'm the lead choreographer. We could smuggle you out, get you to the border, and then you could use your magic to take refuge in West America.*

It seemed too risky. But something stopped me from refusing. It was a plan and I needed one of those.

Would they accept you in West America?

I think they would, I replied, excitement beginning to stir.

And if that doesn't work for you, she continued, *then stay with us on the road, but keep hidden. In two months, once we make it up to the north for our final stop, you can venture up to Canada. It will be riskier to wait that long, but the Canadian government accepts New Colony refugees without question.*

How do you know that?

There was a long pause. *It's a more common subject in this kingdom than those in the palace would like to admit. But anyway, I have a sister who left many years ago for Canada. She sent word back that she'd made it safely. She wanted me to go too, but I couldn't leave the company behind.*

But there's a chance?

A very good chance.

A flicker of possibility danced between us as our eyes connected. She thought I was leaving with her, but it was another thought that burned in me.

I could save Dad.

Lily and Jose weren't going to lose me. I was sticking around to help the Resistance—at least for now. Someone had to stop Richard.

That someone was me.

But I needed to get Dad out of here. It was only a matter of time before he ended up hurt, or worse. Besides, he was the exact kind of leverage against me that wasn't safe for either of us.

Could you get my dad out, too? I wouldn't outright refuse my own escape at this point. She wouldn't understand my reason for staying. I broke our eye contact, guilt coursing through me. But I needed to get her on board with getting Dad away from all this.

I met her eyes again, and pleaded with my own.

Of course, she finally said. *It will be more dangerous but I'm sure we can handle it. Didn't you tell me that your mother and sister are in West America? Your whole family could be reunited again.*

Smiling at the thought, I forced the smile to stay in place. They would be reunited and that was wonderful, but I'd still be here.

Here, until I changed things.

And if I had to stay back for some reason, I asked cautiously, *like if I wasn't able to make it because something happened to stop me, and my dad could make it, would you still help him?*

I'm not sure, she faltered, her head shaking slightly.

His life is in grave danger here, with or without me, he needs to run.

Your life is in danger, too. That broadcast…We all saw it, it was how I was able to convince the others to go along with this plan. Jessa, it was terrible.

We turned around and began stretching the other leg. Now facing away from each other.

I know that, I practically shouted the response in my mind. *Of course I know that. But they're using Dad against me. If I can't get out and he can, it would benefit us both. It could save us both. I need to know if he can come with you, just in case I can't.*

Her soft hand rested on my shoulder, I flipped around.

She nodded.

I exhaled and closed my eyes. *Thank you.*

We're leaving tomorrow night. Do you think you can get out and meet us in time? We will have someone waiting for you at the stage door all day tomorrow. They'll know where to hide you.

I'll find a way, I replied.

Once more, she nodded.

"Are you all stretched out?" she said, her teacher-voice filling the studio space. If anyone was listening in, they'd hear the best ballet teacher in New Colony giving her lesson and that would be all. "Do you feel warm enough for our lesson? I have a tough one planned."

"Let's do it." I gave her a quick smile. "I'm tough." But I was no longer talking about ballet and from the insightful glint in her eyes, we both knew it.

▼

"We're getting you out of here." I tackle-hugged Dad, the sheer excitement of everything causing me to forget about using my telepathy. "For a walk, of course," I added. After letting me go, he stepped back, confusion wrapped in his usually steady eyes.

"Let's grab our coats. It's so stuffy in here tonight," I continued, playfully. After a few minutes, we found ourselves outside, the bitter cold wrapping around our bodies. But the fresh air really did feel amazing. Breathing in deep, I allowed it to steel me for what I needed to do next.

The purple stone, still around my neck, hung warm against my skin. I quickly connected with it and reached out to dad. Once it was established what I was doing, he'd stilled, but let me explain everything to him.

You have to come too, he insisted. *I'm not leaving without you.*

Absolutely not. I need to stay here since I'm the only one with enough power to stop King Richard.

It's not your job! You're only seventeen, Jessa. You don't have to do this.

I glanced behind us, noticing a couple of guards trailing behind us. I turned to dad and wrapped him in a tight hug. The cold was beginning to bite through my clothes, and his warmth poured into me.

You don't have to understand it. But I'm staying.

He shook his head against me. *No. I'm your father. Listen to me. You need to come with us. You have to get out of here. What if I leave tomorrow and never see you again. How am I supposed to live with that?*

"I'm getting cold," I said aloud. "Let's go inside."

Jessa, just listen to me. With a sharp breath, I severed the telepathic link and walked toward the palace doors.

"Jessa," he growled. "We're not done here."

"Yes, we are." I shot a knowing look toward the guards. His mouth fell into a grimace and his eyes narrowed, but he didn't say another word.

We parted without continuing the argument, both upset with the other. I hated going to bed mad at someone, especially him. It was one of those things, that no matter how it happened, it always felt terrible. But one of Mom's old sayings came back to me just as I'd drifted off to sleep. *Things that look scary in the dark always look much different in the morning.* She was right.

The next day at breakfast, he was waiting for me. He'd never said a word as we picked through our food. But as we got up to leave, he'd pulled me into a hug.

"Okay." Was all he had said, but it was enough. The tears burned, and I'd quickly wiped them away.

The hours had moved at lightning speed after that, no matter how much I tried to slow them. My magic seemed utterly useless without control over time. Unfortunately, I didn't get to make the rules.

Classes ended for the afternoon and I found myself pacing back and forward in front of Lucas's suite.

I had no idea how I was going to get Dad out of this palace by myself. The national ballet was located within walking distance of the palace, so that was lucky enough. But with security everywhere, we'd never be allowed off-property, let alone to go downtown in the middle of the day. And even if we could, people would recognize me.

I didn't exactly have a getaway plan.

I could possibly get him out to the street. But that wouldn't end well. He might be recognized. There would be witnesses, adding extra risk to Madame Silver and the others who'd agreed to help me.

▼

I huffed, strolled past the guards with their suspicious eyes, and knocked on the Royal's door.

Nobody answered.

"Can you let me in, or what?" I tossed toward the nearest of the guards. He raised a cool eyebrow. "I need to speak with my fiancé."

He cocked his head, but then with the quick rattling of keys, let me into the royal apartment.

"He's in his room," the man barked after me.

Head up, I strode down the hall, past the family room, past Richard's private office, toward Lucas's bedroom. I knocked softly. No answer.

Okay, don't worry. Maybe he didn't hear it the first time.

I knocked louder, expecting the door to swing wide, but nothing. Was he here? I pressed my ear to the door and heard the faint sound of ruffling bed sheets. My hands began to shake. What if Lucas didn't want to talk to me? What if he wouldn't help me?

I pounded on the door this time, the noise three heavy thuds.

"I don't want to talk about this again, Father. You already know how I feel about it," Lucas called out from the other side in his sharpest tone.

"Um—sorry," I said. "It's me. Jessa?"

Why did I just say my name like it was a question? I wanted to kick myself. Lucas didn't need to know how nervous I was coming to him.

The door flew open.

His pewter eyes, cast in shadows, ran the length of me. "Come in."

I did, closing the door carefully behind me. We stood in the center of his bedroom, a distance between us that felt like we may as well have been on opposite ends of the earth.

I chewed on my lip, gathering the courage to tell him my plan.

"If I asked for your help, would you help me?" I said, my insides twisting.

"Anything."

Expression guarded, shadows still cast over his eyes, he hid his depths from me. But he'd said yes, so it was now or never. My truth burned in my throat.

"Okay." I bit my lip, reaching to my necklace. I connected with the purple. Then crossed to Lucas and placed my hand on his chest.

Showtime.

It's about my Dad, I said, the telepathy snapping to life between us.

He leaned back and studied me with a shocked expression.

"Since when can you do that?" he asked incredulous, "That's rare magic, Jessa."

I hushed him.

Since, I don't know? A week ago? You can talk back to me through the link I've created, I said. *All I have to do is touch you with it once, and it's there to use again and again, depending on the distance between us. It's safer for us to talk this way.*

He eyes flashed when I mentioned the distance but I didn't let myself dwell on the double meaning there.

So you can hear me? he asked, and I nodded slowly, trying not to smile. It was pretty cool, and something I was proud of. *What do you need, then?*

I explained the situation as carefully as possible, making sure not to leave any important details out. I walked to the window, appearing as natural as I could. He followed, his face grew darker and darker.

What's the matter? Spinning on him, anger bubbled up inside me. I knew we were about to argue over this. *You won't do it? I thought you said you would do anything.*

I'll do it, he snapped back. *But why aren't you going along? Isn't that what you want, to leave this palace and never look back?*

Not anymore.

He scoffed. *I'm confused. You suddenly want to stay and marry me?*

No.

So what is it? You just want to stay?

I had my reasons. And he should know better than anyone why I wasn't eager to tell him my secret plans. *Will you help me or not?*

The silence sliced between us, like an impenetrable wall.

This is his chance, Lucas. Please.

He'd gone completely still, watching me like he didn't know me.

Fine, he said, his tone a sharp knife through our link. *But you should go, too. There's nothing here for you anymore.*

I relaxed, exhaling deep. And at the same time, pain buried in my chest, like he'd put the knife there himself.

We don't have time to argue about this, I said. *If he's going to make it in time, he needs to leave as soon as possible.*

I guess I better get my coat. It'll be a cold walk to the theatre.

"Thank you," I breathed aloud. The telepathy waned, and I pushed it back between us.

You want my white magic, obviously, Lucas said. *Guess I'm good for something.*

It's not like that.

He held up a hand. *Tell him to meet me in the garden in twenty minutes and to bring whatever he needs. Twenty minutes should be enough for you to say goodbye, right?*

It wouldn't. But I nodded.

Or if you're as smart as you think you are, maybe it will be enough for you to change your mind.

I guess I'm not smart. I glared, annoyed at his jab at my intelligence.

Suit yourself. He brushed past me to open his door. *Better get moving.*

As I left, I reached out to Madame Silver with my mind, hoping maybe this time she would be able hear me. We'd talked through the link enough times that it had grown. It was almost as if I could feel her, this far-off person attached to a tether reaching back to me. I tugged on it.

Can you hear me?

Jessa? Jessa, is that you? Where are you? Her voice sounded grainy, but it was there just the same. A thrill poured down my body. I was getting stronger. Last time the telepathy hadn't reached that far, but this time, it did. Maybe I would be able to communicate with Dad after he left. Could I be so lucky? We'd established the mental connection, but it was newer.

I'm in the palace, I replied. *I just wanted to let you know that the plan is a go.*

That's wonderful! We'll be waiting for you.

Guilt gripped me as I ended the connection. I couldn't explain to her why I wouldn't be showing up with Dad. There wasn't time and honestly, I didn't have the courage. I hoped she could forgive me.

A heady mix of emotions swirled through me as I walked closer and closer to Dad's door. Gratitude that Lucas was willing to help. Excited that my father was getting out. Nervous at the possibility this plan wouldn't work. And most of all, broken. Broken that I was about to say goodbye to another family member, another piece of me.

But most of all, broken by Lucas's words, now etched into my heart.

There's nothing here for you anymore.

FIFTEEN
LUCAS

We trudged along the sidewalk, arm in arm, invisible and careful. Being that it was broad daylight and late afternoon, people were out and about. As soon as the workday ended, they'd pour out from their buildings in droves. I needed to be back to the palace by then to avoid getting stuck. Christopher and I had already dodged a few unsuspecting bystanders, and also had a near miss. Rush hour would be a nightmare. I sighed; maneuvering through the city streets under the guise of magic wasn't as easy as I'd thought. Especially not with my fiancé's father lumbering against my arm.

"Were you the one who got my daughter out of there?" Christopher asked under his breath.

"Unfortunately, Jessa refuses to leave."

"Oh, believe me, I know all about that nonsense," he said, his frustration matching my own. "No, I'm talking about Francesca. Or, I guess you know her as Sasha." He huffed. "I'll never get used to that new name. Hopefully, it's just a phase. I've missed my Frankie for way too long."

I understood the feeling and my heart went out to the guy. "Oh, yup, it was me who got her out. This invisibility magic is my secret, and now it's yours too." I cleared my throat and tugged him along.

"I'll keep your secret safe," he replied.

"I wanted to help all three of you, but you and Jessa were already en route to the exhibition the night I got Sasha out."

"And now, here we are," Christopher said.

I nodded, though I knew he couldn't see me.

We walked in silence, and I wondered if he knew this part of the city. Was he observing it like it would be the last time he'd ever see it? And if I were in his shoes, would I feel good about the idea? The palace was my home, but the urban city that surrounded it was my backyard. Before things had gotten so crazy, I'd spent a lot of time here. I didn't think I could leave it behind, if it were me.

The city buildings cast cool shadows across the sidewalk as we moved at a steady pace. The architecture was a mix of old and new, though mostly new. And most of the buildings reached up into the sky, pillars of innovation. I looked down at my feet, momentarily stunned that they weren't there. Invisible magic had a way of doing that, no matter how often I used it. Luckily, all the snow had melted, the puddles mostly dried up. That was good for our ability to stay hidden, but I could have done without the prickly wind. It cut against my face, traveling down into my coat despite the zipper being so far up the plastic was nearly in my mouth. I fought the urge to complain. The cold was the least of our worries.

"You're not a bad kid, you know that right?" Christopher's gravelly voice floated gently through the air. He nudged me with his shoulder when I didn't respond. "Jessa seems to think you take after your father, after everything that's happened between you two, but I have to disagree."

My heart twisted into an angry lump. "She told you about us?"

"That girl, she used to tell me everything. We always had a strong bond, you know? And then she kept her alchemy hidden. I wish she hadn't. We would have helped her. After losing Francesca, we would have done anything to keep Jessa. But anyway," he paused. "Yes, she told me about what happened between you two. I can't say I agree with you, but I understand it. What you did...you were blinded by love."

"She doesn't see it that way."

"I know. But I get why you did it. Sometimes we men do stupid things when we're trying to keep our loved ones safe."

"Well, I think it's all too late, anyway."

"Either way, I just wanted you to know that I don't see your father in you. You're his spitting image, yes, no denying that. But your personalities couldn't be more opposite. You're a good kid, Lucas."

"Thanks," I replied, so quietly I wasn't sure if he heard or if it was lost to the wind.

Was he right? Could I believe that about myself? I wanted to, I really did. I had never wanted to be my father. But lately it felt like everything I did ended up hurting someone, usually someone innocent. And that was exactly what Richard did. At least getting Christopher out of New Colony could be one positive strike on my record.

At least I had that.

"We're almost there," I said, changing the subject. "Any last words you want me to pass along to your daughter?"

"No, we already took care of that back at the palace. But Lucas, can I ask you to do something for me?"

I stiffened with uncertainty. "Sure," I replied.

"Take care of her."

Something caught in my throat. "I don't think she wants me to do that. Besides, she'll be back to you eventually," I said. "One day she'll realize the palace isn't what she wants, and nothing will stop her from finding you again. And I'll help her when that day comes."

He was quiet for a long moment.

"I wouldn't be so sure." He tugged on my arm. "This is hard for me to admit, but I don't see how this marriage can be avoided. She's not even eighteen but you're going to be her husband very soon. Just promise me you'll be a good one."

I swallowed hard. "I promise." For months now, thinking about Jessa had consumed me. And now the idea of our future marriage terrified me. Not because I didn't want her, but because she clearly didn't want me.

The theatre loomed in front of us. It stood tall with huge, shiny glass windows and white stone pillars lining the front. We swept around the expansive plaza, dodging puddles, to the alleyway in the back where we found the stage entrance. True to their word, a man stood at the door, tall and lanky in block stage clothes. His brown eyes shifted as if waiting for someone to jump out at him. I doubled-checked we were alone.

"I guess this is it," Christopher said, clearing his throat. "Thanks again."

"Good luck." I released his arm and took several steps back. He materialized instantly. The man at the door startled, rubbing his jaw, his eyes opening wide. "I'm not even going to ask," he muttered.

Christopher laughed then turned back to where I was standing. Even though his eyes couldn't see me, it felt as if he were staring into my soul. Like he knew everything dark there and didn't mind the view. "I meant what I said. You're not your father."

Before I could utter a response, he turned toward the man and they disappeared behind the rusty door.

The white magic flickered through me, burning at my fingertips. The beginnings of exhaustion crept toward the surface. All the practice lately at invisible alchemy had allowed me to go for longer sprints each time, but the magic still demanded a physical payment on my body. Knowing my time was short, I took one last look at the barren alleyway, and sprinted toward home.

Nothing could have prepared me for what I found.

As I neared the palace, lungs burning, I caught the faint scent of smoke. A prickle of panic gripped me, and I ran faster. One hand still in my pocket, the head of the white rose between my fingers, I squeezed at the magic. My thumb caught a thorn, sharp as a tack, but I didn't care. My shoes echoed against the pavement, a mistake for an invisible man, but I didn't care about that, either.

All that mattered was figuring out where the sound of sirens was coming from. They drowned out everything else around me, blaring through the city streets, a rolling thunder. I hurried around another corner, knowing it was a straight shot down the road to the palace. I screeched to a stop. Even from here, I could see the flames.

"No!" I cried, gasping for air.

The palace was burning.

▼

Jessa. **She was** my first thought. My father was my second.

My feet slammed hard against the pavement, toward the gate. I didn't have to wait for a car to come through this time, as it had been left open for the fire trucks and ambulances.

They zoomed through the gate and up the drive in a stream of noise and flashing lights. I followed on foot, holding on to my invisibility for as long as I could manage. Knowing I'd lose my concentration at any moment, I jumped into a cropping of trees to turn myself back and discard the rose. I took off again.

My eyes stayed glued on the raging fire, smoke billowing into the gray winter sky, flames climbing along the rooftop. It was consuming the side of the palace I called home: the Royal Wing.

I'd been there an hour before, resting in my bedroom. It was where Richard usually took his afternoon siesta. Where Jessa might be at that very moment.

I exploded with speed, my morning running habit paying off tenfold as I raced toward the palace entrance.

"You can't go in there!" someone called after me, but I didn't know the voice. I never turned to see who it was, nor did I waver or stop my crusade. I climbed the marble stairs in seconds.

"Jessa!" I screamed, pushing through the doors. "Jessa!" I yelled again, coughing as a wall of smoke hit me. I pushed past it toward her room. Since it was across from our apartment, it had to be on fire.

She could've been in a lesson, in the GC wing, as she most often was.

Or the ballet studio, not quite where the flames raged.

But I wasn't willing to take the chance. Knowing her as I did, she'd have skipped all of that to have a good cry alone in her room after her father had left.

I pressed on. My eyes burned, my throat too, but it didn't matter.

I had to find her. I ran deeper into the palace, the darkness of smoke surrounding me as the heat became suffocating.

The acrid stench of smoke, mixed with the sweat from my own face, filled my nostrils. I coughed over and over again, but I pushed on, arms covering my face. My skin screamed, like I'd been dropped into a furnace. My throat burned. My eyes prickled.

But I was almost there.

Lucas, her voice rang through my mind. *Where are you?*

I stopped, nearly crying out in elation. Her telepathy! I'd never been more grateful for magic as I was in that moment.

I'm coming for you, Jessa. Don't worry. I'll get you out.

No! Don't go into the fire.

It's okay! I fell to my knees and crawled. I should have done it sooner. The heat and smoke weren't nearly as thick down here.

No, Lucas. I got out. I'm fine. I'm with the Guardians. It was just the royal wing that got hit. Arson, they think. You can't go in there.

My vision started to blur.

You're safe? I begged.

Yes! Where are you?

I coughed again. *Where do you think? I had to make sure you were okay.*

I'm fine. Get out of there, Lucas!

Okay. I'm turning back.

I was outside our own apartment. The doors had fallen down and the fire crept up the walls. I coughed, falling to my stomach. I got a hold of myself, turning to leave but the sound of a heavy, hacking cough stopped me.

Dad?

Bear crawling, I bolted into our apartment, toward the coughing.

His body was flat on the floor, one arm over his face, soot covering every inch of his skin, his eyes tightly closed. But he continued to cough; he was alive.

"Dad! Are you okay?" I knelt beside him and shook his torso wildly. The fearful thought that I was about to become an orphan shot through me.

He coughed again and opened his eyes, blinking several times as they searched my face. "I came back for you," he gasped. "When you didn't show up at the evacuation, I came back for you."

"It's okay. I'm here," I said. "Get up. Let's go."

He nodded and rolled to his knees. Another string of hacking coughs followed. When we shuffled toward the entrance of the apartment, the roof caved in directly ahead. The sound was deafening, like fighter jets swooping overhead. Or maybe that was also happening at this moment.

Sparks flew, and we jumped back.

"It's blocked," I said, shaking my head in disbelief. I considered going to a window but we were two stories off the ground and I wasn't sure emergency ladders would be up fast enough. "Let's go into the bunker," I said. Our family's go-to evacuation plan.

"It's locked," he growled.

"No. It can't be locked. It only locks from the inside." My throat burned as I spoke, the smoke growing thicker by the second.

"Then someone locked it," he coughed.

I stared at him, stunned as the realization sunk in. Whoever orchestrated this attack knew about the bunker and blocked it.

"I already tried it after I came to find you," he said. "I exerted myself so much trying to pry open the damn thing that I must have passed out from the smoke."

The fire continued to rage, the heat getting closer and closer now. It was silent, but everything it burned screamed and popped in a sickening chorus.

We were surrounded and there was no way out.

"Let me try," I said. "Maybe you loosened it."

Or maybe it just needs the magic touch.

He ignored me and stumbled away to fiddle with the nearest window.

I approached the door in the paneling, careful to keep clear of the fire. It was mostly on the far wall, but it was moving in fast and would be consuming this wall soon enough. The wallpaper here had yellow in it. I sent out a silent thank you that it wasn't covered in soot, and that yellow was easy for me. I placed one had on the wallpaper next to the doorframe and one hand on the door itself. The heat nearly burned my hands, but I pressed into it.

I glanced back to Dad through the haze of smoke. He was cussing, pushing on the stuck window. I held my breath. It was do or die. I had used my magic in front of him and hope he wouldn't see.

The door burst open.

"Got it," I called back. He turned around, disbelieving before relief washing over him. Together, we dashed inside and down the stairs into the bunker.

"Lily had said an attempt would be made but I hadn't expected it to be this bad," he mumbled behind me as we descended the stairs. The smoke was gone but it still burned in my throat, still stung my eyes. We stumbled downward, arms outstretched, lungs hacking.

Lucas, are you okay? Where are you? I still can't find you. Jessa's panicked voice tumbled through my thoughts.

We're okay, I replied, once again grateful for our connection. I needed to keep practicing that kind of magic as soon as I had time. It was far too useful to continue to overlook. *I found my father. We're both okay. Tell someone to check the bunker. I don't want anyone to know about your telepathy so just tell them I told you about the bunker and you think that's where we are.*

What about my dad? Is he okay? Did he make it to the theatre?

He's fine. He made it.

I don't want him to get blamed for this, she said, her voice rising.

He won't, I replied, but I had no way of actually knowing that. *If anything, we can act like he used the fire as a chance to escape, after his body doesn't turn up. But that doesn't mean he started it. Richard is going to think it's West America.*

Who do you think started it? She put extra emphasis on the you. It was a good question, one I'd give anything to have a definitive answer on.

Could be the Resistance, I said. *Or maybe someone working for West America. Whoever it is, this isn't their first attempt on my life and it won't be their last.*

I don't think it was the Resistance, Lucas, she said. *I honestly don't.*

I wasn't so sure, but didn't want to argue.

Then maybe it really is West America. I don't know.

There was silence, followed by the severing of our connection like a snap in a taut wire.

We took the final two stairs and Richard pulled me into a hearty hug, something foreign to us. My body stiffened and relaxed at the same time. It was the strangest feeling, and one I didn't want to repeat anytime soon.

"Thank God you're okay," Richard said, stepping away. "I really thought I had lost you. And after losing your mother…"

We stared at each other. The soot had turned his face black, his eyes red, but he gazed at me with a renewed sense of purpose.

"What are we going to do?" I asked. "This keeps happening. They almost got us."

"We will retaliate," he said. "If West America wants to turn this into a blood bath then we can make that happen. Until then, the palace is going into lockdown. Nobody will be allowed in or out until we sort through everyone's stories and find out who started the fire."

It made sense, but I doubted he would find the culprit so easily. The front gate being left open was just one reason why. But for the time being, it seemed our royal wing would have to be shut down for extensive repairs. We'd be fine; the palace was massive. But who was to say it wouldn't happen again? Eventually, our luck would run out.

I sat on the edge of a bunk, dropping my head between my knees and breathing in and out as slowly as I could manage without coughing. My skull tingled, and the edges of my vision tunneled into a blur of color. Unable to resist it, I gave into the coughing again. It rushed from me, over and over, as I hacked the thick soot from my lungs. Through it all, the adrenaline still raced through my veins.

An arsonist in the palace...

The fire was expertly done, so quick and all-consuming; so strategically placed. It had to be someone who knew what they were doing. And someone who wanted the job done swiftly and effectively.

Whoever just tried to burn us alive in our own home had to be a trusted member of the staff, or maybe even an alchemist.

"There is an assassin under our roof," my father said, mirroring my own dark thoughts. "I promise you. I am going to find them, and I am going to end them."

SIXTEEN
SASHA

As I sat down for breakfast, I immediately sensed the crackle of tension in the kitchen. Mastin stared at his plate and wouldn't meet my gaze, wouldn't even look at me. Lately, the guy didn't have an issue following me around with those emerald weapons.

Sorry, they were gorgeous. Not my fault.

Nathan appeared the perfect picture of a pensive and angry military leader. His jaw was clenched, and his hands were fisted on either side of his plate. And Melissa buzzed around us all, a ball of nervous energy. She dished the food in little spurts of action followed by long pauses, lost in thought.

I didn't realize how much I'd come to enjoy these breakfasts together until this one, since not a single person was acting happy to be here. This family had showed me kindness when I'd been in need. That had helped me to appreciate the family I'd lost. I wondered what life would be like once we finally had the chance to be together again. Would we ever have a normal breakfast together, too?

Melissa sat in her chair and the silence continued.

Something was definitely off.

Perhaps a normal person would wait for one of them to acknowledge what was going on. Or maybe a normal person wouldn't want to intervene, at all. But I was not that person.

Quickly losing my patience, I set my fork down next to my scrambled eggs, and looked between the three of them, batting my eyelashes. "Is anyone going to tell me what's going on?" I put a strong note of sarcasm in my question.

"She hasn't seen the news?" Mastin asked forlornly, looking to his parents. I shook my head.

The news? Today was the day these men would leave for war. Had that been on the news when it wasn't supposed to be? Or maybe it was that they'd be leaving Melissa today and that's why they were acting so weird. But they hadn't seemed the least bit fazed about the war stuff yesterday or the day before. Well, okay, maybe they'd been a little apprehensive, but they'd hardly acted like *this*.

"King Richard sent out a broadcast directed at America this morning." Nathan sighed, throwing his half-eaten toast onto his plate. "Excuse me, West America, as he calls it." He scoffed. "Apparently there was an incident of arson at their palace yesterday. His son almost died and now he's blaming us. Sure, we've taken our shots, I won't lie about that, but this isn't the first time he's blamed us for something we didn't do."

I mulled the information over in my mind. It was war, right? These things couldn't be out of the ordinary. A sense of relief filled me, knowing Lucas wasn't dead. Even though we were on different sides, he'd proven himself to me.

"Okay, so what's the problem?"

"The problem is the man followed his little broadcast with a raid on Nashville, which just so happens to be near the edge of our border. In his broadcast he said he would be taking his revenge on our military stronghold. But did he? No, the bastard bombed a civilian hospital, ending hundreds of innocent lives."

My blood pulsed through my ears in a whooshing stream. I took a deep breath, trying to settle my nerves. But the anger was building and the fact that I didn't have anything to take it out on coursed through me.

"So what do we do about it?" I finally said, lamely, as if there was anything to be done. Those lives were already gone. Families already devastated. More unsuspecting families torn apart because of the vile King.

"We were leaving anyway but now we're being redirected to Nashville to help. New Colony has already begun to occupy parts of the suburbs and their troops are moving in fast. It won't be long until they completely take over Nashville. This is our first large urban city to deal in this situation and, quite frankly, they're not equipped to handle it. Civilian militias are forming as we speak, and that's hardly going to be the solution."

"It's not your fault, honey," Mel said softly, placing her hand over his fist that seemed to be glued to the table.

"It's my job to protect the citizens in this country," he said. "I'm one of the highest-ranking Army Generals. I am responsible. We should have sent more troops out the second they attacked the first time. All along the border, not just the points where they were already attacking."

I didn't know what to say. I agreed with him.

"We'll make them pay for this," Mastin snarled and stood. "I'll be upstairs," he called over his shoulder as he left us, probably to finish packing.

And as for me? So far, I wasn't slated to travel with them, but I was determined to remedy that little issue.

Melissa wandered off, likely to check on something in another room.

This is my chance. You can do this. You must.

It was the very first moment Mastin had left me alone with his father since the meeting with the President. I'd no doubt he wanted me to stay back on base, to play house with his mother and stay safe. And I also figured he must be temporarily distracted by the news from this morning. Too bad for him; I'd take his distraction and use it to my advantage.

I won't feel guilty for it, I told myself, though the feeling was buried deep.

"Take me with you." I turned on Nathan. "I *know* I can help. You need me."

"We need you here even more," he replied. "We might need you to train alchemists—not kids—but if we can find any willing adults, they'll need a teacher and you're all we've got."

"That's not true. Hank is already on it. He taught me so much about magic. Trust me, he's fully capable and he wants the job," I pleaded, meeting his determined eyes. I would do whatever was necessary to get him to agree. If he didn't come around through begging, he would through magic.

"I would be useless here," I added. "But out there, I could be the difference between winning and losing the war."

"I don't know." He chewed his lip as if mulling over the idea.

"Think about it this way. Those people in the hospital? I bet I could have saved many of them. Green alchemy works quickly to heal flesh wounds, even the worst kind, and I'm an expert with green. There may come a time where I save *your* life." I added for dramatic effect, "Or maybe your son's life."

His eyes zeroed in on me; I had him.

And if he didn't, there was a knife awfully close to my hand that I could use to draw blood. One minute and it would all be over, assuming I still had the ability. If not, I'd be dead. The idea lingered. I imagined jumping into action, slicing him open and using the magic before he could respond. I could have the General healed and cleaned up in moments, unable to remember a thing except for the solid realization that he needed to take me with him today.

I shook the thought away. I didn't want to do it.

It had been years since I'd sworn off the magic. It was a massive risk, and something I never wanted to return to again.

"Well?" I pressed, staring at him head on.

I wasn't here to sit on the sidelines and watch America lose their war, their country, and everyone I knew and loved in the process. There was no way! My pinky finger rested on the edge of the knife, my ring finger beginning to draw closer as well.

"Fine," he said, blowing out a slow breath. My hand snapped back.

"You won't regret this," I replied, filled with anticipation.

He smiled mischievously. "I'm starting to see why he likes you so much."

A new sense of excitement washed through me, this one even more frantic than the first. I bit my lip and looked away, blood rising to my cheeks.

He didn't utter another word about it. He just chuckled, stood, and left the kitchen. I stood and busied myself with the cleanup, emptying the plates and bowls of their half-eaten food into the trash, adding the dishes to the ones already in the sink, and then wetting a towel to wipe everything down.

Through it all, my thoughts hung on Nathan Scott's

comment. I didn't need him to say anything to know that he was hinting at the attraction between me and his son. But I couldn't think about Mastin right now, anyway. It was time to make plans for Nashville and prepare myself for all possible scenarios of what I could do there once we arrived. That's what I need to focus on, but my curious mind had already wandered to the boy upstairs.

▼

We flew in a stream of massive choppers, bigger than the ones we'd been outfitted in for previous missions. These were sleeker, faster, and outfitted to transport an entire squadron of soldiers at once. When I'd first climbed inside the expansive belly of mine, I was struck by the irrational fear that it wouldn't actually fly. It was just so huge. But I kept all wonderment to myself, musing that I might be able to pilot this thing if given the chance.

Okay, maybe that was too cocky, even for me.

Strapped into a seat next to Mastin, I tried to ignore his cold demeanor and the way he avoided talking to me. He was angry that I'd gone behind his back to convince the General of my worth. Either that, or it was the unsaid confessions between us that bothered him. After all the times I'd nearly kissed him, he'd been the one to make the first move, and my response was to run away. We still hadn't talked about it. I watched him from the corner of my eye, studying the way his hair glistened under the lights, the way his jaw moved as he swallowed or talked. He was careful to keep his arm from brushing mine, to keep his body turned away. *Fine by me.*

And on my other side, was Tristan. His scent traveled to me every time I turned toward him, a familiar wash of woodsy forest and sweet citrus. Tristan, the best surprise guest a girl could ask for. The moment I'd seen him approaching the chopper, I'd exploded into a ball of both excitement and worry. I wanted him with me, always. And I didn't want to see him involved in this war, ever.

And isn't that how Mastin feels?

I bristled at the thought. Tristan wasn't an alchemist. He wasn't *needed* out there, though maybe it was me that needed him. In any event, Tristan had also seemed slightly peeved to see me standing at the base of the helicopter. But Tristan didn't let his opinions or moods ruin things. It was one of his best qualities, the easy way he could brush things off. Once we'd strapped into our seats, he'd reverted to his usual adorable self, covering his trepidation with the kind of jokes and teasing that left me in stitches nearly the entire journey. And not just me, the soldiers around us immediately took to him, laughing along.

He provided an element to the group that was greatly needed: comic relief.

The flight took hours and by the time we approached our destination, I was aching to stretch my sore legs on the solid ground. If I could just go for a run, everything would feel better.

"What's the running situation like on these bases?" I turned to Mastin, forcing him to engage with me.

"Running situation?"

"You know? As in, I want to go for a jog when we land. I wondered what the possibility for that is like close to a war zone?"

He frowned. "We're heading into a war zone and you're worried about exercise?"

Tristan laughed, leaning in to join the conversation. "I thought you'd been living with this girl for the past couple weeks? Don't you know, if she can't go running every day, she can't be held responsible for her actions?"

I laughed. "It's true, Mastin. I need my runner's high if I'm going to have to put up with you." I winked, and he rolled his eyes, cracking the smallest of smiles.

There we go!

"You should be fine in a couple of days, maybe even by tomorrow." He shrugged. "These war zone bases are huge. But they're still fortifying this one."

I smirked, leaning into him. "It's your funeral!" I teased.

The group fell into companionable silence as we continued our flight. I noticed a few of the soldiers eyed me with suspicion, and one's glare was downright hostile. I narrowed my eyes on one of the soldier's who'd threatened me my first day on base. He could hate me all he wanted, it wasn't going to stop me from being part of the mission.

I turned away. Most of my critics would come around eventually. I chuckled to myself. Not likely.

"What's the matter?" Tristan whispered in my ear. His nearness sent a shiver down my spine and for a moment, I lost my train of thought.

"I think a lot of these guys hate me," I whispered back.

He sighed. "Yeah, well, they should be focusing on themselves and not worrying about you. But I'm here now," he continued, his lips so close now they brushed against my ear. "I'm not letting you out of my sight."

A rush of relief washed through me, because I knew what he said was true.

Whether or not he'd started this mission because of me didn't matter. He would stick to it, stick with me, because that's what best friends did.

I turned slightly toward him. "I hope one day they see me as another member of the troop, you know?"

He leaned back and studied me, eyes sparked with

admiration.

"It doesn't matter how they see you, but how you see you," he leaned back in to whisper.

I giggled at how corny this conversation had just turned.

"No fraternizing!" a voice called out, teasing. Tristan and I both turned back in our seats as embarrassment crawled up my spine. Mastin bristled in his seat, folding his arms, his biceps flexing.

Being a woman in the middle of all this testosterone was tough.

Not only was I one of only *three* women on board this chopper, I was the only color alchemist in this army. The likelihood that I'd ever fit in was about the same as King Richard turning himself in for crimes against humanity. Maybe Tristan was right about what mattered most. It was my opinion of myself that mattered.

Besides, I like standing out.

There were a few windows in the chopper, and I fiddled with my fingernail as I anxiously watched the scenery below. We would be making up our own base on the other side of Nashville, close enough to the action to jump in when needed, but far enough away for us to have time to fortify a stronghold. Just as we neared the area, the descent of the chopper sending a thrill through my belly, a bomb exploded below. The immediate boom echoed over the land, an audible crack followed by a thunder.

Everyone tensed, ready to move.

"Oh hell no!" a man shouted. Angry cussing erupted among the rest.

"Arm yourselves," General Scott shouted out, his voice loud over the sound of the rotors and angry troops. "We're taking out whoever did that. We'll make them wish they'd never set foot on our soil!"

The men shouted in agreement, pumping themselves up. They quickly unstrapped themselves and loaded their weapons. I watched Mastin do the same as a nervous sensation tugged deep in my chest.

Nathan turned toward the pilot up front, barking orders. "Drop us off as close to the explosion point as you can manage."

The pilot nodded and we began to descend much faster. The inertia of free-fall shot through my body like whiplash, and I grabbed hold of my own gun resting on my hip, grateful someone had finally armed me. Once I'd boarded the chopper, I'd gotten the weapon, and thanks to Hank's training, I knew how to use it. But it was the stone necklace, newly refreshed and fastened under my shirt that I was most grateful for. It was the weapon that would make the most difference down there, and I intended to use it.

We landed softly, the impact a contradiction to the way we jumped out of the chopper. Heads ducked low, we emptied from the machine in a wave of soldiers. We ran, our training taking over as we found cover in the surrounding trees that dotted the base, as well as the few metal-sided buildings that littered the area. A few of the guys took refuge behind a handful of bulletproof vehicles that were parked.

Mastin was at my side even though I never asked for it. Tristan was as well, but that was expected. The three of us stilled behind a tree, assessing the area. Mastin took point, motioning to the rest of his troop with a series of quick hand movements.

"Stay here." He pointed at me.

"Not happening," I replied.

"He's right," Tristan added.

"I'm not having this discussion with you two."

Mastin cussed, and we ran, moving closer to the building,

which was alive with growing flames. Up ahead, a group of people battled. I recognized the black Guardian outfits. Only these were slightly different. They had full body armor attached to their clothes and the alchemists wore full coverage helmets. Bullets would be hard pressed to slow them unless they hit the perfect spot. Stone chokers, in a myriad of colors, wrapped around the Guardians' necks. The color shining in the sunlight most was a yellowish amber.

Super soldiers. Just as Richard had planned.

The way they moved stunned me. These fighters were a sight to behold. They shook the earth when they ran, tore it away in clumps when they jumped, and when they hit someone, the blow was fatal. A body was thrown twenty feet in the air before crashing against a tank, and I had no doubt that life had just ended.

I screeched and ran at them, my own magic blaring to life in my veins.

I pounced on the nearest one, recognizing him instantly through the visor of his helmet. Reed. Popular Reed, the boy who'd had a little fling with Jessa all those months ago. He was a fierce fighter; I'd sparred with him a few times back at the palace. He chuckled as he pushed me to the ground with ease.

"We were wondering when you'd show up." He laughed, leaning over me.

"Here I am!" I shot back, jumping up. "So come and get me!"

"Oh, I plan on it."

He charged, and I met him blow for blow. The second a pain shot through me, I eased it with my green magic. But it seemed he was doing the same; we were an even match and this time, neither one fell. Finally, I ripped off his helmet, tossing it aside. He watched it, momentarily distracted. I swiped at him, gouged my fingers into his skin of his cheeks, fully intending to use my red alchemy and gain the upper hand. But he jumped back and scowled.

"I won't let you do that to me," he shouted, his shadowed eyes two angry black pellets. "Yeah, I figured out your secret after you left, and Faulk told us who you really were, Francesca! I remember you now. I remember your magic. I won't let you be near my blood. I know your sister already messed with me once! She tried--"

I didn't care about his stupid monologue.

I dived at him, reaching out toward a line of blood that dropped down his pale face. A slam knocked me aside and I rolled to the ground, losing my breath. Reed took off running like the coward he was.

"Fall back!" The man who'd tackled me yelled toward the group of alchemists. "Go!"

I recognized that voice, too! Branson, the fighting instructor from the palace. A trickle of fear shot through me as our eyes met. I'd seen this man fight before. He was a machine, and if I didn't manage to use red, I didn't stand a chance. But I pushed that thought aside and attacked him anyway.

He let me. He fell to the ground as if he wasn't even trying. *It must be a trick.*

"Wait," he growled, his voice soft. "I'm Resistance."

I froze, leaning over him.

"What did you just say?"

"Resistance," he spat and then turned to look at his Guardians. Most of them had disappeared but a few were still engaged in combat. One was laying on the ground, their body oddly shaped and a ring of blood around a mess of long blonde hair. He pointed to Reed and widened his eyes at me.

I nodded. That's right, Reed could listen but not if I could counter it. Blocking blue magic was one very useful ability that I did have. Before I allowed myself to question it, I felt for the blue.

"If Reed is listening, he can't hear us now. What do you want?"

"I can't stay or I'm dead," he said in a low voice. "But I'm Resistance and I want to work to help you, help from the other side. I need to make a connection with your leader. Where is he?"

"You can make a connection with me," I whispered firmly at him.

Tristan jumped forward, his gun pointed at Branson, finger hovering over the trigger. I held up a hand and shook my head. He raised an eyebrow but lowered the gun.

"Fine," Branson snapped. "I don't have time for this crap, anyway." He pulled a piece of paper from his pocket and slipped it into my hand. "That's a secure address," he said. "Give it to your highest-ranking officer as soon as possible."

I glanced at the crumpled slip of paper, at a nonsensical email address written in hurried script.

"Fine," I said. "You'd better be the real deal, Branson, or next time I'll kill you."

"I am." He chuckled, as if this was a laughing matter. "I've been working with Jasmine and the others at the palace for years."

"Who are the others?"

"Hank knows." He nodded to Tristan, who towered over us. "He probably does too. You're Tristan?"

Tristan raised his head once in confirmation. Branson used his magic to push us both back. We fell to the ground and before we could react, he was running away at top speed. He slipped behind the nearest building and was gone.

"What was that about?" Tristan knelt beside me.

"He's Resistance," I hissed back. "That's Branson."

Tristan's face lit with recognition, a knowing smile on his lips. "I know the name! Yeah, he's telling the truth. He's been loyal to the Resistance for years."

I shoved the paper into my pocket with shaky hands, still sitting on my butt like a total idiot.

"Sasha," Nathan called out, "over here." His commanding voice and presence embodied every bit the General he was. Soldiers surrounded him, looking to him for direction. The sun glinted off his dark hair, slick with sweat and even some blood.

I sprinted, quickly noticing the body lying motionless in the dirt. Her frame was petite and strong like mine. How easily could it have been me in her place? Blood soaked her tangle of blonde hair and when I pulled it aside, I knew the pretty face below me. Brooke.

"Make sure she's dead. No one wants to touch her," Nathan said with a grimace.

I stilled, studying her. From the looks of it, she was just passed out, not dead. She'd always been such a brat, but she didn't deserve to die like this. She was a product of her environment. *But aren't we all? At what point are we held responsible for our actions?*

I sighed, fell to my knees, and double checked for a pulse. Below my fingers the thick vein in her wrist moved with the faintest of flutters.

"She's alive." I looking up at Nathan.

"Kill her," Mastin added, striding to us with murder in his eyes. Blood dripped down his temple and a dark bruise was already forming across cheek. "She nearly took me out along with the others." I looked over his shoulder at three bodies being zipped into black body bags.

"Can you save her?" Nathan asked.

I nodded. With green magic, it would be easy.

"Do it," he replied. "Don't bring her to full health. I don't want her waking up for a while. Just give her enough to not have any permanent damage."

He turned to Tristan. "Any idea how we can safely put this girl into prison and interrogate her?"

He reached down and carefully unlatched the necklace from around her neck, tossing it aside in the dirt. "Start with removing any color from her." He motioned to me. "But honestly, it's Sasha you should be asking. She just broke out of an alchemist prison, after all."

All the nearby soldiers stared at me. There were about thirty of them altogether, and they glowered at me like I was a bomb about to explode.

"It's true," I said, relenting. "If I can break out of King Richard's prison, then maybe I can help you keep Brooke in ours."

"We don't have a prison for alchemists," someone grumbled from the back of the crowd.

No kidding.

I stood and brushed off the dirt and grass, taking my sweet, sweet, time. The fear that I was making a huge mistake prickled at the back of my mind, but what choice did I have? It was time to show these people just how valuable I was.

"You don't have one *yet*," I said, "but with my help, you'll have the best one on this side of the border. And maybe if you listen to me and we do things the right way, we'll be able to add a few of her magical friends in there to keep her company."

They erupted in shouts of agreement, and I smirked. Mastin stalked away in a fury and Tristan put his hand on my back. I knelt down to take care of Brooke, and as I did, the thought pricked at me again, demanding attention.

Be careful. You might just find yourself locked in that prison as well.

SEVENTEEN
JESSA

Since the fire, the palace wall, gate, and grounds swarmed with security. But on the inside, only the most trusted of the guards, officers, and advisors were allowed to move freely about the palace. Even the newer alchemists weren't allowed to leave the GC wing. No exceptions. They had come from West America, so suspicion was cast upon them. In the meantime, Faulk was conducting interviews. She was shriller than ever, and I didn't envy anyone on the receiving end of that woman.

Somehow, the fire had traveled through the royal wing, but had stopped just before reaching my dance studio. I'd still been permitted to use it, thankfully. And I did, every moment I could. After the stress of everything, my legs were sorer than they'd been in ages, but I didn't care. Dance was my only solace left in this place.

I was back in my old dorm room. Work crews had set out to restore the burned areas of the royal wing, but it would be months before anyone would be living there.

Either way, I wouldn't be in this dorm for long. The morning sun filtered in through the small window, and I stared at the stark white walls. They wouldn't be my walls for long.

Some of the other guest rooms had been taken over for Lucas and Richard. By this time next week, I'd be living with Lucas as a married woman. I could hardly bring myself to think about it, but it was coming whether I was ready or not. The wedding planning was complete. The date was set. Richard refused to let the fire slow things down. He said postponing would show weakness. The marriage was a fast-rolling ball nobody could stop.

I'd accepted it, deciding to enjoy my last week to myself.

Today, however, not so much…

Exhibition number three, the final one, was taking place in the palace's largest ballroom tonight, in the very same place as the first attack. My stomach churned, thinking about what another exhibition would mean. And again, every time I remembered that terrible night Jasmine had died. As I laid in bed, blinking away the sleep, watching the room grow brighter with the rising sun, I knew I'd have face the scene of the crime again tonight.

I rolled over and groaned into my pillow. I still missed Jasmine. She'd been someone I could lean on, someone to tell me what to do. Now I was on my own. Sure, I had Madame Silver. Maybe not at the moment but she'd be back in a few months. And I had Lily and Jose, but they felt more like allies, not mentors. It was up to me to stop the King.

I had to do it. Get Richard *alone*. Use my red alchemy.

An impatient series of quick knocks sounded on my door. I rolled out of bed, stretching as I padded to answer it. The same two cosmetologists from the disastrous exhibition at the lodge stood outside, smiling at me from ear to ear.

"You, dear Jessa, are going to have an amazing day!" the woman said. Her name was Lainey; she did the makeup. Lars did hair. I only remembered because their names went together comically well. I sighed and held open the door.

"Come in."

They pushed past me, assessing the space.

"Oh, this bathroom is quite small," Lars said with a huff. "But I guess it will have to do. Such ghastly news about the fire. So glad your beautiful fiancé made it out okay."

Lainey opened a tiny black folding chair in the center of the bathroom and promptly proceeded to lay out a million makeup and hair products across the counter.

"What time is the exhibition?" I eyed the things they'd brought along today.

"Oh, it's not until five," she replied.

Tonight?

"Then why are you here so early?" I questioned. "I haven't even had breakfast yet. Come back this afternoon."

They shared a knowing look and my suspicion burned deep.

"Don't worry, someone will be delivering your meals today," Lainey said. "We have very specific instructions about how your hair and makeup are to be done and it's going to take quite some time and effort."

"For an exhibition? It hardly seems worth hours of effort."

"Oh, but remember Richard announced there would be a surprise?" Lars jumped on. "Trust me, honey, you're going to want to look perfect for this. Now, we'll step out so you can take a shower. No offense, but you stink."

"Wow, thanks," I grumbled, shooing them from the area that they'd already taken over with their stuff. I probably did stink. I'd danced until midnight and then stumbled back to the dorm to crash in bed.

"Don't forget to shave your legs." Lainey waved at me, winked, and shut the door with a kissy face.

Dread filled me, as I suspected this extra-special surprise would mean the end of my freedom. There was nothing to be done about it now. The shower welcomed me, and as the warm water fell, I allowed my tears to fall, too. Soon, I would have to step out of this shower, and when I did, my tears wouldn't be allowed any longer.

▼

The hairdo was the biggest clue.

The top had been braided back expertly into two loose fishtail braids that met at the back where I usually put my ponytail. Down the back, Lars had somehow managed to curl and braid everything together in such a way it reminded me of a Viking Queen. It was incredible, and he was right, it took hours. Finally, he twisted in glittery, white rhinestone pins down the length.

Lainey hadn't gone for the natural look, like at the last exhibition. She'd given me perfect cat eyes with just the right amount of smoky eye shadow on top. My lips were painted a matte rose color that matched the blush on my cheeks. She called it "ballet slipper pink" and I had to agree. She highlighted my nose and cheeks with pale white shimmer and finished off the look with huge fake eyelashes. I had worn false lashes plenty of times for dance performances in the past, but they always felt strange and heavy. Today was no different. I stared at my transformed appearance.

I still looked like me, so that was good news. But I also looked so much older. It was as if the two had taken an eraser to all my imperfections and to every bit of me that made me look seventeen. I looked at least twenty-five now, like a woman who knew exactly what she wanted in life and just how to get it.

I laughed at the thought.

"Is everything okay, honey?" Lainey asked.

I smiled and lied through my teeth. "It's perfect."

As they finished up, my mind wandered back to Dad. I hoped he was okay. I'd tried to reach out through our telepathy, but I wasn't able to connect that far. I would keep trying. Ever since it was discovered that Dad was missing, I'd expected some kind of retaliation. There hadn't been anything. Not yet. Faulk hadn't even interviewed me. She'd been so absent from my life lately, it was a little odd, but I wasn't complaining. Richard never said a word about Dad to me, either. Lucas had said nobody was blaming me for his disappearance. They suspected that he'd simply used the opportunity of the chaotic fire to run and was in hiding somewhere. That he'd left because he didn't want to be used as collateral against me. It didn't take a genius to assume that. It was true.

"Now for the jewelry!" Lars clapped and removed a diamond necklace from a black velvet jewelry box. He took off my alchemy necklace and replaced it with this imposter. It sparkled brilliantly and ended with a huge teardrop diamond at the hollow of my neck.

He winked. "It's real."

My breath caught as I stared at what could only be royal jewels. More dread spread through me, more worry about what was coming next.

Then he pulled something else out of his bag, a delicate diamond tiara, and fastened it to the top of my head. A pin poked my scalp and my eyes watered.

"Ouch!"

"Sorry, girl. Price of beauty, and all that."

"Okay, what's going on?" I asked. My fingers had gone numb, and my heart felt like it was about to jump out of my chest. Really, there was no question. I already knew.

"Haven't figured it out yet?" Lainey squealed. "We're not allowed to tell you about the surprise but that doesn't mean you can't guess."

"No," I whispered. "No way, he wouldn't."

Oh yes, he totally would.

"Come," Lars said, wagging his finger at me. "It's time to put on your dress."

I stood on shaky legs and followed them back into the bedroom. The dress hung over the closet door, posted there like a warrant. I recognized it immediately and winced. The tailor had measured me for it only a few weeks ago. Shining brilliant white underneath, with fragile lace covering every inch, it fell to the floor in a wide train, the lace just peeking out over the edge.

Even I had to admit it, my wedding dress was stunning.

"I'm not getting married next week. I'm getting married tonight," I said, accepting the truth. I took several deep breaths. They didn't help. The panic began to crawl up my neck, gripping. The heaviness of the diamond necklace, a noose. The ring on my finger, a promise. The tiara perched atop of my head, a cage.

"Yes, you are," Lainey said. "I just knew you'd love this surprise! Now, let's get you dressed. Your groom is waiting for you."

And so was my entire future.

▼

The second I stepped from my room I was faced with cameras. They were everywhere, and more than ever before, as if they'd multiplied.

"Jessa, how are you feeling?" A man shouted from behind one of them.

I smiled, knowing these cameras wouldn't be going anywhere for a while. What did I expect? This was a public event for the beginning of what would be a very public life.

"I'm so excited," I gushed, running my hands along my dress.

"Are you happy about the surprise?"

"I couldn't be more pleased." I stared into the camera, my reflection shining back to me in the lens. "I want to thank Richard for this day. I don't know how I'll ever repay him, but I promise to find a way."

A barrage of security swept me away.

I wasn't brought into the palace ballroom. That plan had all been a ruse. Instead, I was whisked into a town car and driven to the oldest church in the capitol city. Saint Patrick's Cathedral may have been the oldest building in the kingdom, considering so many of others were deemed too patriotic and torn down decades ago. Out with the old, in with the new. There weren't many practicing Catholics left in New Colony, and as far as I knew, this church was used strictly for weddings and funerals. But then again, I wasn't religious. How would I know? Religion was a freedom we had in New Colony, but it just wasn't something people were fanatical about. There were too many reasons for us to stay in line.

As we pulled to the curb, I watched the guards and Royal Officers as they swarmed the area. There weren't many citizens here to gawk, as I'd been expecting and like I'd seen in the old footage of other royal weddings. That was probably because the wedding happening *today* would be a surprise for them, too. Maybe this earlier wedding day was Richard's way of making sure it happened exactly as he wanted. A surprise for everyone else but him.

I climbed out the car, struggling with the tight dress and its long train. A cacophony of people instantly surrounded me, like moths to the flame. My heart hammered, and my breathing picked up, making my dress feel ten times tighter than it had back in my bedroom. Someone handed me a bouquet of white roses, bound in shiny white ribbon. I'd specifically chosen blush pink and pale green for my colors. But looking down at myself and my flowers, everything that touched my body *in any way* was completely white.

I swallowed a shuddering breath, frowning at the genius of it. Just another one of Richard's tactics to keep me from going off-script.

Keep her dressed in white.

Keep her magic inside.

I bit my lip and lifted the flowers to my nose briefly, relaxing in the rose scent. Catching me off guard, not alerting the public ahead of time, what else would King Richard have up his sleeve? He must have been convinced I was going to mess this up somehow, to go to all the trouble.

I wasn't convinced I still wouldn't.

Or maybe he was just trying to throw off anyone with plans to assassinate the royal family during such a public event. Maybe this was all for my protection.

The cathedral loomed ahead. As a kid, I'd loved to study its uniqueness in the city, always picking it out from the modern buildings when my family had come downtown. Now, it would forever be remembered as my wedding location.

It was large, but not as big as I'd pictured. Composed of gray and sandstone bricks, it had gothic-inspired arched doorways and windows. Perfectly manicured hedges lined either side. New state-of-the-art buildings surrounded the cathedral, making it stand out as a gem even more.

The air wrapped around me, still and cold. My usually pale arms turned pink. I shivered and peered up at the large circular stained-glass window embedded above the entrance, trying unsuccessfully to count the number of geometric shapes. Anything to focus on but the reality of the moment.

"Time to go," someone said in my ear.

The ornate crimson front door beckoned to me.

It's going to be okay. This is just a necessary evil to get closer to the King. And it's not like Lucas is going to make you behave as a real wife would. Right?

It was a question that flipped my insides upside-down.

The nerves raged unbearably as I stepped into the church, my sparkly heels clicking against the stone floor. A string quartet played the standard bridal chorus, the music filling the space. A room brimming with people stood and turned in my direction, their gazes heavy as they stared. Someone whispered "now" in my ear, and then Richard slid in to take my arm and walk me down the aisle.

My heart froze. It should have been Dad. None of this was right. If it was right, then Dad would be escorting me down the aisle at my wedding, not this awful imposter who made my skin crawl.

I smiled sweetly despite the angry pit in my stomach. Along the edges of my vision, Color Guardians lined the walls. They stood at attention, manipulating magic in their hands that swirled out and over the crowd. The stunning sparkling colors of sea foam, cobalt blue, lavender, magenta, honey orange, and canary yellow danced around the room. It was magnifying. Stunning.

And absolutely the perfect touch for a wedding between a prince and an alchemist. Just like at the other two exhibitions, the cameras zoomed about the space to catch it all.

Tilting my head, I saw him. Prince Lucas. Lucas to me, and yet to the rest of the world, he was a prince. Today he looked the part, dressed in fine maroon and cream regalia to match the title. Atop of his head, a gold crown, inlaid with pearls, rubies, and diamonds. It was a smaller one than the monstrosity I could see Richard wearing out of the corner of my eye.

We began to walk forward.

The closer I got, the more Lucas's eyes shone. They narrowed on me with a mix of shock and intensity in their gray depths. Love and pain and regret and hope and everything in between flashed across his face as I moved closer with each step. Lately, he'd been so good at covering his feelings, at shadowing his truth. But seeing him now, I *knew* he loved me. I *knew* he was sorry and heartbroken. That he'd nearly given up but so desperately *didn't want to give up*.

Maybe he didn't want to control me. Maybe he just wanted my forgiveness.

Could I forgive him?

I still didn't feel ready. As I walked toward him, my chest ached with the knowledge, and I hated myself for it. I wanted to. I wanted to be with him, to love him, to forget about our past and move forward. But the betrayal burned bright, brighter than ever with Richard on my arm instead of my own beloved father. Things could have been different for me and Lucas. They should have been different.

Richard deposited me in front of his son, then moved to the side.

"You are so beautiful," Lucas's voice cracked as he said the words. Then he took my hand and together we faced the priest.

I didn't pay attention to a word the solemn and elderly

man said as he officiated, but when the time came, Lucas said, "I do." And I said it, too.

"You may now kiss the bride."

The priest's crackly voice rose over the congregation. Lucas and I leaned in at the same time. I expected to recoil at his kiss after all the anger I'd been holding inside. But instead, I fell into his lips as I always had. I breathed him in and a peaceful calm settled over me. I'd missed that. Missed *him*.

It was possible that we were going to be all right. Maybe he wasn't going to turn out like his father. Yes, our love had changed, and we'd probably not be the most romantic couple in the world, but I hoped we'd be able to find mutual respect. Maybe that would transform into something more, something beautiful.

I was relieved, having decided on a place to start.

Respect.

As we strode back down the aisle, hands clasped together and smiling faces beaming back at us, I soon realized the night was far from over. Richard announced that we'd be going back to the palace for a dinner, reception, and dancing.

This time, we rode together in the armored black car. Lucas held my hand softly in his as he explained that he'd had no idea about the surprise wedding, either. He insisted that he wasn't okay about being deceived but looking at him, he didn't seem all that perturbed.

"Are you happy to be married to me?" he suddenly asked with a hopeful expression. A stab of guilt jabbed at me.

I held my breath for a moment. If it was respect I wanted, I needed to start with the truth. "I'm not unhappy about it," I said, my lips twisting as I tried to think of how to explain what I was feeling.

His face dropped slightly, and that familiar shadow overtook him: that shadow not as anger, or as frustration, but as heartbreak.

"It's not like *that*," I said. "Will you hear me out?"

He peered up at me and nodded. The sunlight caught the planes of his face, accentuating his jaw, and I nearly pulled him in for a kiss. I was so attracted to this man, and yet, so conflicted; I hardly knew how to handle myself.

This man is your husband.

I took a deep breath and explained. "After how we got engaged, not the first time but the official time, I thought I would have to be dragged down that aisle kicking and screaming. I was so mad at you, Lucas. You know that. And I can't say I'm totally over it because I'm not. I don't know if I ever will be."

He waited for me to go on, squeezing my hand once. His warm palms sent relief through me.

"I have to admit." I bit my lip, a little embarrassed. "I'm glad you didn't marry Celia. And I think maybe with time, we might be able to build something again. I can't stop thinking about what you did for me that day of the fire." I was talking about my dad, but with no purple near, I couldn't make the telepathic connection. He nodded in understanding. "And about how you went into that fire looking for me," I continued. "I know you care about me. I do."

Silence stretched between us.

"I can work with that." He smiled faintly.

We turned to face forward, and I leaned into him. He stilled for a moment, then placed a gentle kiss on the top of my head.

We pulled into the palace drive and were met with even more cameras. They escorted us into our reception in the main ballroom. It was decked out with white crystals that hung in long strings from the ceilings. White tablecloths were laid over the round tables with rose-flowered centerpieces standing tall in their centers, in the exact shades of pink and green I'd picked with the wedding planner.

The night flew by in a frenzy of food and dancing and talking with nearly everyone I'd ever met in the palace and a few more of the King's closest confidants and families. Even Celia and her parents attended the reception, ignoring the hostile glares people shot their way. They congratulated us on the marriage and left early.

After a few hours of everything, I had to admit, I was starting to get into it. I found myself relaxing, and my cheeks were beginning to ache from all the smiling. Lucas held me in his arms while we danced, my head resting on his shoulder, his face tilted in, breath tickling my ear.

"Are you happy yet?"

I chuckled, teasing. "I guess you could say this feeling is happiness."

I leaned back a little to catch the expression on his face. "Are you happy?"

He nodded once, eyes flicking to my lips. "Yes."

"Oh, you two." Richard stepped in right next to us, snapping us from the moment. "Aren't you a picture?" Lucas still held me as we turned to the King. "You remind me of me and your Mother." His face darkened, pain flickering across it. The crown on his head was a little off-kilter, the red around his eyes a little too noticeable. "We used to be like this, you know? Young, in love, the world at our doorstep..."

Lucas sniffed and furrowed his brow. Richard seemed a tad too drunk, a rare sight, and more than a little unsettling.

"I miss her, too," Lucas said, voice careful.

Richard's face twisted, eyes landing on me. "But we have *you* now." The words came out sharp, sounding like a threat. "Better do as you're told, Princess. This isn't a game."

Then he stalked away, party guests stumbling out of his

way. A prickly doubt coursed through me as Lucas and I continued to dance; the earlier happiness washed away.

A few minutes later, Richard issued more reminders of the truth.

He'd found the microphone, and his voice bellowed out over the crowd. "Friends and esteemed guests, thanks again for coming tonight. I want to congratulate the happy couple."

Lucas and I turned from our dance to Richard, the crowd parting in an arc as they clapped. We stood in the center of the dance floor, the King on the other end.

"This marks the beginning of not just a loving couple's life together, but the beginning of a new era for the Heart family. Jessa and Lucas have united the Royal Family with the alchemists, making our kingdom even more powerful."

I swallowed a lump in my throat. Lucas's arm, draped around my side, grew tighter as his father continued.

"We will win the war, take back what's rightfully ours, and unite West America and New Colony under one prosperous kingdom." His voice was strong, determined, and the guests ate it up. They cheered with shining eyes and nodding heads.

He motioned to us once again, a glass of champagne now in his other hand. He raised it high. "To the happy couple, may you live long and be prosperous." He winked. "And give this kingdom lots of magical little heirs."

"To the happy couple!" The crowd cheered, a few snickering at the joke.

But it wasn't a joke.

Lucas and I smiled wide at our guests, but inside, I burned with anger. Richard's speech had once again shattered the illusion, waking me to my true reality.

I wasn't here to play house with Lucas, or to make alchemist babies for the Heart family. I wasn't here to be friends with the royals and I refused to play right into Richard's hands as

I'd always done.

No. I'm here to complete my mission for the Resistance, gain control over Richard, and end his corruption once and for all.

I owed it to Jasmine. To my family. To everyone who'd lost a life because of King Richard.

"All right you two lovebirds." Richard strolled to us, microphone now gone. He seemed a little steadier on his feet, as if the speech had sobered him. "It's time for you to retire for the night."

But I could still smell the acrid scent of alcohol on his breath.

"I want grandkids, it's true." He laughed, patting his son on the back. "But don't worry, I don't expect any for at least a few more years."

Embarrassment washed over me as Lucas tensed at my side. It wasn't the thought of being intimate with Lucas that bothered me, though I hardly felt ready. It was the fact that Richard was joking about our children as if it were a done deal. And he was right. If things continued the way they were, I eventually would have to produce an heir for this family.

Lucas grimaced and hushed his father. "That's enough, Dad."

"Let's go," I said, tugging him back. I couldn't stand the sight of Richard for another second.

As Lucas and I strode from the ballroom, hand in hand, the guests cheered in a wild frenzy of hoots and hollers. It seemed as if their party was just getting started, judging by the amount of energy they exuded. The second the ballroom doors clicked closed, another flurry of nerves erupted within me.

Lucas took my hand and led me down the palace hallway, a security detail close on our heels. We moved quickly through the palace, toward what I could only assume was his bedroom.

No, not just his bedroom anymore.

Our bedroom.

EIGHTEEN
LUCAS

I never thought I would become a romantic.

The entire notion of romance felt antiquated and too vulnerable for my taste. And yet here I was, asking my wife if I could carry her over the threshold of our shared suite. *Nobody warned me that love came with embarrassing moments like this one,* I grumbled inwardly.

She looked at me like I had completely lost my mind. Maybe I had.

But she also looked gorgeous.

I laughed. "So what? It's our only chance to do something this corny. We have to take it."

She lifted her arms and giggled. "Okay, fine, but if you drop me I'll kill you."

"There will be none of that tonight."

I picked her up, kicked the door open, and stepped over the threshold. Then I set her down gently and closed the door, locking it. "That wasn't so hard, was it?"

She shook her head but smiled the biggest smile I'd seen

all day. That was good. That was more than good. Ever since our conversation in the car on the way back from the ceremony, a flame of hope had rekindled that I didn't know was still there. And I liked it.

"Since when are you such a romantic, Lucas?" she teased back.

I smirked. What could I say? I'd had relationships before. And I wasn't a total jerk, but I'd never fallen in love with any of those girls. "The lovey-dovey stuff is reserved for you, Jessa."

She rolled her eyes. But it was true. She brought something else out in me; I guess that something was romance.

I shook my head, a tad shocked with myself as well. Eight months ago, she'd taken my world and turned everything upside down. And now, she'd made me a married man. She tilted her head to meet my gaze. Some of her hair had fallen from her braid, brushing the side of her neck.

A nervous hush fell over us as she turned to take in the room.

The bed was in the middle, with a loveseat and small desk by the curtained window. Across from the bed a wood fire burned in the fireplace, casting the room in flickering orange light. On one side was the closet door, and on the other the bathroom. But I didn't think it was the layout that had her chewing her bottom lip and her cheeks flushing pink. No, I'd say it was the satin and the red rose petals strewn across the white bedspread.

I gulped, my body instantly tensing.

"Okay," I said, "I swear I didn't have anything to do with that." I motioned in a circular motion at the general area of the bed, but we both knew what I was talking about. "That must have been one of the servants or something." I coughed.

She turned a scathing look on me, and then busted up,

doubling over at the waist. When she looked up at me again, a few loose tears streamed down her face. "Oh my gosh, you should see yourself right now, Lucas," she said between bouts of laughter. "I've never seen you blush like this before!"

I shrugged, but inside I fought a torrent of emotions. I didn't really think any of this was a laughing matter. It was a lot of things, but funny wasn't one of them.

She met my eyes again, and instantly shifted, her laughs catching in her throat as she gasped. I couldn't help it. Her dress fit her like a glove, perfectly cut to show off the curves of her body. Her elaborate hair and makeup were starting to come undone, which was only making *me* come undone.

"Oh," she breathed.

She opened and closed her mouth a few times, so I beat her to the punch.

"You're my wife," I said. "But that doesn't mean I expect anything from you, now or ever. I won't push you into something you don't want, no matter how *I* feel about it."

"And how do you feel about it?" she asked shyly, her eyes fluttering. I groaned inwardly. She really needed to stop that.

"Do you really have to ask that question?" I wanted her. We both knew it. But I also didn't want to be teased for it. I had some pride left in me somewhere.

She chewed on her lip again, and it took everything in me not to pull her into my arms and kiss her until her body agreed with mine. "I'm not ready," she finally said, sighing and walking to the bed. A tingle of disappointment tugged at me, but I ignored it. My feelings didn't matter here. What mattered was winning Jessa back. I wasn't going to blow it.

She sat on the edge of the bed, twiddling her fingers for a moment. Then her face tipped up to study me, a touch of embarrassment rimming her eyes. "But that doesn't mean I won't ever be ready," she added. "It's just that you were my first real boyfriend, you know? And everything happened so fast with us, and then the attack happened…" She paused and studied her nails, the blush in her cheeks growing. "Our engagement was so quick, and the surprise wedding threw me off, too."

"You don't have to apologize," I said. Even though she hadn't, I could hear it in her tone. "This isn't your fault. This wasn't even what you wanted."

Bitterness rose inside me, and I pushed it down to hang out with the disappointment. I'd do anything to avoid her getting upset with me again. We'd finally turned a corner today. I really *was* okay with waiting, given the circumstances, but I wasn't okay with ending the night in another argument.

I stepped forward and gently tilted her head up to me, cradling her warm cheek in my palm. "Let's just get our pajamas on and go to bed." I held her gaze until she nodded.

I strode to the chest of drawers, pulled it open, and tossed cotton pajama pants and a t-shirt at her and found some long athletic shorts for myself. "We'll cross that bridge when we get there. For now, we can do what you said. Let's start with rebuilding our friendship."

"I'd like that." She smiled as she shuffled into the bathroom to change.

I changed quickly and brushed all the rose petals into the small trashcan. I closed the thick curtains and climbed under the heavy comforter, taking the side I was pretty sure she didn't prefer, and tried to relax. The fire was dying down; it wouldn't be long before the room would be completely black. That would help.

A few minutes later Jessa peeked her head out of the bathroom. "You ready for this?"

I sat up. "Umm…"

She threw open the door, sprinted across the room and

jumped onto the bed. She leaned over and kissed me on the cheek, then slipped under the covers. Her sweet rose water smell wafted through me so intensely that I had to ball up my hands. I wasn't going to touch her. As much as I wanted to, I needed to respect her feelings more.

"Goodnight, husband," she said, rolling away and burrowing into the blankets. I stared at the back of her head for a long moment and then closed my eyes. The familiar dragging sensation of sleep tugged at me, as I sank deeper into the mattress. Today *had* been an insane day. Sleep would make everything better.

"Goodnight, wife."

▼

I woke with a start, my heart pounding. I reached out.

Jessa was gone.

Blinking away the sleep, I turned on the lamp. Still gone. Panic prickled at the back of my neck as I stood up and checked the bathroom. I even opened the closet door, but she wasn't there.

Did she already leave me?

No, that was stupid. But the fear was real and the thought nagged, like a little prick in my brain. So small and insignificant, but enough of a sting to demand attention. I went out into the hallway, peering around but she wasn't there either. It was getting late in the night. A guard was posted just outside our door.

"Have you seen Jessa?"

"Said she needed to get a snack." He shrugged, leaning against the wall. One hand was tucked on his gun, the other rubbed the side of his face. He was obviously tired, and that didn't bode well with me. "One of the other guards escorted her and then on her way back Richard stopped to chat, and they left together."

I stilled. "Where'd they go?"

He shrugged again. Useless. I glared at the guard, making a mental note to get him moved to another service, and went out in search of them. Richard's room was just down the hall, so it was the first place I checked. But there wasn't anyone in there.

What's going on?

I grabbed an ugly purple pillow from his bed and tried to reach out to Jessa through our mental link, but it didn't work. I didn't have that ability. It seemed she'd have to initiate the telepathy. But she didn't have her necklace. She'd taken that stupid diamond necklace off in the bathroom earlier, her normal necklace probably back in her dorm.

I threw the pillow at the wall and stormed back into the hall.

I racked my brain for possibilities as I paced the hallway. A faint sound of muffled voices filtered from a nearby room. I pressed my ear to the door, and recognizing Richard's voice, threw it open.

I nearly exploded into a rage at what I found.

Jessa was on the floor, cowering. Her hair was a mess, arms up in defense, whole body shaking. He stood above her, his hands in angry red fists.

"What's going on here?" I yelled.

He spun on me with murderous eyes. "Why don't you ask your wife to tell you what she just tried to do?"

I dropped to my knees to gather her in my lap. Her body still shook wildly, defenseless, and I kissed her forehead. "It's okay, baby," I murmured. She turned into me with a pleading expression and my eyes latched onto the beginnings of a purple bruise blossoming across her jaw.

"Did you hit her?" I glared up at my father in horror. I'd never known him to hit a woman; if this was his doing, it would be his last.

"Tell him what you did, Jessa!" He growled again. "Tell him now!"

"I–I tried to use red alchemy on him," she cried, bursting into tears.

For a split second, I didn't believe it. And then the world lost its balance. "Oh no. Jessa, you didn't."

What was she thinking? Now he would *really* treat her like a prisoner. Or worse. Obviously, whatever she'd done had failed miserably.

"Oh yes," he said, pacing in front of us. He strode to the open door and slammed it closed. We were in another one of the palace bedrooms, this one apparently vacant. "This little witch saw blood on me and assumed it was mine. She said she needed to talk to me about something in private, got me alone in here, and then proceeded to put her hand on the blood, spewing some nonsense about turning myself into West America and ending the war!"

He cursed and glared down at us with a fury that I'd never seen before in him. If I wasn't holding her at the moment, I was sure he'd hit her again.

"You need to get a hold of yourself," I snapped. "This is my wife!"

The silence stretched between us, thick and heady.

"Lucas, you need to take your new *wife* back to your room before I kill her," he finally replied between heavy breaths. "I'll figure out what to do with her in the morning *after* I've had a chance to discuss the ramifications of this treasonous act with Faulk."

That would make things so much worse for Jessa.

But not waiting a second longer for him to change his

mind, I pulled Jessa to standing, half carrying her

"Come on," I hissed at her. "We have to get back."

"Be careful with that one, Lucas. It seems she's a traitor not only to her country, but to her own father-in-law," He spat the words as we stumbled from the room together.

This was bad. This was so bad.

The second we were back in our suite, I wrapped my arms around her in a tight hug. She sobbed against my chest.

"I'm sorry. He seemed a bit drunk and when I saw the blood, I thought the two things combined would be the perfect opportunity to end all this right here and now."

I couldn't emotionally process this disaster. I shut that side of me down, and instead jumped into fixer-mode. If there was one thing that needed to be done, it was to get Jessa the hell out of the palace before morning.

"Use your purple," I whispered against her ear. "We need to talk."

She nodded and walked over to the chest of drawers, rummaging around in frustration until she found her stone necklace. So it hadn't been left in her dorm after all. Her clothes had been moved over since the wedding, luckily, it had been brought along.

Okay, what is it? she asked, and the link between us snapped to life.

I know where a Resistance safe house is, I said. *I also have a few addresses of people throughout New Colony who've agreed to help you. You need to go down to a farm in the south and from there you can make contact with West America. They won't be able to get you out up here; there's just too much going on with the war for you to be safe in the Capitol. But I think they could help you if you make it down there.*

She stumbled back and stared at me in complete bewilderment, her eyes wide. *Lucas, how long have you been planning this?*

Ever since Jasmine died. I ran my hand through my hair and sighed heavily. Then I strode to her and pulled her close to me again.

I'm not ready to lose you. But this was a reality I'd accepted long ago, though I hated it. The only way you'd ever forgive me was if I showed you that the choices I've made really are for you and not just me. She sunk into my chest, brought to tears again. The whole thing with Jasmine had been a stupid mistake, a plea of a man desperate to be with the one he loved.

Her mouth found mine, initiating a kiss, confirming what I knew.

To win her back, I had to let her go. And it ripped me apart. But I took her lips, her body, her soul and held it close, savoring every moment I had, even if they were our last.

Thank you, she said, releasing me. *I'm so sorry. I messed up. I was so close and I had to try. If only that had been Richard's blood I would have been able to do it! That was Jasmine's plan all along, you know? Get your dad alone and turn him around. I actually think she wanted me to reform him, but with the war I thought it would be best just to surrender.*

I wanted to know about the blood, too. Whose was it? None of it made sense. But Jessa's foolhardy idea that Richard turning himself in to West America would make everything better? It was too risky. I wish she would have discussed this with me first. How would surrendering to our enemies be safe for her or for me? We were royals too! I didn't press the issue. It was pointless.

She was going to end up in West America anyway, and soon.

We'll use my white and your purple to get you out, but we have to go now. The safe house isn't far, and the gate should be open, as people will be cleaning up from the reception. A few of the guests probably haven't even left yet, if I know how these events can go. I'm taking you out the same way I took your dad out.

She frowned, questioning. *How do you know where a Resistance safe house is?*

How do you think your sister broke out? I added with a shrug. *I helped her. Anyway, we need to move. I need to get back before I'm locked out and have to climb that damned wall.*

You helped my sister? Her face fell. *I underestimated you, Lucas. I'm sorry.*

I reached out and took her small hand in mine. *It's time to go.*

▼

There was nothing worse than a goodbye kiss.

I delivered her to the safe house and before I took her inside, she kissed me deeply. Her lips curved perfectly to mine, her body following. We stayed like that for far too long, lingering in each other. The regret between us was palpable. It buried me in what might have been. Finally, she pulled away. She reached down and opened my hand, placing something gently in my palm. I felt the cool metal, the cut of the stones, and squeezed.

My mother's ring.

I still love you, you know, she said, her voice breaking. *Thank you for this.*

I love you, too.

Maybe she didn't forgive me entirely but to hear those three words again was like being brought back to life. Brought back, only to have it taken away.

I let her go before I lost my nerve and stepped back. We were in the drive of the house, the night black and silent around us. Her form materialized, and when I saw the agonizing stretch of her face, I nearly ran back to her.

"Goodbye, Jessa," I said, my throat catching on the pain.

She sighed deeply and lifted a hand, then turned and hurried up to the porch, ringing the doorbell and knocking at the same time.

I waited as a house light turned on and a minute later, an old woman swung open the door. They exchanged a few words, and then Jessa was gone.

I walked home alone.

I didn't know if I believed in God, but I prayed to him that night. I looked up at the cold sky and I begged for Him to keep her safe and to bring her back to me one day.

After a while of this, I was back at the palace gate. It wasn't an issue. A van came through right as I approached; I had no problem getting back onto the palace grounds in my invisible state.

I strode up the front steps, my body feeling heavier as the weight of everything pressed down. A few party guests stumbled out, a couple clinging to each other. I moved to the side, watching in disgust as they ran to a nearby car, stopping every few strides to kiss. I hated them. They were happy, unencumbered, and able to do such trivial things when I had none of that.

Storming into the halls of the palace, I checked on our room first. The door was still locked. We'd come out together, locking it behind us and telling the guard we were getting a midnight snack. Before he could bring himself to follow, we'd darted into darkened alcove to turn ourselves invisible.

Now, I stared at the door handle like it was the source of my pain. I wasn't ready to go back in there and lay in a bed that would smell like my wife. The wife I'd only had for not even a night. Who I never really had at all.

I wandered, ending up in the GC wing. It, too, reminded me of Jessa. But didn't everything? The area was silent and mostly dark except for a few lights always on at night to light the halls. Everyone down here was probably fast asleep by now, not that I cared either way.

Something trailing along the concrete floor caught my eye. I squatted down, one hand still on my white rose, and reached the other to touch it. Blood.

Like an idiot, I followed the trail. The little red drips led me around a few corners and into one of the empty classrooms.

I didn't see him at first, not until my eyes adjusted to the darkness. He wasn't moving. He just sat like a statue in a chair.

Who was that? I moved in closer.

His hand snapped out and grabbed me.

Startled, I dropped the rose to the ground. It was the same one we'd taken from Jessa's bouquet earlier. The rest of the bouquet was probably still there, left in the bathroom.

My body materialized, and panic swept over me.

"You!" Mark growled up at me. "How did you do that?"

I snatched my arm away, annoyed but also a little unnerved. Quick as a flash, the man sucker-punched me square in the face. I fell to the ground with a thud.

"What was that for?" I gasped.

He jumped up and kicked me. His heavy boot connected with a rib. It snapped, pain shooting through me and I groaned, curling in on myself.

"You bastard! You broke my little girl's heart. Do you know that? Are you even sorry?" he yelled, landing a blow right in the kidney. I reached toward the nearest plant, desperate for relief, but it was too far.

"And earlier, your father had the gall to hit me when I challenged him. He's put my family through hell and he hit me! *Me!* A loyal servant to him for *years* and this is how he repays me? He humiliated us in front of the whole kingdom!"

I raised my hands in front of my face. "Please stop!"

"So I'll hit *you!*" His voice was wild. "And you're an alchemist? God, just like your whore of a wife! What a match made in heaven. I hope you two will be very happy together."

He chuckled, and I crawled to my knees, the physical pain vibrating through my entire body.

"Oh wait, no I don't," he spat.

Anger clawed at me. He was right to be angry; I would be too in his position. But he had *no right* to touch me!

Then his hulking boot connected with my face. A searing heat enveloped me followed by a confusing heaviness. My vision blurred. Something wet fell into my eyes, and I pushed it away. Blood. I gagged on the salty copper liquid. Once again, I staggered up, forcing myself to stand.

"I'll kill you," he growled. "I'll kill your whole family."

He struck again, kicking me in the same spot, but this time with double the force. I heard it before I felt it. A crack.

"Finally."

I blinked rapidly and fell. My head slapped the cement floor with a wet snap.

A gasp echoed. Was it his or mine? The question faded as my vision turned to black.

NINETEEN
SASHA - TWO WEEKS LATER

"How much longer are you going to hold on to that?" Tristan asked, startling me.

I quickly shoved the small slip of paper back in my pant pocket and turned on him. His eyes squinted at me, shiny black hair hanging in his face. A flicker of challenge passed through his eyes and his lip quirked.

"Shut it," I growled. We'd already had this conversation. I'd turn over the email address when I knew *for sure* that these people could be trusted, that they really weren't going to toss all alchemists in prison once this was all over.

We were walking back from the dining tent toward the barracks to settle in for the evening. The setting sun shone bright against the base, lighting the tents, buildings, and tanks up in a golden tint. Long shadows fell across the scene as a familiar figure jogged toward us.

"You need to come straight away," Mastin called out, motioning with his arm. "It's about your father."

Worry catapulted me forward, Tristan at my side, as we

took off, following Mastin toward a nearby building. Men with enormous guns guarded the entrance. They saluted as Mastin approached and stepped aside.

"He's in here," he said, swinging open the door.

"What do you mean he's in here?" Last I had heard, Christopher was still back at the palace. A jolt of excitement shot through my chest.

Tristan put a hand on my back and ushered me forward.

Sure enough, inside the building, sitting on a chair with soldiers buzzing all around him, was my father. His head was drooped, and he looked beat down and bone tired. But when our eyes connected, the same joy I remembered from back when I was a kid spread across his face. It was as if the years of sorrow melted off of him.

"Frankie!" He jumped up and tackled me in a hug. I didn't bother to correct him. Sasha had been an alias for a few years now, but Francesca was *me*. Eventually, I'd probably have to adopt my old name again.

"Are you okay? What are you doing here?" I asked.

"I just got here a few hours ago," he said. "I came through the border on foot." *He what?* I stepped back and studied him. From the sheen of sweat and the layer of grim and dirt on his clothes, his story seemed plausible.

"How did you not end up getting yourself killed?" I gasped, shaking my head. My hair was braided down my head and the long end of it whipped my shoulders like a rope.

The room had turned on us now, everyone growing quiet. Tristan and Mastin stood the closest, but there were about ten others who were also waiting for an explanation. A few had a hand resting on their holsters, and I glared darkly at them.

"It's a long story for another time. Listen, I have to tell you something. It's time sensitive." Dad's voice turned frantic.

It clicked into place. Jessa had been missing from the palace, everyone knew about the nationwide manhunt Richard was conducting. I was terrified to think of what he'd do to her if he found her.

"You know where Jessa is?" The question came out as incredulous, but hopeful.

He nodded, his eyes round circles of concern. "As I was leaving, she connected with me through her telepathy."

"Her what?" Mastin stepped forward, eyebrows drawn in disbelief.

I nodded. "It's rare magic, but it can be done. She must have learned it recently."

Dad agreed. "She established a link between us before she left, but we have to be in close proximity for it to work. Not the same room close, but a few miles or so. I'd already started on my journey through the border when she connected."

"Is she okay?"

"She's okay, but she's in trouble. She told me where she's staying right now. She's at a farmhouse, not too far from here. We have to get her out of there, out of New Colony. From the way she sounded, I think Richard's officers are closing in."

"Let's go get her," Tristan said.

My eyes shot to Mastin, expecting some kind of argument. He stared at us hard for a couple of seconds before nodding. "Okay, Tristan and I will go."

I held back a laugh. Did he not know me by now?

"No! If I don't go, she won't trust you. She doesn't know either of you."

He motioned to Dad. "Can you tell her we're coming?"

"I'm too far, and besides, she has to start the connection. I can't do it." He rubbed his palm against the side of his head, ruffling his wispy hair.

"So it's settled," I shot back at Mastin. "I'm going. We're leaving the second that sun sets."

Mastin grumbled but didn't argue again. He and a couple other soldiers began to make preparations while dad rattled off the address of the farmhouse.

My mind drifted to Jessa, wondering if she was okay. Sources said that everyone in New Colony was looking for her. There were patrols, random searches, and even helicopters with blaring spotlights roaming the kingdom at night. Richard had even gone so far as to issue a kingdom-wide curfew.

All because Prince Lucas was in a coma. Maybe even dead.

We didn't know for sure what had happened to him. General Scott told us that the prince was rumored to be on the edge of death, in a sleep so deep, not even the alchemists could wake him. But Scott also speculated that was a lie, a temporary cover up for the murder of the only heir to New Colony. Two weeks ago Richard had made a statement that someone had tried to kill the prince, yet another assassination attempt. This time it had come the night of royal wedding, one of the most publicized events in New Colony's history, and yet, there were no pictures, no witnesses, no proof whatsoever.

Speculation ensued like wildfire.

Richard had also said the princess was missing. When he'd issued a massive reward for her capture, people questioned. Had she been kidnapped? Or had she been the one to hurt Lucas? With her disappearance that same night, nobody knew what to believe. I didn't know what to believe!

"Are you okay?" Tristan pulled me to the corner of the room, his hand cupping my elbow. I watched my dad carefully, apprehension building within, as he answered question after question. The soldiers around him didn't seem too keen on the situation. Would they trust him here? Would they help him?

I sucked in a breath and met Tristan's gaze. "Yeah. I'm fine. Is it time to go yet?"

I was suspicious of how they might treat Jessa once we brought her back, but we had to get her out while we had the chance. On base, she was a subject of extreme speculation. I'd felt questioning eyes on me everywhere I went these last two weeks, heard boisterous talk fall to snickering whispers when I walked past. I'd lived in close quarters with plenty of women before, but they had nothing on these gossips.

They called her the blood bride.

That was the one that got to me the most.

I had to admit the nickname was catchy, but it still made me cringe.

I leaned against the metal sheeted wall, leaning against Tristan, and watched as Dad took it all in. I wondered what he thought. Was this place better or worse than he'd imagined? Soon, I'd figure out how to get him back to California where Mom and Lacey were staying. That's where he belonged, somewhere safe.

The door swung wide and General Nathan Stott strode in, his hand outstretched toward Christopher. Nathan was dressed in his usual black and gold uniform, a rainbow of decoration adorning his chest. But even without it, he'd carry himself with the air of importance. The room stood at attention.

"It's a pleasure to meet you, Christopher Loxely," he said, his voice booming. "I hope you don't mind, but I'll get right to the chase. We have to take you in for more questioning before we do anything else; with you coming out of New Colony, you're considered a liability."

"What?" I gaped at Nathan, rushing forward. "Are you

kidding me? He's helping us!"

Nearly all the men in the room reached for their weapons. Nathan held up a hand and glanced quickly at Mastin, as if it was Mastin's job to calm the screaming female. "Not now, Sasha," he pressed. "We did the same due-diligence with you, didn't we?"

That may very well be true, but I still didn't like it.

"He can be trusted," I said between gritted teeth. "He's my father. He's been through enough suffering to get here and now he just wants to help us."

"We just have to make sure he's the real deal. How do we know he wasn't planted here?"

"Oh, you've got to be kidding me!"

I turned to Mastin, waiting for him to back me up, but he stood back, never meeting my eye. So he agreed with dear old dad, did he?

"It's okay," Christopher interjected, meeting me with a sad but knowing smile. "I get it. And I don't have anything to hide."

I shook my head, but he shrugged and willingly accompanied Nathan through a door that led further into the dank building. In a matter of moments they were swallowed up by a cacophony of more soldiers. The door slammed, leaving the three of us left to wait in silence.

"This is garbage." I whirled on Mastin. I strode right up to him and shoved him in the chest. Hard. "You're going to let your dad do that to him? He's been through hell and back getting here and this is how you greet him?"

He was busy looking over my shoulder, ignoring me. I shoved him harder and he finally met my eyes.

"Actually, it was my idea," he said.

Disbelief overpowered me and I stepped back.

"Why?"

"He may be your father, but he's also the father to a royal. A princess. You saw the wedding footage, right? Saw the way those two looked at each other? They were clearly in love. And we don't know what happened after that. This could be a trap."

"It's not!" I felt Tristan coming up behind me. He put his hand on my shoulder but I shrugged him off.

"Be logical. You're getting your emotions involved," Mastin continued.

I wanted to slap him for that comment.

"It makes sense." He frowned and looked into my eyes, pleading with me. "Do you *really* know them, though? I thought you barely made contact with your family again this summer."

He was right, and I hated it. Twisting things around to look a certain way didn't mean they were true. My family was innocent. They were on our side.

"What does this mean for the mission tonight? Are we still going to get Jessa out or what?"

He sucked in a breath. "I'll go, for you. But I'm not risking any of my men on this. It's just going to be the three of us, and a pilot, as planned."

"I can fly the chopper," I snapped. "Even better."

"You're not authorized."

I let out a sharp laugh and turned around to find Tristan's expression. Concern was written all over his face, causing a stab of guilt to go through me. I ignored it and raised an eyebrow in his direction. He sighed and ran his hand through his raven hair, shaking his head ever so slightly.

"Are you still in, or what?" I finally asked.

"Where you go, I go." He shrugged.

"Wow! Don't let me twist your arm," I snapped.

I stood rooted in place. A wash of anger rolled over me.

Anger that they didn't fully trust my judgment on this. But also anger at the small seed of doubt that had been planted by Mastin's logic. He had a brilliant mind for war and strategy, inherited from his father. And what if he was right? What if it was a trap?

Over the last few weeks, I'd witnessed awful interrogation tactics as General Scott had dealt with Brooke, who so far, didn't know much. But his men had certainly exhausted all their efforts in figuring that out. Were they about to put my father through the same? Would trying to be the hero only to put Jessa through more pain? But no, anything was better than Jessa getting caught by King Richard. I didn't know what happened that night between her and Lucas, that was true, but whatever it was, it couldn't be good.

"So let's get out of here." I whipped back around and shoved Mastin with my shoulder as I made for the door. No matter the consequences, it was time to get my sister out of New Colony.

▼

We flew in the middle of the night, the black sky our best asset. And by the way Mastin acted, our only asset. As the helicopter landed silently in the open field, I stood and tensed one hand around the stone necklace, the other rested on my loaded weapon. The three of us peered out the window at the white farmhouse where Jessa was supposed to be hiding. It loomed up ahead, silent and still in the night. I glanced around the farm, looking for hidden dangers. The whole area gave me the creeps. I shuddered. This place was so desolate, so marked with shadow, and dark as midnight.

Mastin nodded, and we jumped out of the belly of the chopper, the three of us running low toward the house—

Mastin on one side and Tristan on the other. What was it with me always being thrown in between these two men? Well, at least they were hot.

I smirked at the childish thought as we trudged on.

We stopped behind a tall oak tree, its shadows long and all-encompassing. Carefully, we cased the area one last time. There wasn't a soul in sight. Just the farmhouse up ahead, empty fields surrounding us, and the moonless sky. Stars watched over the scene. A small critter ran across the lawn.

"I should go," I whispered, already holding up my hand in protest. "Don't argue. She knows me. She might spook if someone else does it."

Before they could reply, I took off. My feet landed softly on the grass, and I imagined I was moving like a cat. Silent. Swift. Predatory.

Dad had claimed that the farmer knew she was here. But the farmer's wife? Not so much. So, we needed to be extra careful as not to draw unnecessary attention to ourselves. Nobody knew if she could ruin this for us or not. With the bounty on Jessa's head, I figured it was more than likely.

Approaching the cellar door, I crouched down and another tingle of nerves swept through me. I knelt at the base of a long sheet of metal, fastened down over a large box like a protrusion coming off the side of the house. I knocked softly three times and then unlatched it. It swung open with a loud creak that pierced the silence like a knife. I cringed.

"Jessa, are you in there?" I whispered down into the dark space. It vaguely reminded me of my time spent in Richard's prison. Pushing the thought away, the feeling still lingered.

There was a moment of silence followed by a soft, "I'm here."

"It's me. We gotta move."

"Frankie?"

"Or Sasha, whatever. No time to debate the pros and cons of that whole name situation right now." I rolled my eyes at my own obnoxious rambling.

She crawled out of the space, her eyes round orbs in the darkness. Her hair was knotted around her shoulders, her clothes threadbare and hanging off her thin frame. She wrapped her arms around her torso and shivered.

"Where's your coat?"

"Lost it."

"How?" I asked before quickly adding, "Never mind." I pulled her into a quick hug, murmuring softly into her hair. "It's okay. You're safe now."

"It's not me I've been worried about. But thanks."

Her body, taller than mine, still felt smaller against me somehow.

"Lucas will be fine," I replied, guessing that it was her comatose husband on her mind. "He's tough. Anyway, he wanted you out of New Colony, right? So let's go."

She nodded and I grabbed her hand, tugging her along. We ran to the oak tree and met up with the boys.

"Who are they?" Her wide eyes tracked up and down the two men. Men who she knew nothing of, but who had become my anchors.

"They're trustworthy," I said, tucking her arm into mine. "They're okay. I promise. But we have to go."

She nodded and the four of us turned to peer out from the shadows. Mastin took point, casing the area one last time and nodding his go-ahead. Just as the four of us were about to sprint back to the chopper, the door to the farmhouse flung opened. A man stumbled out into the darkness, his hands waving.

"Wait!" His deep voice rolled over the cold landscape and I jumped, ready to take action.

"Don't," Mastin said, placing his hand on my arm.

"It's okay," Jessa replied. "We can trust Taysom."

I don't know about that!

"Taysom! Over here!" she called out loudly and the rest of us cussed under our breaths. Was she for real right now? With all our training, we couldn't help her if she was going to pull stupid stunts like this!

"Shh–" I hissed out at my sister. But then, super intelligent girl that she was, she took off running *toward the man*. I began to take off after her, but Tristan yanked me back and slammed me against his hard chest.

"Just wait," he growled. "See what he does."

In the darkness, I could barely make out the farmer's expression. Jessa was the tallest in our family, but this man towered over her. He said something to her, his gravelly voice coming out with a twinge of regret, and she fell to the earth. A sob escaped her, echoing through the landscape.

"Get off me!" I shoved Tristan back and ran to my sister, my footsteps slamming against the ground. One hand on my gun, I ripped it from the holster and pointed it at the hulking man. His eyes flashed when he saw me, and he raised his hands slowly.

"Hey now," he said, nodding toward the gun. His eyes two bright white spots in the darkness. "No need for that. I just thought she should hear it from me first."

"Hear what?" I spat.

Mastin and Tristan ran up behind me, their guns also pointing at the man. I caught the rage in Mastin's eyes, the frustration in Tristan's, and looked away. They had no excuse. I'd come after her. They'd come after me. Same story.

"Lucas is dead!" Jessa cried out, her voice so hollow and pained, it sent an ache through my core. Lucas and I didn't always see eye to eye, but he had proved himself to be a good man. His death didn't please me, but I also didn't have time to dwell on it. None of us did. If Richard's people really were closing in, we should have already left the area by now.

"I'm so sorry." I dropped my gun to my side and squatted next to my sister's sobbing body. "But we have to get out of here. It's not safe. We can talk about it more on the way back to base."

She didn't respond. She continued to cry, as if she hadn't heard a word I said. Either that, or she just didn't care.

"Seriously, Jessa." I grabbed her arm and tried to pry her off the cold grass. "We really have to go. We can't get caught out here or we're all dead."

Tristan strode forward to help, his long arm reaching to tug her up.

"Don't touch me!" Jessa bellowed. She turned on us, her face streaked with tears, her eyes wild. She scrambled back on the grass, pushing away. "I have to go back! I have a connection to him. If I can reach out with the purple I can see if he's still alive."

"But he's dead, sweetie." The farmer looked down on her with pity. For such a large man, his tone was gentle. "There was just a national broadcast about it."

"I don't believe it. Did you see a body? How do you know?" she pressed.

The farmer's dark face was hard to decipher in the night, but even I saw the flash of doubt. "Well, no body. Not yet."

"See! He might not be dead!" Her body snapped to attention and she jumped up. "I'm going back."

"You can't!" I gasped, but she didn't care.

She spun around and took off running, kicking dirt into the air behind her. Her yellow magic must have been coursing through her veins because her speed was unnatural as she tore through the night. I swore under my breath.

"Don't you even think about it!" Mastin said, turning on me.

My eyes flicked once to him, and once to Tristan, before settling on the path ahead.

"I have to," I said simply.

The tug of yellow magic ignited in my veins, the necklace warm against my skin. I bolted forward, legs burning with insane speed as I sprinted out of the yard and into the field, pushing onward.

She wasn't going to endure this alone. I had a family again. For most of my life, I'd let the pain of abandonment push any thoughts of my family away. But really, they'd missed me just as much as I'd missed them. I knew that now. The same blood coursed through us, tying us together, and it always would.

Jessa's head bobbed up in the darkness, a beacon for me to follow. My lungs burned and my breath was labored, but my mind cleared as I gained ground. This was the right thing to do. Helping her, being there for her in her weakest moment, it was what family did for their own. I was ready to embrace what it meant to be a Loxely, what it meant to be a big sister.

Saving Jessa from her grief was the perfect opportunity to start.

END OF BOOK THREE

CONTINUE READING

Thank you for reading The Color Alchemist series. If you liked this book, please leave a review on Amazon or Goodreads. Word of mouth is the lifeblood to an independent author and it only takes a moment.

Thanks again!

Join my newsletter for news on releases, giveaways, advanced reader teams, and more. And be sure to get a copy of *Among Shadows*, a free ebook novella, at **www.ninawalkerbooks.com** today.

Collide, the final book in The Color Alchemist Series, will release in August 2018.

ACKNOWLEDGMENTS

As always, there are so many names that come to mind. My dreams have come true and I couldn't have done it alone. I've felt support from heaven and earth, so thank you. Writing might seem like a solitary effort, and while there is some truth to that, it's hardly a lonesome endeavor. If it weren't for everyone in my corner, there would be no way that Blackout would have happened, let alone the entire Color Alchemist series.

First, I must thank my handsome husband, Travis. Not only do you inspire these love stories, but you are my love story, and that's better than anything in book. Without your help and belief, without your sacrifices, I could never do this passion of mine. Thank you. I love you.

Thank you to my family, blood related and otherwise, you guys are amazing and I'm so grateful to have you.

Of course, a gigantic thanks goes out to all my readers. Since releasing the first book in 2017, I've received hundreds of fan emails and reviews. I do a little happy dance each and every time! Thank you for reading, for supporting the series, and for getting all the way through book three. Haha! That's an accomplishment, so thank you so much and I hope you continue on this journey with me.

Hugs to the team! To every one of my arc readers, proofreaders, my cover designer, and my developmental editor, thank you all so much. Chelsea Moye, Ailene Kubricky, Kate Anderson, Travis Walker, Molly Phipps, and

Kate Foster, you are all such rock stars and I can't thank you enough for all your hard work and heart. I'm picky, you know that, so seriously, thanks for making my job easier.

A huge shout out goes out to the team at Sarah Hershman Rights Management. Thanks for doing such an exceptional job representing the subsidiary and foreign rights. You're all amazing communicators, everything I needed, and you're doing wonderful things for indie authors. I am so grateful to have your agency on my side.

I've been an Audible customer for twelve years, that's how much I love audiobooks. I'm so excited to announce that the The Color Alchemist series has been bought by Audible, with the first two books releasing in April 2018, and the second two planned for later in the year. This is such a dream come true and I am so thrilled for this next step. Many thanks to the awesome team at Audible for not only believing in this story, but for all your hard work in producing the audiobooks. And of course, many thanks to the incredible narrators who've come on for the job. We couldn't be happier!

Thank you to all those who've helped create such an amazing writing community. To Dave Farland, for your amazing workshops. You have truly changed the way I write. To the authors over at An Alliance of Young Adult Authors, you're my favorites! To my author friends and to everyone who has been kind enough to reach out in support, you're the best. And many thanks to all the amazing vendors who offer assistance to indie authors, helping us reach our dreams. I've worked with so many awesome people as I've learned how to do this whole "marketing thing", so thank you!

And finally, a massive amount of love goes out to the dreamers, the writers, the visionaries, and the brave souls who have come before me. You have inspired me. And

I know many more of you are still to come. Keep telling stories, heartbreaking and uplifting, real or imagined, because in this crazy, messed-up world, we need your voice. I need your voice. So please keep speaking, keep writing, keep going.

ABOUT

NINA WALKER lives in Utah with her family, where she spends her time reading, writing, and helping women prioritize their health in online support groups. She also has a mild obsession with Instragram Stories.

Connect with Nina:

Facebook at fb.com/ninawalkerbooks
Instagram @ninabelievesinmagic

www.ninawalkerbooks.com

CPSIA information can be obtained
at www.ICGtesting.com
Printed in the USA
LVHW041221040319
609400LV00001B/61/P